GREEN SHOOTS

A banging mystery loaded with suspense

NICOLA CLIFFORD

Published by The Book Folks

London, 2023

ISBN 978-1-80462-117-2

www.thebookfolks.com

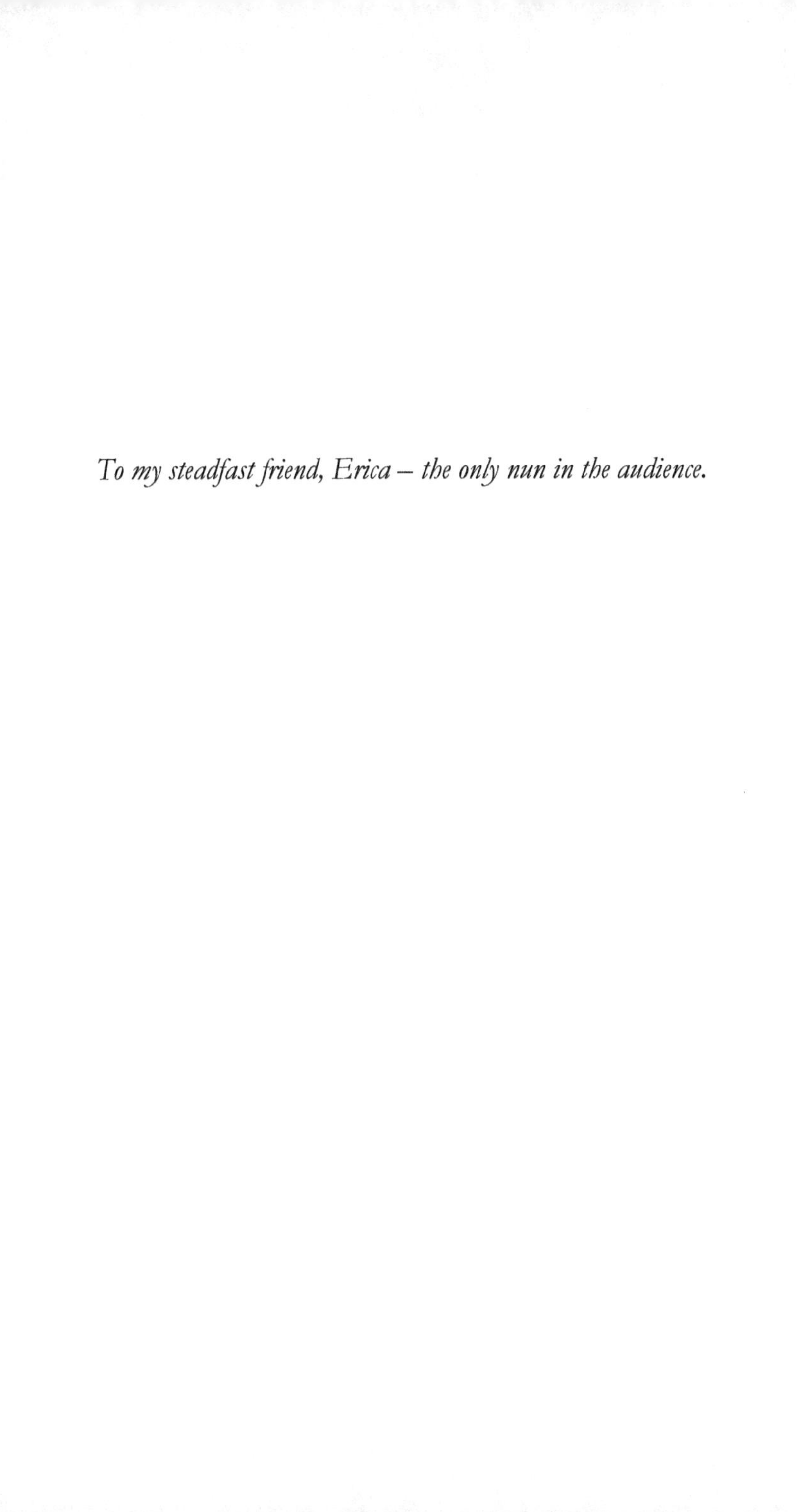

To my steadfast friend, Erica — the only nun in the audience.

Chapter one

Two men dug into the slope of a grassy bank at the head of a green, Welsh valley, using sharply pointed, long-handled shovels. The surrounding area was planted with deciduous trees, sunny glades between their trunks, the air filled with the calls of corvids and the rustle of autumn leaves stirred by a gentle breeze. The rhythmic thunk of shovels was the only man-made sound. The sun was warm for the time of year and the diggers soon removed their fleecy tops and hung them on a low branch nearby.

A couple of hours after the men began work, a child, perhaps eight years old, skipped along the narrow footpath towards them, a wicker basket swinging from one hand. The excavators took a well-earned lunch break, drove their shovels into the mound of soil and sat on a fallen trunk. While they drank cool lemonade and munched on cheese and pickle sandwiches, the little girl examined their efforts. She resembled a foreman of works as she marched from one side of the curiously shaped hole to the other, tiny hands clasped behind her back. The men watched, smiling as she stomped along, pausing every now and again to poke a finger at the freshly exposed earth. She picked up a shard of stone and used it to worry at the back wall.

'Have you found something, Seren *cariad*?' one of the men called.

The girl looked over her shoulder and grinned. 'Treasure,' she said confidently.

Seren had found treasure before during similar excavations, usually ancient bottle tops, maybe a small piece of pottery, and once or twice an old bronze penny, dropped from the pocket of a long dead hill farmer. The man hauled himself upright and groaned, noticing how his muscles had already begun to stiffen. He walked towards his daughter and placed a callused hand on her shoulder.

'So where's this treasure?' he asked.

Seren pointed at a spot about four feet up from the base of the wall. John moved closer, bent at the waist and examined the spot. He had to agree, there was definitely something embedded in the earth. He used the point of his belt knife to scrape dark soil away from a curved piece of dull yellow metal, brass maybe, lost from the bridle of a shire horse during harvest before the age of machinery.

Seren held up her hand. 'Wait a minute, Da. Let me see.'

The second digger, sandwich in hand, walked closer and looked over the girl's shoulder.

'What have you found, Seren?' he asked.

'Told you, Rhys, treasure. I think it's a tiara, covered with diamonds and rubies. A Welsh princess dropped it when she fell off her unicorn.'

Rhys laughed. 'You should write books, young 'un. Was she being chased by a red dragon breathing fire?'

John carefully pried away another chunk of compacted earth and exposed more of the object.

'You know,' he said, 'this might actually be something, a bangle maybe.' He pecked at the soil with his blade as his companions crowded closer for a better look. 'I reckon,' he said, concentrating hard, the tongue poking from his mouth wetting his lips, 'this could actually be gold. Doesn't look the right colour for brass and it isn't tarnished.'

'What's that mean, Da?' Seren asked.

'That some metals lose their shine because oxygen works on them and causes oxidisation. Rust is iron oxide. The clue is in the name.'

'D-a-a, it's not a school day.'

'You're right, but it can always be a learning day.'

John worked at the wall until he could positively identify the buried object as an oval bangle – he could see a hinge and a tiny sparkle in the dark. He took hold of the metal between his thumb and forefinger and tugged gently. No movement. He wriggled his grip up and down, then side to side and detected a slight shift, so he picked up the knife and dug some more. After a few moments, John spotted what looked to be a tree root growing through the metal hoop.

'Have you got a torch, Rhys?' he asked.

Rhys pulled a head torch from his pocket and handed it over. John directed the bright beam at the earthen wall and saw he was right, a thumb-thick root had wriggled its way through the bracelet. He wondered if his knife would cut through, but as soon as the blade touched the obstruction, John knew he had been wrong. The root was a bone. The bangle was still on the owner's wrist.

* * *

The pathologist, Carrie Salmon, straightened up and rubbed her lower back. She turned to face DCI Ben James and DS Jack Trent.

'I can confirm the bones are human, radius and ulna, lower arm. Can't tell you anything else until I've been able to excavate properly.'

'Nothing at all?' Ben asked.

'Only that I think there is something odd with this burial.'

'Odd, how?' Jack asked.

'It's purely conjecture at this stage, but there doesn't appear to be any obvious staining of the surrounding soil.'

'What might that mean?'

'Soil staining is caused by the decomposition of the body. Not seeing any could mean whoever this is might well have been a skeleton when they were buried.'

'That does sound odd,' Ben said. 'Why would anyone bury bones?'

'Smaller hole than an intact body would require.'

'But what would you do with the rest of it?'

Carrie grinned. 'We can go there if you like and I'll amaze you with my knowledge of acid baths, feeding chunks to racing greyhounds, liquidised flesh poured down the toilet…'

Ben swallowed and held up his hands. He'd never been good with gruesome details. 'Point made,' he said. 'Will you start work now?'

Carrie nodded. 'No time to waste. Today's forecast is dry, but squally showers are expected to move in this evening. Conditions are likely to deteriorate. I have a team on the way and SOCO is hovering somewhere nearby with one of their white tents.'

'Any idea how long you'll need?'

'I'll work as fast as I can but I'll need a few hours. I can't rush this.'

'Can you tell when the bones were buried?' Jack asked.

'Soil disturbance appears to be recent, by which I mean sometime during the last eighteen months or so. The natural structure has not quite settled down.'

'Any idea how long the bones were bones before ending up here?'

'I'm fairly certain they aren't ancient and at first glance they don't appear to be decades old either.' She turned and looked at the officers, hands on her hips. 'I can see some fabric, the remains of a cotton bag, a pillowcase perhaps. It's possible the bones were inside it but as I've said, I need to excavate the site properly, and that will take time.'

'We'll get out of your way then,' Ben said, 'go and chat to the locals.'

'Fine with me. I'll give you a shout as soon as I have something for you. I brought flasks of coffee and you're welcome to share. How about we regroup in a couple of hours?'

'Sounds like a plan, thanks.'

The detectives stepped away from the hole and ducked under blue and white police tape. They headed along a narrow path between the trees, where DC Ollie Langdon and newly promoted DC Elsa Duffin stood guard.

'Is there a body, sir?' Elsa asked.

'Early indications confirm human remains.' Ben rubbed his face. 'It looks like just bones. Not able to say how long they've been there. We'll be waiting on Carrie for this one.' He looked at Ollie. 'Make sure you protect the scene, no one allowed inside who hasn't a valid reason to be there. I also want you to extend the cordon behind and above the site. Carrie will need to dig down from above as well as horizontally.'

'Yes, sir.'

'And make sure the uniforms know what to do. Elsa, come with us to speak to the residents.'

'Residents?' Ollie snorted disdainfully. 'Have you actually seen the settlement yet? Bunch of scruffy scroungers. Most of the tree-huggers live underground, like bloody hippy moles. Why would you do that?'

'Don't hold back,' Jack muttered under his breath.

Ben frowned. 'Maybe, Constable Langdon, they'd all had enough of living with their mothers.'

Ollie blushed and stormed off along the path.

'What's bugging Ollie?' Jack asked.

Ben grinned. 'Grapevine says his mother. Now let's get on. How many dwellings are there?'

Jack checked his notebook. 'Five, apparently, at the top of the valley above the trees. Did you know there was anyone living here?'

'No,' Ben said, 'but I've read about places like this in the press. The pictures always look too good to be true, but I've never seen one in the flesh.'

'That's why I enjoy being a copper, a new experience every day.' Jack laughed. 'This is bound to be better than yesterday's adventure.'

'Oh?' Ben asked.

'Stopped a dodgy-looking character at a petrol station off the A40. I made the suggestion that I'd like to search him, and the bugger stripped naked and threw his clothes at me – all of them.'

'What did you do?'

'I rifled the pockets then lobbed his clothes back at him. Didn't find anything so no arrest. A couple of older women filling up found it hilarious. So, on reflection, wandering through an autumn woodland in search of hobbits is much more my cup of tea.'

The detectives followed a twisty path and after a few minutes emerged from the trees into a large, sun-splashed glade. Ben stopped walking abruptly and stared in astonishment at the settlement. Spaced along the grassy bank were the fronts of what appeared to be five small dwellings, with circular doors and white-framed windows. It looked as though the homes had somehow been tucked beneath a turf quilt. Stretching away from the little houses was a large, terraced vegetable patch. A couple in their early thirties worked the plot, harvesting what appeared to be carrots. They straightened up as the detectives drew closer.

Ben stepped forward and held up his warrant card.

'Good afternoon,' he said. 'DCI James, and my colleague is DS Trent. Could we have a word?'

'Of course,' the man said. 'We've been expecting you. I'm John Davis and this is my wife, Sally. Our daughter, Seren, found the… bracelet. Come up to the house and we'll have a cuppa.'

'Most welcome, thanks.'

John led the way to a dwelling with a blue door, red earthenware pots of lavender on either side. He pushed open the door, walked down a couple of steps and glanced back out at his guests. 'Mind how you go,' he said, 'and don't forget to duck.'

'Is there room inside for all of us?' Jack asked.

Sally laughed. 'We'd hardly invite you in if there wasn't.'

Jack shrugged, then folded his large frame and followed John inside, Ben behind him.

'Wow,' Ben said. 'This is just beautiful.'

'Thank you,' Sally said.

Ben allowed his eyes to sweep around the surprisingly sizeable room and saw the walls were clad with planks of golden timber. Light from the front windows shone into the room, enhanced by sunshine shafting through glass panels above his head. He gazed at the kitchen area and spotted a black wood-burning stove sitting on a thick slab of Welsh slate, its metal chimney pipe vanishing through the ceiling.

'Please, sit,' Sally said as she filled a kettle and placed it on the stove to boil.

Jack took up the offer but Ben stayed on his feet, and examined the handmade furniture, packed bookshelves, small wind chimes hanging from beams, and pretty rag rugs on the wooden floor.

'I'm blown away by this,' Ben said. 'No one would ever guess what's behind your front door. Is it just this room?'

John shook his head. 'There's two bedrooms and a bathroom at the back. Genuine Tardis this place, come and have a look if you want.'

'Sure you wouldn't mind?'

John chuckled. 'I'll only complain if you start tossing mattresses about.'

He parted a curtain in the wall to expose a small space and three doors. Ben ran his fingertips along the polished wooden wall and peered inside a compact bathroom and two bedrooms, all lit from above. He stood beneath one of the skylights and stared up through the glass. He saw tree branches waving in the gentle breeze, a pale blue sky dotted with fair-weather clouds, and a lone buzzard riding the thermals.

'What a place to live,' he breathed.

'We like it,' John said. 'Now let's get that cuppa and you can tell us what you've uncovered in Badger's Bank.'

'Does your settlement have a name?' Ben asked.

John nodded. 'We called it *Dolgarrog*, Welsh for meadow of swift-flowing stream.'

Chapter two

After a couple of fairly fruitless hours talking to residents, Ben and Jack hadn't discovered anything to explain the presence of a buried skeleton on their land and returned to John and Sally's house. John Davis, self-appointed spokesman for the group, explained how the small settlement was built with official approval eight years ago, soon after the group had obtained the land. He said the dwellings had been constructed following conditions set out under something called the "Sustainable Development Scheme", run and overseen by the local council. John had helpfully printed out a copy of the terms and conditions for the detectives to read later.

'There's a lot of it,' Jack said as he flipped through the small stack of paper.

'Purposely complicated to put people off,' Sally said. 'It stops too many folk thinking it's possible to build your own home and live off the land.' She smiled. 'If the process was simpler, small, low-impact settlements like this would ease the housing crisis and in turn, help combat the climate emergency.'

'We'll take a read-through, thanks,' Ben said.

'Where does your electricity come from?' Jack asked.

'I'll show you if you're interested,' John said. 'It's just a short walk up the hill behind the houses.'

'I'm game.'

'I'll stay here,' Ben said, 'catch up with Ollie then head back to the scene.'

'OK, guv, I'll meet you there.' Jack ducked his head and followed John up the steps and into the sunshine.

'John,' Sally called. 'I'm going to check on Seren, she's playing with the other girls. Teatime soon so don't be too long.'

John nodded then set off up a narrow flight of stone steps next to his home and onto a grassy slope. He walked through a group of statuesque Scots pines; the ground was littered with pine cones which crunched beneath his boots. A pair of glossy-feathered ravens perched in the high branches and chattered to each other. When the men moved closer, the birds took flight and soared out over the valley on stiff, squeaky wings.

'Just up here,' John called. 'Not much further.'

The grassy incline steepened. John covered another few yards and halted on the edge of a man-made pond surrounded by reeds and a few bulrushes. A small stream fed the pool from higher up the hill and John pointed at the running water.

'Our swift-flowing stream,' he said. 'The pond is effectively a header tank. We collect the water here, then run it through earthenware pipes laid across the grass and down the incline, gaining speed and building pressure.' He pointed down the steep slope to a wooden cabin with turf on the roof. 'There's a turbine in there. The water spins the turbine, electricity is generated and sent to our homes. Any excess is stored in lithium batteries.'

'That's impressive,' Jack said. 'No leccy bills to pay then?'

'No, thank God, the way the prices are heading. As I told you, Dolgarrog is completely off-grid. As well as this turbine, each house has its own system of solar panels and batteries.' He smiled broadly. 'We all keep a few candles for emergencies, but doesn't everyone? We're about to upgrade the hydro; we have to as we're adding a couple more homes.'

'Is that difficult to do?'

John smiled again. 'Luckily for us we have our own genius-boffin on site, Will North. He has a cabin in the wood. We offered to build him one of our designs but he said he couldn't live underground.' John shrugged. 'It's not for everyone.'

'Is Will around? Can I talk to him?'

'He went out this morning to pick up parcels from the local post office. It's a long walk so he won't be back till late.'

'Do you walk everywhere?'

'As much as possible, but we own a small electric vehicle parked on the lane at the top of the valley.'

'OK, we'll catch up with Will tomorrow. Right, better get down to the dig site. It would be a good idea if you could keep the children away from the cordoned area.'

'We'll do our best. Do you have kids?'

Jack nodded. 'Twins, boy and a girl, they'd love living here. I think I would too.' He chuckled. 'I grew up in the East End of London, moved here several years ago and never thought I'd get used to the wide open spaces. Even the sheep bothered the hell out of me. Got a place on the Epynt now with the wife and kids and when I think of London my palms sweat.'

John grinned. 'I'd never have guessed, not a trace of cockney in your accent, more like you've stuffed half a pound of plums in your mouth.'

'I went to a good school,' Jack said. 'Come on, let's go down. My guv will be looking for me.'

* * *

Ben and Carrie perched side by side on a fallen log, sipping coffee and surveying a small mound of walnut-coloured bones lying on a plastic sheet.

'This is good, thanks.' Ben waved his mug at the bones. 'Can you tell me any more about this?'

'Nowhere near as much as you would like, but I'm fairly certain the bones belonged to an adult, edentulous female.'

Ben raised his eyebrows.

'No teeth,' Carrie explained.

'Are they still in the grave, dropped out?'

'No. She lost her teeth a few years before her death. I detected some shrinking of the jaw, but I've asked for the surrounding soil to be removed and collected. Easier to search through at base than out here. Until I spread out the bones I won't know whether I have all two hundred and six.'

'Any chance of DNA?'

'Obviously I'll look, but DNA molecules like cool, dry and dark, not cold, wet and dark.'

Ben sipped more coffee. 'The bones are nearly black, they look old. Do you still think she was buried in the last year and a half?'

Carrie smiled. 'I'm fairly sure. It only takes a couple of months for organic compounds to stain bone.' She hauled herself upright. 'I'm going to leave SOCO in charge of the digging while I take the remains to the lab and make a start. I should be able to provide an interim report sometime tomorrow.'

'Marvellous, thanks. Any thoughts on the bangle?'

'I've left it in place for now, worried it might snap.'

Carrie carefully wrapped the skeleton in the plastic and placed the bundle in a plastic crate, then she stripped off her protective suit, rolled it up and stuffed it in a rubbish bag. 'Did you learn anything useful from the residents?'

'Quite a lot, to be honest, but nothing about the burial on their land. We'll return tomorrow, still a few to speak to.' Ben got to his feet. 'We're waiting on you to find some clues or better still, provide an identification and cause of death.'

Carrie snorted. 'No pressure then? You know I'll do my best but I don't think you should hold your breath.'

She bent down, took hold of the crate and headed down the footpath to her car.

* * *

Stacey Logan stomped bad-temperedly through the streets of Brecon after a meeting with Sam Jenkins, editor of *The Mid Wales Times*, and her boss. The chat had taken longer than anticipated while he grouched and grumbled about the lack of news. Stacey glanced at her watch and frowned, school had finished for the day and the supermarket would be heaving. Needing to fill the larder and stock up on essentials, Stacey had little choice other than to move her car from one car park to another, grab a trolley and enter the busy food aisles. She dodged harassed mothers and tantruming children for forty minutes before gratefully escaping back outside.

She began to feel better as soon as she drove out of town. Better still when she made the turn at Llywel and crawled up the steep lane to the range road which twisted and turned over the Epynt towards Llanagethin and home. For the last couple of weeks, Mid Wales had been enjoying a warm Indian summer with plenty of sunshine, but the daylight hours were shrinking while nights grew noticeably longer and cooler. There had even been a couple of sharp frosts which scorched the leaves of any remaining tender vegetables.

At the end of the range road Stacey slowed, turned left and drove carefully down the steep lane to the edge of the village. She passed by the houses and was surprised to see Ben's car parked next to the grassy verge outside her cottage. She pulled up in the drive, collected her belongings, left the car and walked around to the back garden.

'Wow,' she said as she pushed open the kitchen door. 'Something smells amazing.' She hung her kitbag on the back of a chair.

Ben looked up from the Aga and smiled. 'Game pie from Dave the butcher. You know I couldn't make a pie.'

'How come you're home so early? No bad guys to catch?'

'There are always bad guys.' Ben opened the door of the Aga and checked on a tray of roasted vegetables then walked across the kitchen and kissed Stacey on the cheek. 'Glass of wine?' he asked.

'Sounds good.'

'Tell me,' Ben said as he removed two glasses from an overhead cabinet, 'what do you know about hobbits?'

'Small humanoids with hairy feet who live in holes and fraternise with elves and wizards.' She grinned. 'And of course, they're not real.'

'How about folk who live in houses that resemble hobbit holes?'

Stacey removed her coat and sat at the table. 'I met some a year or so back. I was writing a piece on sustainable living and visited a couple who'd built a place on the edge of the Preseli Mountains. Why are you asking?'

'Jack and I were called out today to a small settlement not far from Brecon. We saw five hobbit-type houses dug into a slope at the top of a valley.' He grinned. 'They had round doors. I managed to get a guided tour of one — incredible place. Peaceful, organic.'

'Why did you visit an off-grid settlement? Are residents growing crops they shouldn't?'

'It's more interesting than that,' Ben said. As he dished up supper, he told her what had been discovered.

'Any sign of foul play?'

Ben laughed. 'Carrie didn't find a dirty great hole in the skull if that's what you mean.'

'Just be sure to give me the heads-up if there is a story here.' She sipped from her glass. 'The editor is on my back.'

When the meal was finished, Stacey piled the dirty dishes in the sink.

'I was going to suggest an evening stroll,' she said, 'but it looks like the weather is on the turn.'

'Rain is forecast. I hope Carrie's team managed to finish the dig.'

'Evening by the fire then? Can't say I'm disappointed.' She headed to the living room. 'Blimey,' she said, 'you cooked supper and lit the fire. You must have knocked off hours ago.'

'As I said, I can't really begin an investigation until we have more to go on.'

Stacey dropped onto the sofa and put her feet up. 'Tell me what the hobbits are like.'

'They seemed like decent folk.' Ben swigged from his glass. 'John and Sally Davis; their daughter Seren discovered the bones. Then there's Matt and Maxine Ansell, younger couple in their twenties and have no children. Janet Crabtree is a single mother with two little ones, Holly and Heather, and a couple of single blokes, Rhys Evans and Geraint Jones.'

'A few living there then.'

Ben nodded. 'We haven't managed to catch up with everyone yet.'

'Do they all live underground?'

'Yes, except a guy called Will North, who lives in a log cabin in the wood. Haven't met him either. He keeps the settlement supplied with green energy.'

'Sounds fascinating. Where did you say the settlement is?'

Ben grinned. 'I didn't and I'm on to you and your journalist's wiles. You know I'll share when I can so knock it off. Now, fancy a film or an early night? Up to you.'

Stacey drained the last of her wine. 'I'm pretty knackered, to be honest. Sam wore me out with all his grumbling so an early night would be good.'

'I agree,' Ben said. 'You go and warm the bed. I'll lock up and make some hot chocolate.'

Chapter three

Stacey woke to the sound of rain splatting on the bedroom window and the whistle of wind in the pipes. Ben's side of the bed was empty and the sheets were cold. She hauled herself out from beneath the duvet, pulled on her fluffy robe, and after a quick visit to the bathroom, wandered downstairs to the kitchen. Ben was sitting at the table and glanced up.

'Morning, Pumpkin,' he said. 'Coffee?'

'Please.' Stacey sat on the wooden carver and rested her bed socked feet on the bottom rail of the Aga. 'Our Indian summer has come to an abrupt end. Doesn't look very nice out there.'

'Not so bad for those who can curl up next to the Aga.'

'Till Sam rings and sends me out to take photos of someone holding a big cheque made out to a donkey sanctuary.' She sipped from her mug. 'How about I come out with you and meet some hobbits? The paper's about due for another zero-carbon story that doesn't include greenwashing and planting shitloads of trees on agricultural land.'

Ben raised his eyebrows. 'Are you serious?'

'Yes, I am. Three local farmers have recently been offered life-changing sums and sold up. The money came from outside Wales I understand. Where have the hobbits come from?'

'You should stop calling them that; anyway, my plans have changed. Carrie sent a text, wants me at the lab first thing. Seems she's been up all night trying to identify the remains we found.'

'Did she tell you anything?'

'No, that's why Jack and I are going over, and even if she had, I wouldn't tell you.'

'Ooo, snappish. Everything OK?'

Ben got to his feet and wrapped his arms briefly around Stacey's fleece-clad torso. 'If I were you,' he said, 'I'd work hard to come up with good reasons for not going out in that. Stay cosy indoors, research something.' He kissed the top of her head. 'If I had the choice, that's exactly what I'd be doing. I'll text you later.'

Stacey returned his hug and watched as he shrugged into his jacket and left by the back door. She heard his car start in the lane, then she opened her laptop and began looking into sustainable and alternative living. It didn't take long before she discovered mention of a settlement outside Brecon, together with photos of cute houses which did look like she imagined hobbit holes to be. The group had a website and Stacey was interested to see that Dolgarrog offered various courses – one on foraging caught her eye. The phone rang, she recognised the number and picked up the handset.

'Morning, Heidi. I was just thinking about you.'

'Really?' Heidi asked. 'Why?'

'Wondered how you were getting on in your new home.'

Heidi had recently inherited a large house with land on the outskirts of Abergavenny, left to her by an elderly friend.

'I haven't really moved in yet. Lots of meetings with Felicity Savage's solicitor regarding the charitable trust she put me in charge of.'

'How's that going?'

'It's going,' Heidi huffed. 'Buckets of paperwork.'

'Is Erica well?'

'She's fine. Working hard but she has some leave coming up, and when she goes back to work it will be in Brecon. Her transfer finally came through.'

'That's good news. So, why did you ring?'

'I need to sort out the mad library at the house; I wondered whether you fancy giving me a hand if you have any spare time.'

'Yeah, I'd be up for that.' Stacey sighed heavily. 'I remember seeing the place for the first time when Fliss told me there was no such thing as too many books.' There was a pause in the conversation as they remembered their friend before Stacey continued. 'The reason you crossed my mind was because I'm considering going on a foraging course and wondered if you'd like to come with me.'

'Why did you think I'd enjoy a foraging course?'

'It's run by hobbits.'

Heidi snorted. 'Sounds like you've already been on the mushrooms.'

'I'll ignore that. The course is run on a sustainable settlement not far from Brecon. The houses appear to have been built mostly underground, hence hobbits.'

'Is this for fun or work?'

'Bit of both. Strictly between you and me, Ben was called out there yesterday. The residents discovered a skeleton buried on their land.'

'Sounds intriguing,' Heidi said, 'but I really am up to my ears at the moment. You go and tell me all about it when you come over to help with the books.'

Heidi hung up and Stacey glared at the phone, wishing – not for the first time – that her friend wouldn't be so abrupt. Maybe the grumpy weather was rubbing off on everyone.

* * *

Ben and Jack stood side by side in the pathology lab and gazed down at an anatomically correct skeleton resting on a gurney. Carrie Salmon stood on the opposite side.

'Let me start by telling you what I haven't found,' she said. 'No teeth, no dentures, no sign of decomposed flesh and so far, no DNA. I'll try to obtain a sample from the petrous bone behind the ear. Might recover some there if we're lucky. I'm also missing a few small bones, the hyoid – tiny bone in the throat – and several toe and finger phalanges.'

'So, tell us what you *have* found,' Ben said.

Carrie picked up a clipboard and began to read. 'Adult female, forty to fifty years old. Five foot five inches tall. Parturition pits on the inside of the pelvic bones tell me she was a mother. Seemingly good health, no arthritis, rheumatism or similar, just an old fracture of the wrist. The distal radius is the most common of these breaks, usually occurs when people fall with their hand outstretched. Two broken fingers on the same side confirm that scenario. I was also right about the missing teeth. Calculating the shrinkage of the jawbone they were probably removed five years or so prior to her death.'

'Any idea how she died?' Jack asked.

'None at all,' Carrie said and put down the clipboard. 'Absence of the hyoid means I can't say whether she was strangled, and I haven't found any nicks on the bones that may indicate a stabbing or a bullet wound.'

'Any chance the missing bones were left behind during the exhumation?' Ben asked.

'None. We recovered a large quantity of soil from the site, which has been sifted, and we found nothing. In my mind, it's more likely these bones went missing prior to the burial, maybe during the excarnation process. We may never know for sure.'

Ben swallowed. 'Any indication of how that was accomplished?' he asked.

'Not so far.'

'Has the bangle told you anything?'

'Not really. It is gold and set with a single diamond, half a carat maybe. The item hasn't been hallmarked, so it was either made outside the UK, or inside by an independent jeweller.'

'Maybe it isn't gold,' Jack said.

'It's gold, I tested it. Fifteen carat, another reason to think it might have been made abroad. The bangle weighs fourteen grams, half an ounce of gold, worth a few quid even at scrap value.'

Ben groaned and rubbed his face. 'I must admit I was hoping for more,' he said. 'Do you still believe the bones were buried in recent times?'

'Yes, I do.'

'Any suggestions about where we go from here?'

'Well...' Carrie hesitated. 'Do you know I volunteer at HMP Heatherlea? The women's prison over the border in England.'

'No, I didn't,' Ben said. 'As a pathologist?'

Carrie laughed. 'No, you idiot, as a prison visitor. I spend time with inmates who have no one or have been ex-communicated by their nearest and dearest.'

'Where are you going with this?'

'During the years I have visited a few lifers.'

'And?' Ben asked.

'This is a bit out there, but two women I met had their teeth removed before they were released.'

'What? All of them?'

Carrie nodded. 'Full clearances. When prisoners are eventually released, the last thing they want is awkward questions from dentists. A new dentist would want sight of their dental records.'

'Yeah, I reckon I get it. So what are you suggesting?'

'It's a long shot but in the absence of anything else, why not check the records of any female LTI – long-term inmate – who was released over the last couple of years.

Once you have a shortlist, find out if any had broken their wrists while they were incarcerated.'

'That is a long shot,' Jack said.

'Best I can come up with,' Carrie said and yawned. 'Sorry, but I really need to get off now, grab some sleep, but I'll return later and take another look. That's all I have for now, except...'

'Except what?'

Carrie held up a plastic evidence bag containing the bangle. 'This bothers me. At current scrap value, this piece is worth approximately £28 per gram, total value just under £400, plus something for the stone. If someone killed this woman, why not take the bracelet? Why bury her with it on her wrist?'

* * *

Ben and Jack strode into the incident room and Elsa glanced up from her screen as they entered.

'How did it go with Carrie?' she asked.

'Not great,' Ben said, breaking the seal on a bottle of Dŵr Cymru. 'Didn't get much but we do have some ideas of how we might try to identify the skeleton.'

'So where do we look?'

Ben sat at the head of the long table and removed a sheet of paper from a cardboard file, together with the plastic bag containing the bangle.

'I need you to check missing persons, female, forty to fifty, who went missing during the last couple of years.'

Elsa made a note on a legal pad. 'Then what?'

Ben sighed. 'Carrie thinks it's possible the woman may have spent a considerable time in prison, lifer maybe.'

'How did she get that from the bones?'

'That's not important, but I also need a list of women LTIs, released during the last two years.'

Elsa picked up the evidence bag and peered at the bangle. 'This is really pretty, looks expensive too. Was it really still on the owner's wrist?'

'Yeah. Surely if the victim was murdered the killer would have taken the gold?'

'I agree. Perhaps this is just a burial,' she said thinking out loud, 'but where did the rest of her go? If it's a murder, where did that happen? How would whoever did this remove the flesh?'

Ben groaned. 'I bloody wish people would stop saying things like that. I can't imagine what sort of person would do something so horrid.' He glanced up at Elsa. 'You're right though. We need to know where the woman died, but where do we begin to look? We're surrounded by hundreds of thousands of acres of rural land, a lot of which is mountainous.'

'I reckon we should go back to Dolgarrog. We need to know more about the residents, backgrounds, that sort of thing. As the bones were found practically on their doorsteps, someone must have heard something, seen something, even if it was only a patch of disturbed earth,' Jack said.

'I agree,' Ben said. 'We'll take official statements from all of them, something might shake loose. Have we received the SDS records from the council?'

'Yeah. I'll take a look through on the way if you don't mind driving.'

'No problem. Go and lay claim to a car, I'll be down in a minute.' He turned to Elsa. 'When Tegan Hughes comes in, ask her to start digging into the Dolgarrog residents. As much background as possible.'

'Yes, sir.'

Ben slipped on his jacket and headed downstairs.

Chapter four

Ben left from the rear of the station, got behind the wheel of a dark Mondeo and headed for the A40. Thirty minutes later, he turned onto a narrow lane and navigated a long slow hill, tall hedges either side. Near the top he saw a woman and two children, standing on the verge picking what looked like hazelnuts. He slowed, pulled past them, and raised a hand. They waved back.

'Find anything useful in the council stuff, Sergeant?' Ben asked.

'Not so far. All I'm seeing are records concerning regular visits made by officials to ensure the rules were being followed.' He sighed. 'There's a lot of stuff that's above me. What's a "grey water reed bed"?'

'My understanding is that if you're off-grid you need to get rid of waste water. Reed beds will clean that water naturally.'

'How do you know that?' Jack asked.

'I read up on sustainable living last night. Spent some time looking at similar places on the net. I can't get over how lovely the interiors of the houses are.'

'I'd live underground for a couple of weeks,' Jack said. 'It'd be a great way to spend a summer, the kids would love it, but I'm not sure I could do it full time.'

Ben pulled up behind a white EV parked at the top of the lane in a lay-by. The detectives left their car and began walking down a footpath towards the settlement.

'Bugger,' Jack said, 'I didn't bring any wellies. Bloody weather. I hate rainy days.'

'At least it's backed off a little, but yes, wellies would have been useful.'

They picked their way along the path, dodging a myriad of deep puddles. After a few minutes, Ben stopped and pointed off to the right at a small group of individuals.

'What do you reckon is going on over there?' he asked.

Jack peered through the murky morning air. 'Dunno, guv, but that's where John took me yesterday to show off the header pool which powers the water turbine.'

Ben left the path and set off across the grass. As he drew closer, John Davis saw him, raised a hand and walked over to meet him.

'Morning,' John called. 'Didn't expect to see you again so soon, but I'm glad you're here.'

'Why, what's going on?' Ben said.

John groaned. 'The hydro system has been vandalised – not for the first time, unfortunately. Come and take a look.'

Ben followed the man and shuddered as cold water finally made its way through his leather shoes and soaked his socks. From the bank of the pool John pointed down the steep slope towards the turbine shed. The line of earthenware pipes had been smashed and scattered. Water spilling from the pool ran over the grass and created more mud before rejoining its original path. A young man, probably in his early thirties, was working at the base of the slope, almost knee-deep in mud, gathering and stacking unbroken sections of pipe.

'Bloody hell,' Ben said. 'That's a mess.'

'There's more damage inside the shed. I'll show you, but make sure you watch your step, boys.'

'You said your system has been attacked before?' Ben asked.

'Yeah, a couple of times over the last year. Bloody nuisance. We have enough to do without this.'

'Any idea who is responsible?' Jack asked.

'Not really. Some of the locals don't like us being here and we're too far out for it to be kids.'

'Anyone in particular?'

'Take your pick. The farmers aren't keen, even though none of them ever used this land for anything much, and the folk in the large house at the top of the valley definitely wish we weren't here.' He chuckled. 'They inherited the place about eighteen months ago. Ironically, it was their father who sold us the wood and land.'

'Why don't they like you being here?' Ben asked.

'They have a long list of petty gripes. We do our best to ignore them and thankfully they don't visit very often.'

After a slippery journey, John reached the door of the garage-sized cabin and pushed open the door. Ben and Jack followed him inside and at first glance the damage wasn't obvious.

'I'll give Will a shout,' John said. 'He can explain things for you. I'm better at growing things than building things.' He leaned out of the door. 'Will!' he yelled. 'Can you spare a couple of minutes, please?'

The young man dragged his boots out of the growing morass of mud, stamped his feet to dislodge the worst clumps and walked closer. He was about five foot ten, had short, wiry hair, and was wearing oil-stained jeans and a dirty, hi-vis, yellow jacket. He looked at the officers.

'Are you cops?' he asked.

Ben nodded and introduced himself and his sergeant. 'Can you tell us about the damage in here?' he asked. 'Explain what has been vandalised?'

'Yeah, no probs.' Will moved closer to the turbine and began to speak rapidly. 'See this? The observation panel has been smashed, made of Perspex so it's easy to break. Underneath is the propeller, with vanes attached. See those small, spoon-shaped things? Some of those have also been trashed and it looks as though the metal disc which holds the lot has been bent out of shape.' He pointed across the room to large metal boxes sitting close to the wall. 'Those are the batteries. Power runs through the cables from the turbine to the batteries and then on to the houses. The wires have been cut more than once. I'll need a whole new length. I can't solder so many breaks.'

'Can you fix it?' Jack asked.

Will nodded. 'I built it, so I can fix it. I can fix pretty much anything. We need new parts though, and they aren't cheap. Over five hundred quid to replace all this, and a day's work.' He rummaged in a toolbox, removed an adjustable spanner and began working at the bolts holding the observation panel onto the turbine.

'Before you get too involved,' Ben said, 'could we have a quick word about something else? We need to take a statement from you concerning the discovery of the skeleton in Badger's Bank yesterday.'

'No good asking me for one of those,' Will said without looking up. 'I can't read or write.'

'Not a problem,' Ben said. 'My sergeant can take care of that. He'll write down what you tell us and you can sign it. Could we go to your place? It'd probably be easier to talk there.'

Will shrugged. 'I guess. Can't do much with this until I've got the parts.' He returned the spanner to the toolbox and called John over. 'See this?' Will asked. 'You need to order a new cover, there's a serial number on the old one, and a new set of spoon-shaped cups. I can probably repair the metal disc they are attached to so don't order one of those, but I'll need another roll of wire too. Use the place we always do. Have it sent express delivery then I can get on tomorrow.'

'OK, Will, I'm on it,' John said. 'The rest of us will concentrate on resetting the pipework.'

Will nodded and glanced at the detectives. 'Come on then, I'll make some tea.'

Will left the turbine shed and strode off through the trees. Fallen leaves covered the muddy track making the going easier and as the group entered an open glade, sunshine broke through the clouds. At the back of the clearing was a log cabin, long and thin with windows at regular intervals. A black chimney pipe poked through a turf-covered roof, from which a thin trickle of wood smoke twisted skywards, before being dispersed through the trees by a gentle breeze. Will shoved open the door.

'Come in,' he said.

The officers sat next to a table covered in random bits and pieces – tools, rolls of electrical wire, a vice clamped to one end, a soldering iron close by; more of a workbench than a table. Will opened the front of a wood burner, put two brick-shaped lumps inside and closed the door, before lifting a kettle from the top.

'What do you run your stove on?' Jack asked. 'That didn't look like wood.'

'It isn't,' Will said. 'I make eco blocks from cardboard.' He placed a pair of chipped mugs on the bench. 'Sorry,' he said, 'got no milk but plenty of sugar. Help yourselves.' He perched on a tatty wooden stool. 'So, what do you want to ask me? I don't know anything about the bones you found. Wasn't me who buried them.'

'We're not suggesting you did,' Jack said. 'We just wondered if you saw anything strange going on at Badger's Bank over the last year or so. We don't think the skeleton was buried much longer than eighteen months ago.'

Will shook his head. 'I can't see the bank from here and don't go up there much. I'm usually working down here. There's always stuff to do.'

Ben sipped from his mug. 'When did you come to live here?' he asked.

'Seven years ago. When John and Sally began building Dolgarrog, they needed someone to help with the off-grid stuff. I used to live in a caravan a couple of miles away. One day they turned up, said they'd heard I could build solar panels, and asked if I could rig up something for them. They offered me a place on their land if I'd build and maintain the power supply.' He grinned. 'They didn't want the caravan on their land, so I built this place. Got more room here and no rent to pay. No-brainer.' He slurped loudly from his mug then got to his feet. 'I ought to get on,' he said. 'Even more to do now the turbine's been trashed.'

'John told us this has happened before. Any idea who might have done it?' Ben asked.

'Not really, but I wouldn't put it past those bastards in the big house, on the other side of the lane at the top of the valley. Not nice people.'

'Can you give us some names?' Jack asked.

'The Lloyds. Two sisters, Shirlee and Joanne, and their brother, Darryl. They were left the place by their dad.' Will sighed. 'Mr Lloyd – George that is – was a nice old guy; he often used to pop down to see what I was doing and have a cuppa. I miss him sometimes. Shame his useless kids aren't more like him.'

Ben stood. 'Thanks for the tea, Will,' he said. 'We'll let you get back to work, but if you think of anything about the bones, or have any thoughts about who vandalised the turbine, give us a ring.' Ben removed a card from his inside pocket and handed it to the younger man. 'Any one of the numbers on there will find me.'

'Ta. I'm OK with numbers, words are my problem. What about the statement?'

'We'll type it up and pop back with it, thanks.'

The detectives left the cabin and walked through the dripping wood, back towards the main settlement.

'What a fascinating character,' Jack said. 'Imagine being able to put all that kit together without knowing how to read. Amazing.'

'I agree with you. If he keeps on like that he'll end up a wealthy man. Right, let's have a quick word with John, then we'll find our way to the Lloyds' and hear what they have to say.'

Chapter five

Stacey made an omelette for lunch, sat at the table to eat and opened her laptop. A new email had arrived and she smiled when she saw it had been sent from Dolgarrog. Someone called Sally had written to confirm a booking on a foraging course at the end of the week. Sally had advised waterproof, "sensible" clothing and sturdy footwear. Stacey sent a short acknowledgement.

Lunch over, she carried her plate to the sink and noticed the rain had stopped. Craving some fresh air she laced on her boots, grabbed a jacket from the newel post and left her cottage by the front door.

At the top of the lane on the far side of the cattle grid, she paused to catch her breath and gazed out across thousands of acres of untamed mountain land. As autumn progressed the landscape had changed from shades of green to rusty browns and yellows; the grasses and bracken hunkered down in preparation for the cold of the oncoming winter. Stacey heard dogs barking and removed a small pair of binoculars from her pocket. She scanned the open country and spotted a farmer bouncing along on a quad, two Welsh collies galloping alongside as he checked on his flock. Having always enjoyed watching sheepdogs work, Stacey tracked the quad until it vanished from sight over a rise.

She replaced the binoculars with a camera and captured a series of panoramic shots, including some of a long stand of beech trees, golden leaves luminous in the sunshine. Glancing at her watch, she was surprised how much time had passed since she'd left home and began the trek off the mountain just as another squadron of rain-heavy clouds obliterated the sun. She made it back to her cosy kitchen before the rain arrived, put a kettle on the Aga and posted a couple of logs into the firebox as the phone rang. She picked up the handset.

'Stacey Logan.'

'So you are there,' Sam Jenkins grouched. 'I've been ringing all morning.'

Stacey chuckled. 'Must have dialled the wrong number then cos I was here for most of it.'

'Whatever.'

'So, what can I do for you?'

'I've got a couple of stories to pass on. A local woman has been in touch to tell me she has a book launch tomorrow evening just down the road from you. Might be worth covering.'

'OK, email me the details and I'll make sure I attend. What else?'

'An environmental group is planning a demo later in the month. I've got some contact numbers for you, there could be a story in it.'

'I'll put it on the list.'

'Anything newsworthy your end?'

'Not much. I'd like to write a piece on sustainable living – I'm visiting an off-grid settlement this week – next to an investigation into the buying up of agricultural land to plant trees to offset carbon emissions. Some locals are grumbling about recent purchases and calling it greenwashing.'

'It doesn't sound like much of a story to me.'

'Won't know until I've had some time to dig around.'

'Well, don't be long about it, readership is dropping off. We need some decent stories to put brakes on the decline. Keep in touch,' Sam said and disconnected the call.

Stacey poured boiling water into a small teapot, carried it to the table, woke her laptop and got to work.

* * *

After parking the car outside an imposing manor house on the edge of the Bannau Brycheiniog, Brecon Beacons, the detectives strode across an area of gravel and Jack rang the bell next to a large front door.

'Let's hope the Lloyds are in,' he said, 'and we make some progress. We still haven't been able to speak with all the residents down the hill yet.'

'Not a murder investigation though,' Ben said. 'We're still in the "making enquiries" stage regarding the bones. We can however investigate the recent vandalism and that gives us the perfect excuse to call here.'

Jack rang the bell again. 'Must have been foul play,' he said, 'otherwise the woman would have been buried in a graveyard, not halfway up a bloody mountain.'

Ben was about to answer when the door swung open and a man in his twenties looked out.

'Yes?' he asked.

Ben held up his warrant card. 'DCI James and DS Trent,' he said. 'Are you Darryl Lloyd?'

'Yes, that's me. What can I do for you?'

'We'd just like a quick chat, sir. Won't take up much of your time.'

'Can you give me a clue what about?'

'An incident on your neighbours' land. Dolgarrog.'

'Oh, that lot! Yes, come on in. I'll help you if I can.'

Darryl turned away from the door and led the way to a large living room, with enormous oil paintings on the walls and filled with antique furniture. He waved his hand towards a pair of sofas facing each other in front of a large fireplace. Ben and Jack had just taken their seats when the door opened and two women entered.

'Ah, my sisters,' Darryl said as the officers got back on their feet. 'Shirlee and Joanne.' He turned towards them. 'Two gentlemen from the police,' he said. 'Here to ask us about the eco-warriors living in the valley.'

'What about them?' Joanne said and perched on the arm of one of the sofas.

'They've been the victims of an act of vandalism,' Ben said. 'They own a water turbine system which was smashed up during the night. We wondered if you heard or saw anything.'

'Not likely,' Joanne said. 'We can't see their squalid little shacks from here.'

Ben bit his tongue. 'You can see the lane though. Perhaps you noticed a vehicle parked there last night?'

'No,' Shirlee said, 'we didn't see anything. We keep well away from those awful people.'

'Awful?' Jack asked. 'They seem pleasant enough to me.'

'They should never have been allowed to build there. God knows what the council was thinking when they gave them permission.'

'John and Sally, two of the founders, told us your father sold them the land. I guess he wasn't set against them like you are,' Ben said.

'They groomed him,' Joanne snapped. 'He was an old man and shouldn't have been making such huge decisions without input from us.'

'Are you saying he was mentally infirm when he sold the land?' Ben asked.

'Certainly confused,' Shirlee said.

'Not the fizziest drink in the fridge,' Joanne added. 'Anyway, from what I remember, those people put pressure on him.'

Darryl nodded. 'We didn't really know anything about the sale until after everything had been signed and sealed.'

'So how do you know he was pressurised?' Ben asked.

Joanne ignored the question. 'It devalued the estate without a doubt,' she said. 'Can't say having a commune of dropouts on our doorstep is enjoyable either.'

'So where were you all?' Jack asked.

'When?'

'When your father sold the land. Eight years ago, wasn't it?' Jack glanced up. 'How old are you, Darryl? Mid-twenties?'

'Twenty-four.'

'So if not here, where were you living when you were sixteen?'

'I was sent to boarding school in England when I was eleven and apart from holidays, didn't come back to live here until I was eighteen. My sisters were at uni.'

'What's the name of your school?'

'Orchard Lea Academy. Look, what's with all the questions? I thought you were here to talk about vandalism.'

'We are. We're just collecting some background information – important in any investigation.'

Ben cleared his throat. 'We are also looking into another matter you may be able to help us with.'

'Oh? What?' Darryl asked.

'This isn't the first time we've been out to Dolgarrog.'

Darryl shrugged. 'More vandalism I'm guessing.'

'No, actually, something much more interesting. A human skeleton was discovered. Buried close to the border with your land. Badger's Bank, to be exact.'

Shirlee's hand flew to her mouth. 'You found a body?' she squeaked.

Ben shook his head. 'No, just the skeleton. Our pathologist believes the bones had been excarnated before burial.'

'It means the flesh had been removed,' Jack said.

'I know what it means,' Shirlee snapped. 'I'm not stupid.'

'Do you have any information regarding this burial?' Ben asked.

'Of course not, I don't know anything about it,' Shirlee said.

'Nor me,' Joanne said. 'I'm not even sure I believe you.'

'We're not making it up,' Ben said and glanced at Darryl.

'Don't look at me,' the lad said. 'I've already told you. I wasn't here eight years ago.'

'The burial is more recent. Examination of the remains proves the bones haven't been in the ground much longer than a year or two.'

'How awful,' Joanne said. 'I hope you've asked the squatters where they were, what they were doing.'

Shirlee giggled. 'Human sacrifice perhaps. Witches and warlocks rather than warriors.'

The living room door swung open and a tall, thin, almost cadaverous man stomped in. He was dressed in a tweed jacket and wore a flat cap, greasy at the front. Jack's instincts kicked in when he spotted a shotgun in the newcomer's grip. Jack got to his feet, stood protectively in front of his boss and held his warrant card high.

'Police, sir. I must insist you put the gun down.'

'It isn't loaded, Constable.'

'I'm not a constable and I am ordering you to put the weapon down. Tell me who you are.'

The thin man shrugged and placed the gun on a pretty inlaid side table. 'I'm the estate gamekeeper, Gill Baird, and before you ask, the gun is licenced, all my guns are.' Gill looked past Jack to the Lloyds on the sofa. 'Everything OK in here?'

'We're fine, Gill,' Joanne said. 'They've been asking about some bones dug up on the hippies' land – human, apparently. Do you know anything about that?'

'Human bones you say? No, never heard anything about buried bones. There's no burial site on the estate. All your ancestors, your father included, are resting in the graveyard behind St David's Church at the bottom of the valley.'

'Might have been a suicide,' Shirlee said, 'bound to be, really. Years ago, people who killed themselves committed a mortal sin and couldn't be buried in consecrated land.'

'True,' Jack said, 'but normally they were placed just outside the churchyard walls, not miles away.'

Darryl got to his feet. 'I'm sorry, officers, but as nice as this has been, we're busy. The estate shoot is fast approaching and Gill and I have work to do. Busy time, autumn.'

'Mr Baird,' Ben said as he rose from the sofa, 'I guess your occupation means you are up and about at all hours. Did you see any vehicles parked in the lane last night? Hear anything in the valley?'

'No, everything was quiet. No one around that I saw.'

'You might want to keep your eyes open,' Jack said. 'Dolgarrog has managed to attract a vandal who has caused a fair amount of damage.'

'I'm surprised, we're a bit off the beaten track for stuff like that.' Gill stuck his hands in his pockets. 'Don't get taken in by that lot. They're all a bit economical with the truth.'

'In what respect?' Ben asked.

'You only have to consider how they bought the land and managed to build on it. Getting planning permission around here is like climbing Everest without oxygen – bloody difficult and often impossible, no matter how many times you try.'

'It doesn't sound as though you're enamoured with your neighbours.'

'That's because I'm not. Old Mr Lloyd was blinded by what he called their "vision". He was pressurised into selling the land.'

'We've already discussed that,' Darryl said. 'Now we really must get on and I'm sure the police officers are busy men too. I'll show them out and we can finalise our plans for the shoot.'

Darryl escorted the visitors to the front door, said his goodbyes and went back inside. Jack opened the car door and sat behind the wheel.

'Witches, warlocks and warriors? Really?' he asked as he fired up the engine.

'Too much *Dungeons & Dragons* at uni, I reckon,' Ben said. 'The Lloyds really don't like their neighbours though and I don't fully understand why not. They can't even see them from the house, or the garden, come to that.' Ben fastened his seatbelt. 'Mind dropping me at Noddfa?' he asked.

'No worries, guv. I'll even pick you up in the morning.'

'Hopefully by then, one of us will have worked out what's been going on in the valley over the last year or so.'

'Yeah, hopefully,' Jack said as he pulled away from the house, 'because I know something isn't right. I just don't know what… yet.'

Chapter six

Ben walked in through the back door of the cottage and discovered Stacey at the kitchen table, laptop in front of her, scribbled notes and scraps of paper scattered around. She looked up as he entered.

'Hey, Sherlock. Are you early?'

'A little, it feels like it's been a long day though.'

He draped his jacket on the back of a chair and poured a shot of whisky into his favourite glass, before slumping on the carver by the Aga. He pulled off his damp shoes and socks and replaced them with his old, leather slippers.

'What have you been doing?' Stacey asked as she tidied her mess and closed the laptop.

'Been out to the settlement to collect statements from the residents.' Ben went on to tell her about meeting Will North, the vandalism and his visit to the Lloyds.

'They don't sound very nice,' Stacey said getting up from the table. 'Is a stir-fry OK for supper?'

'Great, thanks. I can cook if you're busy.'

'No need, you'd make a mess of my kitchen.'

'Fair enough. Must say, I didn't warm to the Lloyds, any of them.'

'How much damage was done? Any clue who is responsible?'

'Will said he can fix it but it'll cost about five hundred quid. As to who the guilty party is' – he sighed – 'someone who doesn't like them living in the valley, I guess.'

'Like the Lloyds?'

'Possibly but I need to be able to prove that with evidence. Can't just nick them cos I don't like them.'

'Anything new on the bones?'

'Nope. I'm at Dolgarrog again first thing. I'll pop in to see Carrie on the way back through. Have you got anything planned?'

'I have as it happens,' Stacey said as she added noodles to a wok already containing diced chicken and vegetables. 'I'm over at Dolgarrog myself in the morning.'

'You're kidding, aren't you?'

'No, and it isn't what you think. I'm not going to doorstep anyone. A woman called Sally advertised a foraging course and I've booked a place.' Stacey added black bean sauce to the pan and stirred vigorously. 'It was going to be at the end of the week, but we brought it forward, the forecast isn't great. She didn't mention anything about the vandalism.'

'Have you finished?'

'What?' Stacey turned from the stove and stared at her partner.

'I don't like how this makes me feel, you muscling in on cases I'm working on, talking to people I've been talking to. Even chief inspectors can get into trouble for leaking to the press.'

Stacey tipped supper into a pair of shallow bowls and placed them on the table together with two pairs of chopsticks.

'Ben,' she said, 'we've been through this so many times I've lost count. I have never caused you any trouble because I know where the line is and make sure never to cross it.'

'You say that, but I'm not so sure. I tell you about the skeleton – never mind I shouldn't have – and a few days later you're taking a course on how to pick mushrooms. Stealth doorstepping, I call it. Make bloody sure you don't ask anyone about the bones.'

'Of course I won't, I've been at this a long time and… I know where the line is.'

They ate in silence. Ben collected a bottle of wine from the larder and poured two glasses.

'Has something happened?' Stacey asked. 'Have you got trouble at work?'

'Not that I know about and I want to keep it that way.'

More silence until Stacey asked, 'Fancy coming to a book launch with me tomorrow evening? We could have supper in the Neuadd?'

'It'll depend on how the day goes.'

'Just send a text then. If you are going to be late, I could bring a takeaway home with me. These things never usually go on for very long.'

'Yeah, I'll text you.'

* * *

The next morning, Stacey somehow managed to avoid bumping into Ben at Dolgarrog. She hadn't seen any cars on the lane when she'd parked, so reasoned he had probably got caught up at the station. She was glad. After their discussion the night before she didn't feel up to going another round. Sally had met her at the top edge of Dolgarrog and after introductions, and a cuppa in Sally and John's beautiful home, the one-on-one course got underway.

It began in the terraced vegetable plot, and Sally showed off an extensive herb patch and explained how she had gathered seeds from the wild to cultivate the same plants closer to home. After the garden, Sally headed beneath the trees of the wood, explaining how to find fungi and how to tell which were poisonous. A pair of pheasants suddenly burst out of a thicket and made Stacey squeak. Sally laughed.

'They do that to me all the time,' she said. 'There are so many around at this time of year.' She pointed towards the head of the valley. 'The manor house estate runs a shoot and always overstocks.' She bent at the waist and ran her fingers through the mass of fallen leaves. 'Look,' she said, 'beech nuts. It's been a good year for them.' She sifted through more leaves. 'So, Stacey, what do you do for a living?'

'I'm a journalist based at *The Mid Wales Times* in Brecon.'

'That's interesting. Have you always been a reporter?'

'Ever since I moved onto the Epynt, just outside Llanagethin village. Very different landscape to this. Our forests are mainly larch and spruce plantations, so your deciduous woodland makes a lovely change.'

'You do seem to be enjoying yourself. Let's walk to the edge of the trees and pick the last of the blackberries from the hedges. Fill our freezers with sunshine.'

A little later, when Stacey heard the first gunshot, she left the ground by at least six inches and a thick briar raked the back of her hand. She held the torn skin to her mouth and sucked beads of bright blood from the wound.

'I should have warned you,' Sally said. 'Sorry. Not only are most of our neighbours field sports enthusiasts, but one of the farmers sets up a crow scarer not far from the edge of the wood.'

'A crow scarer?' Stacey repeated.

'A device that fires at intervals to keep the birds away. They're perfectly legal, unfortunately.'

'Certainly disturbs the peace and quiet. Does it go on for long?'

'Hours sometimes.' She grinned. 'It's quieter in the houses thankfully, good insulation. John and Rhys tried to discuss it with the bloke but things didn't end well. Rhys really doesn't like being called a townie, he was born up north in a tiny village miles from anywhere.' Sally sighed. 'We receive a fair amount of insults.'

'Like what?'

'The usual, useless hippies, scroungers, work-shy, terrorists–'

'Why terrorists?'

Sally smiled. 'Your lot – the press – tend to refer to us as eco-warriors; it makes us sound like a foreign army, dangerous.'

Another loud explosion split the air and Stacey ducked.

'Let's go back into the wood,' Sally said.

Stacey nodded. 'Tell me more about your "warriors",' she said, 'and how the settlement was conceived. Did you all arrive at the same time?'

'Most of us have been here since the beginning but there have been some changes. Geraint, who lives on his own in the farthest house from the veggie plot, arrived about a year ago. The original members had to leave for family reasons and Geraint took over their place. Our oldest resident died a couple of years ago and left her home to her nephew, Matt. He moved in with his partner, Maxine – both in their twenties and committed activists. They've been involved in many protests. They're climbers so they get a kick out of scaling enormous, prominent buildings, to unfurl banners warning folk about the climate emergency – amongst other things. You should meet them, maybe write an article.'

'I'd like that, thanks,' Stacey said.

Sally suddenly stopped walking and beneath a small patch of larch, pointed out three oversized fungi. The caps were a rusty brown and looked velvety, like mole fur, supported by broad, trunk-like stems as thick as Stacey's wrist.

'Look at those,' Sally said. 'Penny buns, my favourite. Some people know them as ceps, Latin name *Boletus edulis*. We'll take these back and cook them for lunch.' She removed a knife from her pocket and sliced through the stems just above the soil so as not to damage the subterranean mycelium. She tucked the treats into her wicker basket. 'After we've eaten, we'll pay Matt and Maxine a visit. You'll enjoy talking with them.'

'I'm sure I will, and I'm really glad I spotted your ad. This is a great day, just what I needed.'

Chapter seven

Once again, Ben and Jack stood facing Carrie in the pathology lab, the recovered skeleton resting between them on an examination table.

'Still no DNA then?' Ben asked.

'Sadly not,' Carrie said, 'but I haven't given up. A colleague of mine from the lab says he'll pop over tomorrow and take a look. A second pair of eyes never goes amiss.'

'So you've nothing to tell us?'

Carrie smiled. 'I didn't say that. Let me show you something I've set up on the microscope.' She crossed the room, put her eyes to the lenses and checked the image then waved Ben closer.

He bent, copied her actions and peered into the scope.

'You'll have to give me a clue what I'm looking at,' he said. 'Science wasn't my thing at school.'

'Which is why you became a copper,' Carrie teased. 'Can you see three strands, side by side at a forty-five-degree angle?'

'Yeah, I see them. What are they?'

'Fox hairs. I found them stuck on the femur.'

'Where do you think they came from?' Jack asked. 'Were they in the soil?'

'Wait for the reveal, Sergeant.' She winked at him. 'Finding the hair sent my investigations in a completely different direction. Come back to the table. I've something else to show you.' She handed Ben a magnifying lens. 'Concentrate on the femur near the top. Tell me what you see.'

Ben did as she asked. He bent low over the table and held the lens above the bones, moving it up and down to obtain the best focus.

'Well,' he said, 'bone obviously, stained a deep brown by the soil, but nothing… oh, hang on. I can see some lighter marks, like faint scratches.' He worked his way along the bone towards the knee cap. 'There's a fair few. What's caused them? Insects? Something that happened during the removal of the flesh?'

'Not insects, but definitely something to do with the excarnation.'

'So how was it done?' Jack asked. 'Acid bath or surgical?'

Ben paled and swallowed hard.

'Neither. More likely red kites and ravens, with the odd fox thrown in.'

'Someone fed her to the local wildlife?' Jack asked.

Carrie laughed. 'Highly unlikely. No, I think she died somewhere out in the open, somewhere quiet, a mountain perhaps. After her death, nature did what it does and began cleaning up. The marks on the bones were left by scavengers – teeth, beaks, and claws.'

'Misadventure?' Ben asked. 'Natural causes? What?'

Carrie shrugged. 'Not a clue. It could still be murder but until we can identify the woman, the investigation goes nowhere.'

'We're doing what we can, but all we've been able to confirm is that if she went missing locally, no one reported the fact.'

'Which could point to a killing,' Jack said, 'rather than her getting lost on a mountain and having her bones picked clean. She could have been dumped, or even killed where she fell and we've very little chance of discovering where that was.'

'We're following up on your idea about her being an ex-prisoner.' Ben sighed. 'Seems HMP record-keeping isn't the best but at least we know what we're looking for.'

'All we can do is our best,' Carrie said and stripped off her gloves. 'I'm hoping my friend will be able to tell us more; not only is he mister go-to for DNA sampling, but a bit of a bone-nut too. I can't do any more, but he might. I'll keep you informed.'

'Thanks,' Ben said. 'We'll do the same. It always disturbs me, unreported missing persons and unnamed, unclaimed bodies.'

'I'm with you on that. Time for a coffee?'

'Not really, but thanks for the offer. We'll talk again soon.'

* * *

Stacey had been right – the book launch was well attended but didn't go on for long. She shook hands at the door with the smiling author and returned to her car just after eight. She saw a text from Ben saying he was busy at work and would stay the night at his place so she dialled Heidi's number.

'Hey, you,' she said when Heidi picked up.

'You said you were coming over to the house days ago,' Heidi grumbled, 'and I haven't seen you yet.'

'Sorry, stuff going on… not so much work-wise though.'

'Oh?'

'This and that, all very boring.' Stacey changed the subject. 'The foraging course was great, you should have come with me.'

'Where are you now?'

'Just about to drive home for a quiet evening on my lonesome.'

'That doesn't sound much fun, why not get yourself over here? Erica has some leave and it's about time we all got together. Been a while.'

Heidi and Erica had met when Heidi had joined the force as a newly recruited DC. When Heidi walked away from the job, Erica had stayed on and they had married almost a year ago.

'I don't know…'

'Rubbish! Go home, pack a bag and leave a note. If you get a move on, you'll be here in time for the bedtime brandy snifter.'

'Go on then, you've convinced me. I'll be there before ten.'

Nearly an hour and a half later, Stacey turned onto the narrow lane and soon pulled up behind Heidi's truck. Some of the lights were on in the building and made the place look even more like a giant doll's house. Stacey tooted the horn, then gathered her belongings and walked up to the front door. Heidi and Erica stood on the steps, arms around each other's waists.

Stacey smiled. 'The perfect picture of married life.'

Erica stepped forward and hugged her friend. 'Don't be fooled,' she said.

Stacey returned the hug. 'Nonsense. Heidi's smiling and she doesn't do that often.'

'You're letting the heat out,' Heidi grumbled and took hold of Stacey's bags. 'Go to the library. There's a fire in there, just about the warmest place in the house.'

The women settled themselves in front of the large fireplace sitting next to each other on a long Chesterfield. They held balloons of brandy and stretched their feet out towards the flames.

'So,' Stacey said, 'all OK with you two? You should be in your honeymoon period, still a couple of months until your first anniversary.'

'We are pretty much,' Heidi said. 'It's Erica's job that's causing friction. Unpredictable shifts, double shifts, and it's dangerous being a copper.'

'I'm perfectly safe,' Erica said. 'Rank and file protect sergeants if there's trouble.' She grinned. 'That and the fact we stand at the back.'

'You should resign,' Heidi said, 'and help me run this place.'

'I know, you've said before, but I don't want to be a kept woman.'

Heidi smiled and brushed her fingers across Erica's cheek. 'Bad luck,' she said. 'You're my wife and I'm definitely keeping you.' She laughed. 'Chained up in the cellar if I have to.'

'Too much information,' Stacey said and got to her feet. 'Fancy a trip to Dolgarrog in the morning? A walk would do us good. I've got an open pass and I'd like you to meet my new friend Sally.'

'Yeah, why not? No rain forecast.'

'Brilliant. Now off to the cellar, both of you, but be warned, I'm on breakfast duty. If you're not at the table by eight thirty, I'll eat everything myself. Sleep well, ladies.'

Stacey blew kisses then left the library and climbed the wide staircase to her room at the front of the house. She cracked open the sash window and a damp, slightly mushroomy smell blew inside the room, the scent of autumn. She cleaned her teeth in the en suite, changed into pyjamas, and finally slipped into a bed with linen sheets, woollen blankets and an old-fashioned quilt affair on the top. She listened to the breeze outside, rustling brown oak leaves on a nearby tree and the occasional scream of a fox calling for a mate, and soon fell asleep.

Chapter eight

After breakfast the next morning, and a quick call to Sally to warn her of their visit, the women left the house and Heidi drove her truck to the bottom of the long, wooded valley. Sally had told Stacey there was a footpath from a lane below the trees and that it was a pleasant walk up to the houses. She also invited her visitors to lunch and Stacey gladly accepted.

'The estate has a shoot today,' Sally had warned, 'you'll hear the guns but they'll be miles away, so don't be concerned.'

The weather wasn't as warm as the last few days. A fine white mist crawled between the trees like dragon breath, and a large murder of crows sailed above the wood cawing loudly. Heidi locked her truck and Stacey led the way onto the footpath at the end of the wooded valley. She walked in front, and Heidi and Erica held hands behind her.

'This really is a lovely spot,' Erica said. 'Good idea of yours to come walking, Stacey, especially after that enormous breakfast.'

'Work on our appetites for the promised lunch,' Heidi said. 'I'm looking forward to meeting the hobbits.'

The group ambled, rather than walked. Stacey showed off her new skill of fungi identification, and even picked a few to take to Sally. The occasional barrage of shotgun fire disturbed the peace and quiet, but the racket wasn't constant. The women moved steadily through the trees and paused in a large, sunny glade to catch their breath. Suddenly, a single shot rang out; it sounded closer and different to the blasts of shotguns. Stacey paused to look back at her friends and saw Erica stumble and fall. She watched as Heidi dropped to her knees by her wife's side, and knew something was very wrong. Stacey ran back, saw Heidi place a hand on Erica's throat and spotted a crimson splash on Erica's chest. Blood! Without taking her eyes off Heidi, Stacey snatched her phone from her pocket and stabbed at the screen. Her call was answered quickly.

'Ben,' she said. 'Where are you?'

'Dolgarrog.'

'We're in the wood below you. Erica's been shot. It looks bad and you need to be here.'

The phone slipped from Stacey's fingers as she knelt on the damp earth facing Heidi, Erica lying on a thick carpet of leaves between them. Stacey reached out, gently took hold of Heidi's tiny hand and lifted it from Erica's throat.

'Heidi,' she said quietly. 'Look at me, *cariad*.' She squeezed her friend's hand, noticing how cold the skin was. 'Look at me and take a breath.'

Heidi did neither. She tore her hand away and replaced it on her wife's neck. Stacey was wondering if she should tap Heidi's cheeks, pull her away, do something, when Jack crashed into the clearing, Ben on his heels. They skidded to a halt and with horror in their eyes, surveyed the shocking scene. Jack knelt close to Erica's body, placed two fingers next to Heidi's hand and hunted for a pulse. He glanced up, caught Ben's gaze and gently shook his head. Ben moved a couple of steps away, yanked a phone from his pocket and called in the troops. That done, he walked back to the group and placed his hands on Stacey's shoulders.

'Pumpkin,' he said. 'Are you or Heidi injured?'

Stacey shook her head, her eyes still fixed on Heidi's face.

'Stand up and move back a little.' Ben slipped his hands beneath her arms. 'Up you come now.'

With Ben's help Stacey made it to her feet. The ground beneath her boots seemed to shiver and shake and she stumbled into him.

'Erica…' she said.

'This way,' Ben said. 'Sit on this lump of rock and stay here, OK? I need to help Jack.'

Satisfied she would do what he'd asked, he walked back to the gruesome scene, blinking moisture from his eyes as he stared at his fallen colleague. Erica was stretched out on golden leaves, her pale skin and almost black hair a striking contrast. She was dressed in a bright orange, long-sleeved T-shirt, and on the left side of her chest, a large, ominous, red circle resembled a fiery sun. The image burned itself into Ben's brain and he knew it would haunt him as long as he drew breath. He heard a sound, not unlike a herd of Welsh black cattle approaching at speed, and turned to see Tegan and Elsa, together with four uniformed officers, running towards him, Ollie at the rear of the pack. A couple of metres away, they halted en masse and froze. Ben cleared his throat.

'Is this all of you?' he asked.

'No, sir,' Elsa said. 'The pathologist is on her way, more uniforms too, and an ambulance parked up on the lane.'

Ollie moved closer. 'What the fuck… is she…'

'Yes,' Ben said, 'she is. Now we must do our jobs.' He bent low, tucked a finger beneath Heidi's chin and encouraged her to look up. Her pale grey eyes bored into his and turned his soul to ice. 'Heidi. Tell me, how many shots?'

'One,' she said, her voice small and tight. 'Rifle.' She turned her head towards the crest of the hill on the east of the valley. 'Came from up there.'

'Did you see anyone?'

'No. As I said, somewhere up there.' She flapped a hand at the ridge and pinched the bridge of her nose. She suddenly sprang to her feet and fixed Ben in her gaze. 'Make sure you take care of Erica,' she said, then she turned and began to run in the direction she'd indicated.

'Heidi! No!' Ben yelled but she didn't break her stride. 'Jack. Go with her!'

Jack set off hoping he could keep up. His legs were much longer than Heidi's, but being so small she didn't have to move a bulk like his own. He didn't shout her name. He knew nothing would stop her and that he needed the breath.

Ben watched him go. A female officer perched on the rock next to Stacey and draped an arm around her shoulders. Ben moved back to Erica and squatted on his heels. He knew he shouldn't touch her, not without gloves, but reached out anyway and gently closed her eyes, his brain struggling to make sense of the new reality he found himself in. He'd worked with Erica many times in the past, she'd been a great cop. He covered his eyes with his hand and left it there until he heard his name called.

'Ben?'

He looked up and saw Carrie Salmon staring down at him. He gave his face a scrub and got to his feet. Carrie placed a hand on his arm.

'Why not sit with Stacey,' she suggested, 'while I spend some time with Erica? Go on, you'll be in the way here.'

She nudged him gently and he took a few steps towards his partner just as a high-pitched child's scream barrelled down the valley and sliced through the air between the trees. Ben froze. He snatched a quick reassuring glance at Stacey, then ordered Ollie and two uniformed officers to follow him. The distress siren sounded again and Ben quickened his pace. Brambles snagged his trousers and thorns pierced his skin but he didn't feel them.

Bursting out of the wood, he scanned the slope. The terraced garden was empty and a couple of round front doors stood open. He caught sight of movement by the turbine shed, saw figures standing by the door. He hesitated. Had another act of vandalism caused the scream? The scene in the wood flashed through his mind and he knew that's where he should be, then another wail filled the valley so he ran on up the slope.

By the time he reached the doorway of the wooden building, his lungs were burning, throat desert-dry as he gasped for breath. He rested a hand on the door jamb to steady himself and looked inside. He saw a dark puddle of blood on the floor and a man face down in the centre. Ben stepped through the door and saw three more men in a tight group. John and Rhys stood on each side of a smaller, younger man with blood on one of his hands, and grasped his arms tightly. On the floor, close to the turbine was a large hammer. Trying to kick-start his brain, Ben glanced back out through the open door and saw Seren, arms wrapped around Sally's waist, face buried deep in her mother's woolly jumper. Ben turned his attention back towards the awful scene.

'Who's that on the floor?' he asked.

'Will North,' John said. 'Looks like he was repairing the turbine when this toe-rag' – he shook the younger man angrily – 'smashed him in the head with a fucking lump hammer. This is Geraint, lives in the last house.'

Maxine suddenly appeared, a first aid kit clasped in her hands, her partner Matt with her. She squatted on the floor trying to avoid the sticky puddle and gently checked for a pulse.

'Is he dead?' Ben asked.

'Not quite,' Maxine said, opening the kit and removing a bundle of sterile pads to press against a large wound. 'His breathing isn't great and it's slowing. He's lost a massive amount of blood and needs an ambulance, right now!'

'There's one up on the lane,' Ben said.

'I'll go and fetch them,' Matt said, anxious to leave the horror inside the shed.

Ben stepped closer to Geraint, still held tightly by Rhys and John, and glared at the young man.

'Is that right? You hit Will with a hammer?' he asked.

'Of course not, he was my friend. I don't even kill wasps, never mind people.'

'Why did you have the hammer in your hand?'

'I heard Seren scream. I was the first adult here.' He swallowed. 'I saw Will, and on the floor, near the blood, was a hammer.'

'You're saying you picked it up? Why did you do that?'

Geraint shrugged. 'I'm not sure.'

Ollie spoke quietly into Ben's ear. 'Air ambulance on the way, sir, paramedics outside. We should nick that boy and get him to the station.'

Ben nodded. 'I agree. Read him his rights and have one of the uniforms take him back to base. Any word from Carrie? Jack? Anyone?'

'No, sir.'

Ben stepped outside. Geraint was taken from the shed in handcuffs and marched up the hill as paramedics from the ambulance on the lane rushed in. Ben tried ringing Jack but his call went straight to voicemail. Once again, Ollie stepped closer.

'I can handle this, sir,' he said. 'I know you want to be down there.' He nodded towards the wood. 'Reinforcements are on the way, so go back to Erica. Not much to do here as soon as Will has been taken to hospital, other than protect the scene.' He took a deep breath. 'Do you think he'll make it?'

'I sincerely hope so,' Ben said, 'so he can tell us who did this to him.'

'I reckon we've already got the scumbag in custody. Go on, sir. Like I said, I can handle this.'

Ben nodded and headed back down the grassy slope to the wood. As he moved beneath the trees, he heard the thump-thump of rotor blades as the helicopter pilot searched for somewhere flat to land. When Ben entered the clearing it didn't seem as though much had changed. Elsa and Carrie still knelt by Erica's body, Stacey and the female officer were still perched on the rock. He walked closer, brushed a kiss on his partner's cheek, then went to stand next to Erica's feet.

'Elsa, any sign of Jack or Heidi?' he asked.

'No, sir,' she said.

'What can you tell me, Carrie?'

'Single rifle shot to the heart. Probably died before she hit the ground,' Carrie said. 'No exit wound so the bullet is still inside.'

'We should move her,' Ben said. 'There's been a serious incident in the settlement and things are going to get busy. I don't want the others to see her like this.'

'Nor me,' Carrie said. 'Was that the air ambulance I heard?'

Ben nodded.

Carrie addressed one of the uniformed officers. 'Leg it up the hill, Constable. Fetch the paramedics who arrived in the ambulance and tell them to bring a stretcher. Don't hang about and don't speak about what's happening here to anyone. Got it?'

'Yes, ma'am,' he said and hurried away.

Carrie recorded the scene on a camera, and then removed her coat and spread it gently over Erica's upper body and face. She got to her feet and stood next to Ben.

'No need for the white tent,' she said, 'any evidence will be with her. Do you know much about what happened yet?'

'Heidi said she'd been shot by a rifle, fired from the ridge.' Ben pointed to the east.

'Heidi was with her? Oh my God! So where is Heidi now?'

Ben shrugged. 'She ran off, up the side of the valley, probably thought she could catch the killer. I sent Jack after her.'

'Any word?'

Ben shook his head.

'What happened in the settlement?'

Ben brought her up to date while they waited. The ambulance crew soon arrived and they lifted Erica gently inside a body bag which they loaded onto the stretcher, then began the long trek up to the lane. Carrie knelt and searched the patch of leaves where the body had lain but came up empty-handed. Once again she placed a gentle hand on Ben's arm.

'If you want my advice, you should put Elsa in charge here and take Stacey up to Dolgarrog. You need to get in touch with Jack and drink at least one cup of strong, sweet tea – you're the colour of leftover pasta. Sort yourself out, Ben, you're no good in this state.'

'No, I can't. I must stay here.'

'No, Ben. There's nothing you can do for Erica right now, so take Stacey away from this place and go and help the living.'

Chapter nine

Ben and Stacey walked up to the settlement, his arm around her waist. Sally was in the garden and ran to meet them. 'Oh,' she said, 'are you two together? I didn't realise. Are you OK? Is it true that your friend has been shot?'

'How do you know that?' Ben asked.

'We heard the guys in uniform talking, but we'd already guessed something awful had happened in the wood when so many coppers turned up.'

'I can't talk about it,' Ben said. 'Not yet. I have an important call to make and I need to track down my sergeant. Would you take care of Stacey for me, please?'

'Of course, bring her to the house.'

'Where's John?'

'He went in the helicopter with Will. Seren is with the other girls and Janet is looking after them all.'

Sally pushed open her front door. Ben helped Stacey down the steps and onto the sofa. He bent low and wrapped his arms around her.

'You OK, Pumpkin?'

'I'm not sure,' she said, voice quavering. 'Where's Heidi?'

'With Jack. I'm about to go and find them. Sally will make tea and you must wait here with her. Please don't wander off, it'll make things more difficult if I don't know where you are. I want to be sure you're safe. Do you understand?'

Stacey nodded. 'I'll wait here for you.'

'Good.' Ben kissed her forehead and straightened up. 'Thanks for this, Sally. I'll be back as soon as I can.'

'No rush,' Sally said and handed Stacey a mug of tea. 'She'll be fine here with me.'

Ben left the house and returned to the sunshine. He walked a little way away, pulled out his phone and tapped the screen. While he waited for his call to Heidi's father to be answered, he tried to work out what he was going to say.

'Milebrook Manor,' a deep male voice said. 'Frederick Holtz speaking.'

'Freddie. Morning. DCI Ben James here.'

'Ben. Good morning to you. This is a pleasant surprise.'

'No, sir. I'm afraid it isn't.' Ben's voice stuck in his throat. 'It really isn't.'

'My, dear man, what's wrong?'

'I have some terrible news and I'm very sorry.' Ben took a deep breath. 'DS Erica Bevan was shot less than an hour ago.'

'Christ! I wasn't expecting that. How is she?'

'I'm so sorry, she died at the scene and is on her way to the morgue in Brecon.'

'How is my daughter? Is she with you?'

Ben groaned. 'No, sir. Heidi was with Erica and Stacey when the shooting took place. She ran off to look for the shooter. Jack Trent went after her.' Ben rubbed his eyes. 'To be honest I don't really know how she is, but you should be here.'

'I'll leave immediately. Where will Heidi be? At her place in Brecon or at the house near Abergavenny?'

'Once I've tracked her down I'm planning to take her to Stacey's cottage in Llanagethin.'

'Right. Good plan. I'll meet you there.'

'I have no idea how long I'll be, there's other stuff going on. You'll find a key to the back door beneath the watering can in the greenhouse. If you arrive first, let yourself in. I'll be in touch again as soon as I can.'

'Is there anything I can do to help?'

'No, thanks, Freddie, just get yourself over to Wales.'

Ben ended the call, then tried Jack's mobile number and was surprised when he answered.

'Yes, guv.'

'Where are you?'

'Down on the bottom lane beneath the wood. Heidi's with me and we're about to get in her truck and drive up to you.'

'Stay where you are. I'll send one of the uniforms to you with Stacey. I want you to drive the girls to Noddfa. Freddie Holtz is on his way over from the Cotswolds. Might be a couple of hours before he arrives.'

'Yeah, I've got it.'

'How is Heidi?'

Jack lowered his voice. 'Not great.'

'Where did you find her?'

'Top of the ridge on her hands and knees in the grass.'

'Did she say anything?'

'Nothing. It took me a while to get her on her feet. I could see her truck from where we were and it seemed the easiest option to walk downhill rather than drag her up to Dolgarrog.'

'Probably right. Just sit tight, then drive the girls to Noddfa and stay there. I've got my hands full here, but I'll follow you over as soon as I can.'

The conversation stalled until Jack asked, 'How are you doing, guv? You OK?'

Ben caught his breath. 'No, not really, but we need to find whoever killed our friend. I can't worry about myself until we've done that.'

'There is something,' Jack said. 'I don't know how she did it, but Heidi found a spent cartridge, had it in her fist. Good chance it might have come from the rifle used.'

'Bloody amazing!'

'Fired from a .22. You need to round up the shooting party, we might get lucky. Could have been a terrible accident.'

'I'm not convinced. Take care of them, Jack. Might be hours before I can get to you.'

'No worries, guv. See you later.'

Ben hung up and arranged for Stacey to be driven to Jack, then headed back towards the turbine shed. Blue-and-white tape had been strung across the path and, as he approached, a constable lifted it high so Ben could duck underneath. He nodded his thanks and walked on. Ollie stood by the door, face grim and looking as though he had aged ten years.

'Where are we with this, Ollie?' Ben asked.

'Victim on his way to hospital, suspect on his way to Brecon nick.' He jerked his head towards the shed. 'Carrie Salmon's inside taking a look, SOCO on the way. The hammer has been bagged and tagged. All under control.'

'Good job. Where's Rhys?'

'I sent the residents home, can't have random people wandering about.'

'Did he say much?'

'He only repeated how he'd seen Geraint with the hammer in his hand, standing over Will.'

'OK. I've spoken with DS Trent. He has Heidi and is going to drive her and Stacey to Llanagethin, which means I'm an officer down. So… this is your crime scene. You've made a bloody good start, so don't cock it up. I want Elsa Duffin with me taking statements – if she's up to it.' Ben scrubbed miserably at his face. 'Such a fucking awful thing to have happened,' he mumbled.

'Sorry, sir?'

'Nothing. If you hear from Elsa before me, let her know where I am.' He sighed. 'We also need to question the members of the shooting party. Get some of the uniforms on to it and make sure no one leaves the estate until we have their details.'

Ollie nodded and Ben turned, ducked back beneath the tape and went in search of Rhys Evans. It didn't take long before he found him with Matt and Maxine, sitting on a bench outside their home. Rhys spotted Ben and got to his feet.

'Do you know how Will is?' he asked.

Ben shook his head. 'No, he's been taken to Hereford County Hospital.'

'If he dies,' Rhys said, 'I want some time alone with Geraint. I didn't like him when he moved in, it seems I was right not to. How can anyone smash someone's head in with a hammer?'

'Geraint said he wasn't responsible.'

'Course he did! You wouldn't admit doing something like that.'

'Maybe not, but we'll question him at the station. What I need to do now is start collecting evidence and I can begin by taking your statement.'

Maxine handed Ben a mug of tea as he removed a notebook and pen from his pocket. He glanced up at Rhys.

'So,' he said, 'tell me everything that happened after you heard Seren scream.'

* * *

Nearly three hours later, Ben gathered his officers together. He could see how tired they were so sent his team home to rest and take some time to process the events of the day. On the walk up to his car, he popped in on Sally to let her know what was happening.

'Have you heard anything from John?' Ben asked.

'Just a quick call. Will survived the trip and was sent straight to surgery.'

Ben nodded. 'What can you tell me about Geraint? Could he have done this?'

'I can't see why he would. I haven't known him as long as the others, but from what I've seen he's very sensitive and a bit of a loner.' She smiled. 'Not in a creepy way, more like a hermit way.'

'John told us he found Geraint standing over Will holding the hammer.'

'I have no idea about that, sorry.'

'OK,' Ben said. 'Thanks for taking care of Stacey. I'm off now but will be back in the morning. You've got my number so if you need anything, call.'

Ben ducked beneath the low lintel and walked up to his car on the top lane. He opened the door, slipped behind the steering wheel and rested his forehead on the leather cover, before raising his eyes and staring into the gathering dusk. The temperature had dropped as soon as the sun began its descent and the evening star became visible. He rubbed his face and realised he was sweating. He struggled to believe Erica was so suddenly gone and might never have moved if his mobile hadn't vibrated.

'DCI James,' he said.

'Jack here, guv.'

'Everything OK at Noddfa?'

'About as you'd expect it to be given the circumstances. Freddie has arrived, but to be candid, Heidi doesn't seem to be doing very well.' He sighed. 'Difficult to be sure though as she hasn't really said anything.'

'And Stacey?'

'Better than Heidi, but not great. I just wanted to check in. Carrie Salmon called here on her way home and collected the brass casing. She said she'll deliver it to the lab and convince them to work on it overnight, so that's something. How is it with you?'

'I'm about to leave Dolgarrog. I'll fill you in when I get there.'

'OK, guv.'

Ben tucked his phone away, started the car, and began the drive through the Bannau Brycheiniog to the cottage on the Epynt.

Chapter ten

Ben pushed open the back door quietly and saw Jack, a white tea towel tucked into his belt, standing by the Aga stirring a large pot. He glanced up and pulled a face.

'Bloody hell, guv, you don't look great. Sit down and I'll pour you a drink.'

Ben sat. 'How are things here?' he asked.

'Much the same. I was about to find out if anyone wanted some of this chilli. No rice though, I'm crap at cooking rice so there are some jacket spuds in the oven.'

Ben gulped from his glass and removed his jacket. 'I'll go and ask.' He padded down the hall and pushed open the door of the living room.

Freddie Holtz was sitting in an armchair on one side of the fireplace, Heidi curled in the other wrapped in a blanket. Stacey, who was lying on the squashy sofa, sat up as Ben entered.

'Hello,' Ben said. 'How are you all doing?'

'Surviving,' Stacey said, 'but I'm worried about Heidi, she still hasn't said much.'

'It's shock,' Freddie said. 'She just needs some time.'

'What about calling a doctor?' Ben asked.

'No, thanks. She's strong and doesn't need a doctor.'

Ben thought he sounded as though he was trying to convince himself. 'Jack's cooked supper,' he said. 'Why not come to the kitchen? You may not feel like eating but it will help.'

Freddie offered a weak smile, hauled himself out of the chair and took Heidi's hand. 'Come with us, darling girl.'

Heidi didn't stand but turned her head to look at Ben.

'Where is she?' she asked, her voice sandpaper scratchy.

'With Carrie in Brecon,' Ben said. 'The shell casing is with ballistics. Amazing you found it.'

'Have you recovered the weapon?'

'Not yet. We're planning to question those who attended the shoot first thing tomorrow. By then, I'm hoping we'll have the ballistic report.'

'She wasn't shot by accident!'

'How do you know she wasn't?'

'A marksman made that shot with a rifle, not some moron blasting shots at game birds.'

'Who would shoot Erica?'

Heidi surged to her feet. 'How would I know who shot my wife?' She stepped closer to Ben. 'One thing's certain, you better find who did this terrible thing before I do.'

'Heidi,' Freddie said, 'you know Ben. He's a good copper and he's got Jack by his side. They'll find Erica's killer but you need to give them some space to investigate this business properly.'

Heidi glared at her father and dropped back onto her chair. 'I loved her. Nothing made sense until I met her.' She pulled her feet up beneath her, wrapped her arms around her petite body and closed her eyes.

Stacey got to her feet. 'Ben, take Freddie to the kitchen, feed him supper, and ask Jack to bring two bowls of food in here.'

Ben nodded and left the room with Freddie. Stacey perched on the arm of Heidi's chair and gently stroked her friend's short hair.

'I won't leave you alone with this,' she said, 'I promise. I'll be right by your side for as long as you want me there.

Freddie's right, you are strong, probably the strongest person I've ever met. You will get through this.'

The door opened and Jack walked in carrying a tray which held two bowls of chilli, two glasses of brandy and some bread and butter.

'No spuds, I'm afraid,' he said. 'Turns out I'm pretty crap at cooking those too. Give me a shout if you need anything else.'

'Thanks, Jack,' Stacey said.

He backed out of the room and closed the door. Stacey handed Heidi a glass and she gulped down the spirit.

'I can't eat anything,' Heidi said, 'but I need to lie down. I'll stay in here tonight.'

'I'll keep you company.'

'I know you mean well, Stace, but no thanks. I just need to be alone with this for a little while.' Heidi held up her hand. 'Before you ask, yes, I am sure.' She helped herself to the second brandy.

'OK. I'll fetch a quilt and if you need anything in the night, you must call me.'

Heidi nodded. 'I will.'

Stacey delivered the bedding to the living room. She forced herself not to fuss and returned the food to the kitchen. Ben looked up as she shuffled in.

'Where's Heidi?' Freddie asked.

'She's settled herself in the living room, says she needs some time alone.'

'Perhaps I should keep her company?'

'I think you should leave her.' Stacey rubbed her eyes. 'After all, she's lost her first and only love in utterly tragic circumstances.'

Freddie nodded sadly.

'Sit down, Pumpkin,' Ben said. 'You look exhausted.'

He slid a bowl of chilli across the table and with little enthusiasm she dipped a piece of bread into the sauce.

'We should contact Erica's family,' she said. 'Tell them what has happened.'

Ben shook his head. 'From what Erica said in the past, they more or less disowned her when she joined the force. Her folks had a very poor opinion of the police. One of their number was clobbered by a copper policing a picket line during the miners' strike.' Ben sighed heavily. 'Heidi's next of kin; it's her decision, not ours.'

Ben's mobile vibrated on the wooden table and he answered the call.

'Evening, Sally. Something up?'

'Hi, Ben. No, we're OK, just to let you know John is home from Hereford.'

'How's Will doing?'

'He's out of surgery but has been placed in a medically induced coma. The doctors won't know if he's suffered any significant brain damage until they begin to wake him up, and that won't be for a while yet.'

'Thanks for the update. I'm busy with interviews in the morning, but as soon as I'm done I'll come and see you.'

'How is Stacey doing?'

'Better, thanks. Try to get some rest, Sally, and we'll talk tomorrow.'

'Yeah, I will. Good night.'

Chapter eleven

At exactly eight o'clock the next morning, Ollie Langdon led the prisoner into interview room one at Brecon police station. Ollie removed Geraint's handcuffs and he sat as Jack set the recording machine in motion. Ben was surprised to see that Geraint appeared calm and well rested. He'd even smiled at the officers and wished them a good morning as he was brought in.

Once Jack had stated the date, time and names of those present in the room, Ben began the interview. 'Before we really get going, do you understand why you are here?'

'I do, yes.'

'Is there anything you'd like to tell us regarding your arrest?'

Geraint smiled. 'Only that I'm not particularly enjoying the experience.'

'No need to be cocky,' Jack snapped.

'I'm not. I answered the question.' Geraint folded his arms and stretched out his legs.

Ben continued. 'You have been offered, and declined, legal representation. Are you still happy to be interviewed under those circumstances?'

'Perfectly, thank you.'

'So then, for the tape, will you tell us what happened yesterday morning?'

'Same routine as usual. Nothing about the day was different until I heard Seren scream.'

'What is your "routine"?' Jack asked.

'Up at five, an hour's meditation followed by a run down to the end of the valley. Home for breakfast then work in the garden. I was on my way back for a cuppa when I heard Seren, so I changed direction and ran to the turbine shed.'

'Tell us what you saw,' Ben said.

'The first thing was little Seren, standing in the doorway screaming. I looked past her, saw Will and the blood. There was a hammer on the floor and as I told you, I picked it up, just before Rhys and John turned up and pinned me to the wall. Then I dropped the hammer.' He glanced at Ben. 'You know the rest, you were there.' He held out his hands, palms uppermost. 'I didn't do this, I'm not a killer, quite the opposite.'

'Meaning what?' Jack asked.

'I'm a Buddhist, we don't kill anything.'

'Some of you do, look at Myanmar.'

'But are they Buddhists?' Geraint asked, a faint smile on his lips.

Ben changed tack. 'Tell me how you came to live in Dolgarrog. Sally told me you moved in about a year ago, is that right?'

'Yes, it is.'

'Where did you live before that?'

'Everywhere and nowhere.'

'Meaning what?'

'I dropped out of university. After a year of being talked at and racking up debt, I knew it wasn't for me. Cut my losses and ran.'

'What did you study?'

'Mechanical engineering.'

'Where did you run?' Jack asked.

'I travelled the UK.' Geraint smiled. 'Pretty much all of it except Northern Ireland, never quite got there.'

'How long were you travelling for?'

'A couple of years or so, mostly tramping. I found Dolgarrog by chance, camped for a couple of weeks and loved it.' He sighed, lost in the happy time. 'Anyway, it turned out one of the residents and his wife had to leave for family reasons. I moved in the day they left.'

'So you bought the place?' Ben asked.

Geraint laughed. 'No. One of the conditions of the council-run SDS is you can't sell the home you build. I just live there for now.' He smiled. 'I couldn't believe my luck. I knew it was the perfect place for me.'

'Tell us about your relationship with Will North,' Jack said.

'Will's a great guy with the most incredible brain. He can fix anything, design and build pretty much anything too. The kids love him. He always has time for them and they enjoy watching him work. Dreadful what's happened. He didn't deserve that, no one does.'

'Had you fallen out? Argued recently?'

'I don't fall out with anyone.'

'Never?' Jack asked.

Geraint smiled. 'I've made it my mission not to.'

'Where are the folks who own the house?' Ben asked.

'I have no idea. I got the impression they were going abroad but didn't ask where. None of my business. I'll live in and look after their place until they return – as I promised I would.'

'Does anyone in Dolgarrog know where they are?'

Geraint shrugged. 'You'll have to ask them. I can only speak for myself.'

Jack leaned forward in his seat. 'We need you to work a bit harder with us on this,' he said, 'because we're not making much progress.'

'You should know why that is, Sergeant.'

'Tell me why.'

'Because you've arrested the wrong person. I'm innocent of this awful crime but there is someone walking around out there who isn't – someone dangerous.' He looked at Ben. 'You really need to catch that individual, and soon.'

* * *

Taking a break from interviewing Geraint, the detectives went upstairs to the squad room and found Tegan working at her screen.

'How did the interview go?' she asked.

Ben groaned and dropped on a chair. 'Don't ask me. I can't make up my mind whether Geraint did attack Will and is ridiculously calm about it or, as he said, he didn't do it. What's your take, Jack?'

'I don't think he's calm,' Jack said. 'I think he's smug cos he reckons he can get away with it.'

'Why do you think that?'

'He doesn't seem bothered enough about what's happened to his friend, or being accused of doing it.'

'That's a bit thin. Everyone reacts differently.'

'Maybe, but Geraint is an odd fish. Can't say I warmed to him.'

'You should talk to the child,' Tegan said. 'Seren was first on the scene. Ask her what she saw.'

'She's very young,' Ben said.

'I know, but it's not like you're going to haul her into an interview room. Have Elsa talk to the girl, with the mother present obviously. Elsa has a great interview technique and is brilliant with kids. She has a whole herd of young nieces and nephews.'

'That's not a bad idea.'

'What shall we do with Geraint?' Jack asked.

'We've nothing like enough to charge him, so he'll have to be released under investigation for now.'

'We've got his prints on the hammer.'

'And he told us he picked it up off the floor. As I said, not enough. Go and sort out the paperwork and we'll drive him back to Dolgarrog with us.'

Jack nodded and left the room. Ben turned to Tegan.

'What are you working on?' he asked.

'Still trying to put a name to the skeleton we recovered. I finally got hold of HMP records and I'm working my way through.'

'Maybe you should put that on the back burner, while so much else is going on.'

'I don't agree,' Tegan said, 'the remains of the woman deserve to be identified.'

'You're right of course. Any word from Elsa or Ollie?'

Tegan nodded. 'Ollie rang a little while ago. He's spoken to the members of the shooting party and arranged for them to assemble at the Lloyds' place in a couple of hours. It saves us having to traipse around the country trying to speak to them. The owners and the estate's gamekeeper will be there too.'

'Good move. As soon as Geraint has been bailed, Jack and I will make our way over. Any news from Hereford Hospital?'

'Nothing's changed. Will is still in ICU, serious but stable I was told.'

'OK. How about ballistics?'

'Full report is in. If you find the rifle they'll be able to match it with the brass. How on earth did Heidi manage to find that casing?'

'Not sure, pure luck I guess.'

Jack re-entered the room. 'All done, guv, shall we get off?'

Ben nodded. 'The sooner the better.'

The weather had turned from autumn sunshine to mild and drizzly. Visibility on the country roads wasn't great and Jack drove accordingly. Geraint sat on the back seat and gazed through the side window at the passing scenery as though he was on a day trip. Ben still couldn't make up his mind whether that was because the young man was innocent, or just incredibly skilled at keeping up a front.

A while later, Jack pulled up in the lane at the head of the valley. He opened the back door and let Geraint out, then got back behind the wheel and turned onto the drive leading to the manor house. The expanse of gravel was covered with shiny four-wheel-drive vehicles and a handful of tatty Land Rovers belonging to members of the shoot. The detectives left their car, walked up to the front door and Jack rang the bell.

Chapter twelve

After Freddie Holtz had set off for home in the Cotswolds, Stacey went to the office, fired up her computer and gave her editor a call.

'Jenkins,' he said when he picked up.

'Hi, boss. I've got a story for you.'

'That's good news, but you don't sound very enthusiastic.'

Stacey took a deep breath. 'My friend, and Heidi's wife, DS Erica Bevan, was shot and killed yesterday.'

'Christ!' Sam said. 'Is that the subject of your story?'

'It is, yes. I'm just about to start work but wanted to talk to you first.'

'So talk.'

'We cannot release Erica's name. Her family haven't been informed yet and Heidi – as next of kin – has asked us not to name her. I'll describe her as a "serving police officer".'

'Fair enough. Terrible thing to have happened. I know you were close. How are you coping?'

'Barely, but holding it together for Heidi's sake.'

'Any clue who might be responsible?'

'Much too soon for that.' Stacey hesitated. 'I'm finding it difficult to get my head round it.'

'Do you have any idea whether Erica was targeted?'

'None at all. I'll write what I've got and let you know as soon as I have something more.'

'As soon as possible, OK?'

'I'll do my best.'

Stacey disconnected and wrote a headline at the top of the screen.

Local Police Officer Shot Dead

She stared at the words and experienced a wash of misery flood her heart. Being with Erica when she had died was sickening, and writing a piece for the paper wasn't going to be any easier. She took a deep breath and began typing.

A couple of hours later she read through her work. With a click, she sent the article to her boss hoping she'd done enough, and had captured the right tone without being too emotional. Hearing a sound in the hall, she turned and saw Heidi padding down the stairs.

'Hey, you,' Stacey said. 'I didn't expect to see you so soon.'

'I managed a few hours,' Heidi said. 'Won't sleep later if I have too much now.'

'Would you like something to eat?'

'Yeah, maybe. What have you been doing?'

Stacey hesitated then said, 'Writing tomorrow's front page. Would you like to look through it?'

Heidi shook her head. 'No need. I trust you.'

'Let's go to the kitchen. The Aga is warm. No sunshine today so it can be chilly.'

Heidi shuffled along the hall and curled up in the carver.

'I have a theory,' she said, 'about what happened.'

'Oh? Fancy sharing?'

'Like I told Ben, I'm sure Erica wasn't shot by accident but she may have been mistaken for someone else.'

'Who could she have been mistaken for?'

'What if the killer thought they were picking off one of the hobbit-hole dwellers?'

'It seems a bit of a stretch. Running a crow-scarer to annoy neighbours you don't like is a whole different thing to shooting them.'

'It's not so different from bludgeoning one to death – or trying to.'

'How do you know about that?'

Heidi shrugged.

'So you think the incidents are linked? That the shooter was also Will's attacker?' Stacey shook her head. 'It's not possible. The events happened within minutes of each other.'

'No,' Heidi said, 'they didn't. Will was discovered within minutes of…' She took a breath before continuing. 'We don't know when he was hit on the head.'

'That's true.'

'There's too much we don't know.' Heidi got to her feet. 'I'll go and get dressed and after lunch we'll drive over to Abergavenny. You can collect your car and pick up your stuff, then I'll have a dig around in cyberspace.'

'I'm not sure any of that is a good idea.'

'Why not?'

'Lots of reasons – all of which you know – but mainly you should take some time with this. You've experienced a dreadful shock and need time to grieve.'

'Do I? Isn't that what I did last night?'

'Well…'

Heidi took a deep breath. 'I don't want you to think that because I'm not weeping and wailing I don't care, or don't feel the loss. I will always feel that. I will always miss Erica.'

'Even so, why not stay here tonight, take a breath, and we'll drive over to your place in the morning?' Stacey smiled sadly. 'I'm not keen on being on my own.'

'Then come and stay with me. Ben's going to be busy.'

'So why do you need to dig about online?'

'To keep us up to date with the investigation and look for a possible link between the attacks.' Heidi sat back at the table. 'You know I'm different,' she said. 'Most of the time I don't understand people, why they act the way they do, but I make allowances so I can interact with them. What I can't do is be like them, so stop fretting, pack your laptop and some more underwear, and we'll decamp. Keeping busy will be therapeutic.'

'OK, then, but soup first.'

* * *

While a group of uniformed officers collected preliminary statements from those who had attended the shoot, Ben and Elsa questioned the Lloyds in the large living room. Jack and Ollie took Gill Baird to a smaller room off the hall. Once they had settled around a low table, Jack began the interview.

'The first question is, where were you between 8am and noon yesterday morning?' Jack asked, pen poised above his notebook.

Gill leaned back in his chair, stretched out his legs and folded his arms. 'The simple answer is here, there and everywhere. I'm always extremely busy the morning of a shoot, lots to do to ensure the guns have a good day and the event is run safely.' He smiled proudly. 'I've been running shoots for many years now with only one minor accident.'

'Tell me about that,' Jack said.

The gamekeeper laughed. 'One of the gun dogs shot his owner – didn't kill him fortunately but the man had to miss the rest of the season.'

'How is that even possible?'

'The chap stowed his still-loaded guns in the back of his vehicle. The dogs jumped in and one stood on the trigger.' He smiled again. 'Dopey prat! Not a natural sportsman.'

Jack made a note. 'OK, so tell me what you were doing before and during yesterday's shoot.'

'The usual. I made sure the beaters had turned up – they don't always do. Then I checked they knew where the drives would take place, where to spook the birds out of the bush.'

'Doesn't sound very sporting to me. Where did you hold the drives?'

'Above the valley, west of here. Four drives in all before… well we heard things weren't good down below. I saw the police and the air ambulance and, for safety reasons, called off the rest of the shoot.'

'So you're saying that from eight until noon, you were with the guns the entire time?'

'Yes, that's correct. There are many folk here today who will confirm that if you ask them.'

'You didn't go to the other side of the valley for anything?'

'No, I can't walk away from a shoot. City boys often attend these events, which means shoots can quickly disintegrate into a free-for-all.' He made a rude noise. 'They turn up here in 4x4s that have never seen mud, brand new, expensive guns, and partially trained dogs. Can't take my eyes off any of them.'

'Who are these folk?'

'All sorts. Lawyers, bankers, consultants…' He rubbed his stubbly chin.

'You don't appear to have a very high opinion of your guests,' Ollie said.

Gill snorted. 'That's because I don't. Lots of posh boys from England with too much money, who want to play lord of the manor and have something to talk about at their gentlemen's clubs.'

Jack nodded and made more notes. 'Did you see anyone on the opposite side of the valley from where the drives were?'

'I had a lot to keep my eye on as I'm sure you'll appreciate, I'm not running a tea party, but I didn't notice anyone up there.'

'Have you seen anyone in that area during the last few days?'

'Not that I recall.'

'What about any strange vehicles parked in the lane that morning?'

Gill shook his head.

'Spot anyone by the turbine shed, or someone other than a resident of Dolgarrog walking in the valley?'

'Not that I noticed.'

'Did any of your guests bring rifles?'

'Wouldn't have thought so, we use shotguns. I suppose it is possible someone brought one but they wouldn't have used it.'

'Do you own a rifle?'

'Yes, I have two, locked in the gun cabinet in Keeper's Cottage.'

Jack got to his feet. 'I'd like to take a look.'

'Fine by me.'

Gill hauled himself upright. The officers followed him through the back door of the manor house and along a narrow shingle path towards a patch of trees. As they walked around a bend, a small, whitewashed cottage came into view. The roof was constructed of good Welsh slate which shone a deep blue in the wet weather. On one end of the cottage was a slightly overgrown kitchen garden, at the other a group of sheds and dog pens, and as the men approached, the animals began to bark and howl.

* * *

Ben and Elsa sat in the manor's living room. Opposite sat Joanne and Darryl.

'Where's your sister Shirlee?' Ben asked.

'Upstairs, lying down,' Darryl said. 'This business has been too much for her.'

'She has mental health issues,' Joanne explained.

'Oh?' Ben raised his eyebrows. 'Something we should be aware of?'

'I wouldn't have thought so. Not really any of your business.'

'We are investigating the murder of a police officer,' Ben said, 'amongst other things.'

'None of which have anything to do with Shirlee,' Darryl said.

'We will need to speak with her,' Elsa said.

Darryl glared at her. 'Not now though. I won't allow it.'

Ben decided not to push the issue – for the time being.

'Let's make a start,' he said. 'Can you tell us where you all were yesterday morning during the shoot?'

'I spent most of it with Gill,' Darryl said. 'The girls were in the house, preparing lunch for the guns.'

'All morning?'

'Pretty much. I left the house early to set up the drives and then welcomed the guests.'

'Do you shoot?'

'Sometimes.'

'Did you have a gun in your hands yesterday?'

'Briefly. I took part in the first drive.' He chuckled. 'Show the townies how it's done.'

'You're a fair shot then?'

'Not bad.'

Elsa glanced at Joanne. 'How about you, madam?' she asked. 'Do you shoot?'

'Not yesterday,' she said. 'Too much to do in the kitchen for shooting.'

'Do you all shoot?' Ben asked.

'As I said, sometimes.' Darryl took a deep breath. 'I don't know what's going on here, but it feels as though you are trying to accuse us of killing your colleague. I can't say I like that much.'

'We are – as you know – investigating two serious incidents which occurred on your doorstep. We need to discover who is responsible,' Ben said, 'so we can protect the local community, yourselves included. Aren't you concerned there's someone capable of such crimes on the loose?'

'Of course we are,' Darryl snapped, 'but I don't enjoy being pestered like this.'

'No one does, sir,' Elsa said. 'We don't enjoy doing the pestering much but it's part of our job.' She changed direction. 'Do you all own guns?'

'We have a shotgun each,' Joanne said. 'Our father used to take us clay shooting when we were young.'

'Are your weapons in the house?' Ben asked.

'They're upstairs,' Darryl said. 'There's a gun safe in the smallest bedroom.'

Ben got to his feet. 'We'd like to take a look.'

'Suit yourselves,' Darryl said.

He left the drawing room and headed up the wide staircase, followed by his sister and the detectives. He walked along a carpeted landing to the far end, while Ben and Elsa shared a look. Darryl pushed open a door and went inside with Joanne. Ben brought up the rear and closed the door. Elsa would try to find and speak to Shirlee while he talked to the others. Luckily, neither of the Lloyds seemed to notice her slip away. Darryl removed a key from the top drawer of a small dressing table in the window, unlocked the metal cabinet and swung the door wide.

'There you are. Three double-barrels, just like I said.'

Ben leaned closer and examined the weapons. He couldn't tell whether they had been shot the day before, but they looked clean and didn't smell of gunpowder.

'They are fully licenced,' Darryl continued. 'No ammo in the house. Gill keeps that at his place.'

'Do you own any other guns?' Ben asked.

'No, just these. Seen enough?'

Ben nodded, Darryl relocked the cabinet and turned back.

'Hey,' he said. 'Where's your mate?'

Ben shrugged. 'Using the toilet?'

'Bloody nerve,' Joanne snapped. 'She can't just wander off on her own. This is our home.'

'Sure I heard her ask…'

'Well, I didn't,' Joanne said. 'I think it's time you left.'

'I'll just have a quick chat with Shirlee, as we're up here.'

Joanne shook her head. 'I've told you she isn't well and I will not let you disturb her. She's very distressed and not in a fit state to be interrogated by you.'

Joanne stepped to the door and stretched out a hand just as it opened and Elsa walked in to the room.

'Where the hell have you been?' Darryl asked.

'Powdering my nose,' Elsa answered.

'Well, we'd like you to leave now,' Joanne said.

'We haven't finished taking your statements.'

Joanne grinned. 'Then you should have made better use of the available time. We are busy people and have wasted enough time on you. Take your investigation somewhere else. If we're not suspects, and didn't witness anything, we don't have to talk to you.'

Elsa opened her mouth to speak but Ben sent her a warning look.

'I'm sorry you feel that way,' he said and looked at Darryl. 'If you could show me those gun licences, we'll be on our way.'

Five minutes later, Ben and Elsa stood at the front of the house and looked out over the wooded valley.

'Well?' Ben asked. 'Did Shirlee tell you anything useful?'

'No, sir. I checked all the rooms and she wasn't in any of them.'

'She wasn't there? I wonder why those two' – he nodded back towards the house – 'told us she was resting in bed.'

'Maybe they thought she was.'

Ben groaned and rubbed his face. 'I really don't want to arrest them to get them to talk, but they do need to make statements. I didn't even get the chance to broach the subject of Will North.'

'Let's go and find out how the uniforms are getting on with the shooters. I'll pop back here later. If Shirlee has returned home, she might to talk to me. People do.' Elsa grinned.

'You're right, they do. Interviewing seems to be your superpower. Which reminds me, I'd like to ask Seren what she saw in the turbine shed, with her mother's permission obviously. Tegan tells me you're good with kids, so fancy giving it a go?'

'Of course, sir.'

Chapter thirteen

Ollie was the last to arrive in the incident room at the end of the day and puffed slightly as he dropped onto a chair.

'Sorry, sir,' he muttered. 'Got caught up downstairs.'

Ben nodded. 'Let's get on then. Jack, tell us about your chat with the gamekeeper.'

Jack leaned back in his chair. 'As far as we've been able to ascertain,' he said, 'his alibi checks out. He didn't leave the shoot until he cancelled the last few drives and shepherded everyone back to the house.' He smiled. 'Gill does own a couple of rifles though, Sauer 202s. Same calibre as the bullet used to kill Erica so we brought them back with us. Ollie's just dropped them off with ballistics.'

'What was your opinion of Gill Baird?'

Jack snorted. 'Bit of a snob if you ask me. You've met him, guv, he dresses like a country gentleman, has an overinflated ego and is protective of the Lloyds.'

'Any idea why?'

'His family have worked on the estate for three generations. Guess he feels it's his duty or something. He is also unmarried and childless, so maybe he looks on them as a surrogate family.'

'Do you think he could have killed Erica?'

Jack shrugged. 'Instinct says not. Foxes maybe, but humans...?'

'He really doesn't like the residents in the valley,' Ollie said.

'Any particular reason?' Ben asked.

'No.' Ollie grinned. 'Other than just about everything. He made his feelings plain in his statement.'

'How did it go with the Lloyds?' Jack asked.

'So-so,' Ben said. 'The younger woman, Shirlee, wasn't at home, even though her siblings told us she was resting upstairs. They mentioned a problem with her mental health – but they weren't specific.'

'Did the other two have anything enlightening to say?'

'Not really.' Ben updated the team and told them how he and Elsa had been asked to leave. 'However,' he said, 'we caught up with Sally and John, and were able to speak to their daughter.'

'What did Seren have to say?' Jack asked.

Elsa took up the narrative. 'Lots about how horrid it was finding Will like she did, but she gave us a couple of valuable snippets of information. Firstly that Will had been spending his nights in the turbine shed to keep the equipment safe, and second that Geraint did pick up the hammer when he came to her rescue.'

'That's him off the hook then,' Jack said.

'Seren adored Will,' Elsa continued, 'all the children did. He always took time to explain what he was doing, show them how things worked. Seren called it "doing magic".'

'The overnight thing chimes with an early report from SOCO,' Tegan said and held up a document. 'The pool of blood exhibited drying and evaporation consistent with hours, not minutes.'

'So Will was probably attacked early morning?' Jack said. 'Maybe before it was light?'

'Could be. More test results to follow.'

Jack nodded. 'And who was out and about early that morning? Who is out and about early every morning? Geraint Jones, that's who.'

'We mustn't jump to conclusions,' Ben said. 'Less than a minute ago you were saying he was off the hook.'

'Think about it, it's a perfect set-up. Geraint clobbered him on his early morning run then "discovered" him hours later when Seren sounded the alarm. He picked up the hammer to provide a legitimate reason for his prints to be on it, and made sure Seren saw him.'

'What's the motive, Sergeant?'

'There will be one, guv. That's what we're here for, to uncover what it is.'

Ben rubbed his eyes. 'You're right of course, so we'll double down.' He glanced at Ollie. 'When did ballistics say they'd have some results?'

'First thing in the morning.'

'OK then we'll call it a day. Early start tomorrow.'

'One more thing, sir,' Tegan said.

'Yes?'

'I reckon I might be closer to putting a name to the bones.'

'Really?' Ben walked closer and sat next to her workstation. 'Show me.'

'OK, so…' Tegan tapped the keyboard and a screen full of names appeared. 'All these women served ten years plus and, in most cases, were released under licence.'

'Why not all cases?'

'Lifers are given life licences. Probationers are monitored under licence. LTIs, having completed two-thirds of their sentences, are released without supervision.'

'What, none?'

'None.'

Ben took a deep breath. 'There's a lot of names on that list.'

'There are, but if I remove those who are too young or too old, it shrinks dramatically.' She rattled the keyboard.

'Still leaves a good few,' Ben said squinting at the screen.

'Watch while I take out all those who were released on licence. They would have been supervised by probation officers and if any went missing that would have been recorded.' She tapped some more and the list shrank again.

Ben smiled. 'That does make a difference. Five names.'

'Now all I have to do,' Tegan said, 'is to get hold of their HMP files and health records. I'll look for removal of teeth and a broken wrist and fingers.'

'We ought to be able to get DNA too from police records,' Ben said.

'Not a given, sir. In 2003 England and Wales were granted permission to routinely collect DNA samples from those arrested. At least three of the women on my list were arrested prior to that date, so no DNA on file.'

'Blimey,' Jack said, 'that means they served in excess of eighteen years. What were they convicted of?'

Tegan flipped pages on a yellow legal pad. 'One got life for arson with intent, tried to burn out an ex she accused of abusing her four-year-old daughter.'

'Did anyone investigate her claim?' Ben asked.

'Not enough info here to determine that.'

'OK, so what about the others?'

'One was convicted of killing her two young children, the third stuck a knife repeatedly into her husband and claimed self-defence.' Tegan glanced up. 'Over twenty stab wounds said "frenzied attack" to the jury and she was found guilty of manslaughter. Served longer than the minimum fourteen-year tariff.'

'Why?'

'It could be that she failed her probation interview, or misbehaved and no remission was granted.' Tegan smiled. 'Pretty safe bet I'll only find one broken wrist amongst them.'

'You've made good progress,' Ben said. 'Did your jeweller friend manage to take a look at the bangle we found?'

'She did. Confirmed it was made by an artisan jeweller. She discovered a maker's mark near the hinge but hasn't been able to track down whom it belongs to. She said that could mean the jeweller wasn't based in the UK, but that she'll keep looking. She was impressed with the stone though. A blue diamond apparently, third of a carat. A top-grade gem could be worth as much as fifteen thousand dollars.'

Jack whistled through his teeth. 'That's a shitload of money. Why was it left on the woman's wrist? Why didn't whoever buried the bones take it?'

Tegan laughed. 'Unfortunately, Nirjana couldn't tell from looking at the bangle, and couldn't properly assess the stone. We need to talk to a gem dealer.'

'All we can hope,' Ben said, 'is when you put a name to our Lady of Bones we'll have a better chance of answering those questions.'

* * *

The journey to Abergavenny had been uneventful and when Heidi pulled up outside the building, her shoulders dropped and she let out a huge, shuddering sigh.

'Are you OK?' Stacey asked.

Heidi nodded. 'Glad to be home. Odd though, isn't it? I haven't really settled in here yet, but already I'm calling it home.'

'I don't think it sounds odd. You and Fliss were so alike I'm not surprised you've fitted in so well.'

Heidi opened the door of the truck. 'If you unload the gear I'll go and light the fire in the library.'

'Any food in your cupboards?' Stacey asked, removing bags from the back seat.

'Yeah, probably. Check out the freezer too, bound to be something edible in there and I'm not fussy what.'

'I'll do my best,' Stacey said and carried the luggage into the hall.

A little while later, Stacey loaded up a large tray in the kitchen and headed for the library. She bumped the door open with her hip and saw Heidi curled on the huge Chesterfield in front of the fire, laptop open by her side.

'Managed to find something to eat then?' Heidi asked without looking up from the screen.

'Yeah, freezer curry, looks like jalfrezi to me.'

Heidi caught her breath and glanced up. 'Was it in a blue Tupperware box?'

'It was, yes,' Stacey said. 'Smells fabulous.'

'It will be,' Heidi said. 'Erica made it.'

'Oh God.' Stacey hesitated. 'Sorry, I'm sure I can find something else.'

'Why? Do you think I should keep it in the freezer forever?'

'Well... I...'

'Don't be daft. We'll eat it and remember our remarkable, beautiful friend.'

Still unsure, Stacey picked up her bowl, dipped a small piece of bread into the fiery orange sauce and posted it between her lips.

'It is very good,' she said.

'Shame to waste it then,' Heidi said.

They ate in silence, listening to sparking logs in the grate, the tick of an elderly long-case clock, and the odd creak from the rafters as the old building settled some more. Stacey nodded at the open computer.

'What have you been doing?' she asked.

'Getting myself up to speed with Ben's investigation.'

'Have you found anything?'

'I have. It looks like the team hasn't quite managed to put a name to the bones, they haven't made the connection.' She grinned. 'Well, I have.'

'Wow, so who is she? Uh... was she?'

'A fifty-one-year-old ex-con, name of Katrina Randall. Served nearly twenty years after being convicted of killing her two young sons. Left prison just over two years ago.'

'Gosh! Do you think the boy's father took revenge after she was released?'

'As far as I can tell – mainly from press clippings – it seems he stood by his wife. Never wavered in his belief she was innocent.'

'So perhaps he killed the boys, let his wife take the blame, then stayed close by in case she dropped him in it?'

'Honestly, Stace, you have a very fertile imagination. You should write fiction.'

'How would you explain it?'

'OK, here's the twist. After spending years inside, labelled as a child-killer, and no doubt having a ghastly time, her conviction was overturned and she was released.'

'Bloody hell.' Stacey took a moment to digest what Heidi had told her. 'She was innocent after all?'

'It certainly looks that way but more research is needed.'

'Are you sure you've got the right woman?'

'I took a peek at her HMP medical records. Katrina was treated for a broken wrist, five years before her release.'

'That poor woman. Accused of killing your own children and then spending so many years inside, knowing you were innocent. How did the boys die?'

'I haven't been able to discover that.'

'What happened after she was released?'

'I have no idea. I'll resume the search in the morning.'

'You haven't found an obvious link with the other incidents in the valley?'

'None, but that doesn't mean there isn't one.' Heidi yawned. 'It's no good, I can't think straight while I'm this exhausted.' She hauled herself upright. 'I'll have a bath and get my head down.'

'I'll be close behind you after I've tidied the kitchen.'

'Leave it, I'll do it in the morning. Just make sure you ring Freddie, tell him where we are and how well I'm doing.'

'Are you? Doing well?'

Heidi paused in the doorway. 'I reckon,' she said, 'as long as I keep my brain occupied I can repel the demons. How about you?'

'Same, pretty much. Need to keep busy.'

'I'm sure we'll be fine – in the end. Sleep well.'

Heidi slipped through the door and pulled it closed behind her. Stacey, determined not to stare into the grate feeling miserable, picked up the phone and dialled Freddie's number.

Later, after she was tucked up in bed, a heavy rainstorm rolled in off the Bannau and pounded on the slate roof. At times it sounded like a rushing wind, at others a deep, thrumming vibration. The rooms beneath the roof acted like soundboxes creating a deep, low-register hum which Stacey focused on. The change in the rain's intensity caused ebbs and flows and altered the overhead percussion and she eventually slipped into a deep sleep.

Chapter fourteen

The next morning, having arranged a troop of uniforms to conduct a fingertip search of the area where the brass casing had been found, Ben instructed Jack to drive to the head of the valley above Dolgarrog. The detectives left the car parked outside the manor house and followed the narrow path through the small patch of woodland sheltering Keeper's Cottage. The day was grey and mild, the air saturated; branches and brambles were dripping, and birdsong muted. Wood smoke mingled not unpleasantly with the scent of fungi and leaf mould. Rounding the bend, the detectives spotted Gill working next to the woodshed, sleeves rolled above his elbows, splitting logs for the stove.

'Morning, Mr Baird,' Ben called.

The man put down the axe, removed a handkerchief from his trouser pocket and mopped his sweating brow.

'Morning, gents,' he said. 'What brings you out this way again so soon?'

'Few more questions to ask,' Jack said.

'You'd better come in then.' Gill peered up at the sky. 'More rain on the way.' He collected an armful of freshly chopped firewood and carried it inside. 'Take a seat and I'll get the kettle on.' He grinned. 'Never met a copper who said no to a cuppa.'

'You have now,' Jack said. 'We're a bit pushed for time.'

'Fair enough.' Gill perched on a corner of the kitchen table. 'What can I do for you?'

'I'd like to talk about the rifles you own,' Ben said, 'the ones we took from you yesterday.' He opened his notebook. 'A pair of Sauer 202, lightweight, bolt-action weapons, .223 calibre.'

'Yes. What about them?'

'I was wondering if anyone other than yourself has access to your gun safe.'

'No, of course not. I take safety very seriously.' He reached into his waistcoat pocket and removed a small metal ring from which dangled a single key. He held the object high. 'Always with me,' he said.

'Do you ever lend out your rifles?' Jack asked.

'Never have, why? Is there a problem?'

Ben nodded. 'We have a report from ballistics. They have matched a spent shell case – discovered on the day of the shooting – to one of your weapons.'

Ben watched Gill's face carefully but didn't see any kind of shock or nervousness, just the flicker of mild surprise behind the eyes.

'Where was the shell case discovered?' Gill asked.

'At this point in the investigation I can't divulge that information.'

Gill chuckled. 'Then I'm afraid I can't be much help, Chief Inspector. I use my rifles to control vermin, part of my job. I'll have left spent shells all over the estate.'

'What sort of vermin?' Jack asked, notebook open and pen ready.

'The usual – rabbits, foxes, the occasional deer. Muntjac were becoming a bit of a nuisance a while back. A rifle is cleaner, more accurate than a shotgun.'

Ben tried a different approach. 'We recovered a bullet from the victim's body. The lab has confirmed it is the same calibre as the recovered shell case which matches your weapon.'

'I don't really see your point, unless of course you can prove the lead came from the brass you found.' Gill stood, filled a kettle and placed it on the stove. 'I have to say, I don't like the way this conversation is going. It feels like you're working up to accusing me of shooting your colleague.' He glared at Ben. 'Is that the way it's going? Should I have a solicitor?'

Ben didn't answer Gill's questions and shrugged. 'You will appreciate why we have to ask.' He smiled. 'If a cuppa is still on offer…'

Gill frowned but dropped an extra teabag in the pot.

Ben continued. 'My sergeant tells me your family have lived and worked on the estate for generations, that you worked for Mr Lloyd senior.'

Gill seemed to puff out his chest and stood straighter. 'I did, yes, man and boy. My father and grandfather were keepers before me.'

'What was Mr Lloyd like?'

'A proper gentleman, clever and decent.' He smiled. 'Bloody good shot too.' He poured the tea and handed out mugs.

'Thanks,' Ben said. 'You must have seen some changes over the years.'

'Yes, indeed.' Gill smiled sadly. 'The local hunt used to meet at the house and ride on the estate, but that all stopped a few years ago.'

'Do you know why Mr Lloyd sold the woodland and head of the valley for a development of sustainable residences?'

'Not a clue. He didn't discuss the matter with me, but I know he spent a lot of time with the tree-huggers.'

'Were you upset the land was sold?'

'I'll admit I was. The wood offered perfect cover for the game birds. I used to rear them in pens beneath the trees.' He sighed. 'These days we mainly import what we need from Europe.'

'His children seem to think he was leaned on. Darryl used the word "groomed".'

'I'm sure there was some of that. Bad business decision, that's for certain.'

'It seems to me the younger generation want the land returned to the estate.'

'It was sold too cheaply and has gone up in value now. A company involved with carbon offsetting offered the family a large sum for it – not realising the land had already been sold.'

'Do you know what the company planned to do with it?'

'Plant more trees, I guess. A fair amount of local land has been bought up recently for the same purpose.'

'Do you have a view about that?' Jack asked.

'Not really, not my land, but planting trees on agricultural land doesn't seem like a great idea. You can't eat trees.'

Jack scribbled in his notebook.

'Were you surprised that Mr Lloyd's children moved into the house and kept the shoot going after their father died?' Ben asked.

'Not really, this is their home after all.' He chuckled. 'They never really left apart from during their educations. The girls lived in Sri Lanka for a little while but returned after their father's death.'

'Are they decent employers? Do you all get on well?'

'Of course. I've known them since they were born.'

'An uncle figure then?'

'I suppose.' Gill stood even straighter.

'Bit of a guardian angel maybe?'

'I don't understand where you're going with this.'

Ben shrugged. 'Just wondering.'

'Wondering what?'

'Whether you'd help the family drive out the residents of Dolgarrog. Whether you'd commit acts of vandalism to achieve that aim. Whether you'd attack a young man and near enough kill him… or murder a police officer.'

'What?' Gill's face flushed red then darkened with anger before he exploded. 'How bloody dare you come here and accuse me of such atrocity!' He leapt to his feet and towered over the officers. 'I'm a respectable man, law-abiding. I have a reputation to maintain – and to lose. As if I'd do such a thing.' He took a deep breath. 'You should leave – unless you intend to charge me.' He glared at the detectives. 'Didn't think so, I'm guessing you don't have any real evidence. I'm sorry you've lost a colleague, but that doesn't give you the right to charge around the district accusing all and sundry.' He took a deep breath. 'I've had enough of this, so get out!'

Ben got to his feet and Jack followed suit.

'When am I going to get my rifles back?' Gill demanded.

Jack turned at the door and glanced back at the agitated man. 'When we're finished with them, sir,' he said and stepped out of the cottage into steady rain.

Gill slammed the door and the detectives began the trudge back to their car, collars turned against the weather.

'Bloody hell,' Ben said, 'he's right. We don't have enough evidence to nick him.'

'Not yet, but maybe the fingertip search will turn up something. I reckon we ought to find out more about the offer to buy the land.'

'Not a bad idea. The Lloyds seem very unhappy the valley isn't still part of the estate. I wonder how much the offsetters put on the table.'

'I'll have a word with Elsa, she might be able to find out. She's a bit of a whizz in cyberspace these days.'

'Got to be worth a try.'

'So what's next on the list, guv?'

'I can't make up my mind whether to try and talk to the Lloyds again or wander down the hill to Dolgarrog.'

Jack grinned and removed a coin from his pocket. 'Heads or tails?' he asked and flipped the coin high into the air.

* * *

Following a breakfast of toast and coffee, Heidi and Stacey left the kitchen and made camp in the library. A few small embers nestled amongst the ash in the grate and after some careful coaxing, a couple of fresh logs were encouraged to ignite. A strong wind chased around the old building, rattling doors and driving rain against the window. Heidi shivered.

'I hate this bloody weather,' she said. 'Give me frost and sunshine any day. This too-mild-to-be-true stuff is a bit freaky.'

'I agree,' Stacey said. 'Following the drought in the summer, primroses and Herb Robert are flowering again. I even saw a violet yesterday, it's like a second spring. I've seen heaps of frogs and toads wandering about – they're usually hibernating at this time of year.'

'Things are definitely on the change,' Heidi said.

'I'd be happy if the rain would just stop. I'm sure a walk would do us good but no way am I going out in that.'

'Can't say I'm keen.'

'Shall we make a start sorting out in here then?'

'Might as well.' Heidi got to her feet. 'I think we ought to weed out any duplicate books, obviously checking for signed copies and first editions. I've spotted quite a few clones and removing them will make space for those on the floor and tables.'

'How do we go about finding them? I haven't been able to discern any order in here.' Stacey chuckled. 'Fliss obviously wasn't a fan of Dewey decimal.'

'By using your eyes, like playing a monster-sized game of "pairs". You make a start. I want to dig a bit deeper into

Katrina Randall's case, see if I can track down her husband or any other family members.'

'I told Freddie you'd ring him today, so make sure you do.'

'I will.'

Stacey began walking along the shelves, running a finger over the spines of the mass of books, and soon found a couple of matching editions. After a couple of hours, Stacey went in search of elevenses and returned from the kitchen bearing coffee and crumpets dripping with butter. She placed her burden on the low table next to the sofa and Heidi looked up.

'Coffee. I'm ready for that,' she said.

'Me too. The books are so dusty, my tongue is stuck to my teeth.' Stacey filled mugs and passed one to her friend. 'Found a fair few replicas though. You were right, it is just like playing "pairs". How have you got on?'

'Not great,' Heidi grouched. 'Many of the records I want to search don't appear to have been digitised.'

'Which ones are you talking about?'

'Most of the HMP stuff, massive gaps everywhere.'

She nibbled at a crumpet, butter dribbling down her fingers. Stacey handed over a piece of kitchen roll.

'For example,' Heidi said, 'I can find Katrina's release date but nothing about how she left. No travel pass issued, nothing about anyone collecting her at the gates, or where she went.'

'Any sign of Katrina or her husband in the real world?'

'No, it's as though they ceased to exist. More than likely, they changed their names and began again somewhere else.'

'Although they didn't, did they? Something bad happened and the only trace of Katrina is her skeleton buried in Badger's Bank.' Stacey sighed heavily.

'I'll have a chat with Ben, let him know what I've uncovered.' Heidi drained her mug, shut the laptop and hauled herself upright. 'Rain's stopped,' she said. 'I think better on the move, so let's take a wander around the grounds and find a suitable resting place for Erica.'

Chapter fifteen

Ben and Jack were navigating their way down the flight of stone steps leading to the settlement, when they heard angry voices floating up on the breeze and quickened their pace.

'You've been nothing but trouble,' a deep Welsh voice yelled. 'A huge pain in the arse, the lot of you.'

John and Sally stood outside their house, toe to toe with a short, stocky man. He had tight curly hair liberally streaked with white, and was wearing wellies, waterproof trousers and a tatty, waxed cotton jacket. Standing by his side was a younger man, no doubt his son as they shared looks and stature. Both men carried shotguns, and a hairy-looking dog – part deerhound possibly – stood between them, fur spiky from the rain.

'You should calm down, Mr Griffiths,' John said.

'And prove those guns aren't loaded,' Sally added. 'There are children living here and you know it.'

'Living here?' Griffiths spluttered. 'Nothing like it! You're just piddling about, scratching a living from the mud and diverting streams, while your little bastards run riot.'

'That's enough!' Jack snapped and stepped closer, warrant card in hand. 'Do as the lady asked. Show me those guns are empty.'

The younger man opened his mouth to protest and Jack glared at him.

'Do as you're told, boy.'

Ben stayed out of it. He knew a wise man wouldn't tangle with his sergeant, although one or two had tried in the past. He smiled as the Griffithses broke open their guns, displayed the empty chambers, and offered little resistance when Jack removed the weapons from their hands.

'Right,' Jack said, 'one of you better tell me what all this is about.'

'None of your business,' the older man said, 'and don't call my son, "boy".'

'Anything that happens in and around this valley is my business. In case you haven't heard, the chief inspector is investigating the murder of a police officer.' Jack pulled out his notebook. 'Now, your names.'

'I'm Gwilliam Griffiths. My son is Dewi.'

'Address?'

'Brynmelyn, the land west of here. We share a border with the estate – and this godforsaken place.'

Jack nodded. 'Now tell me what the problem is.'

Gwilliam swept a stumpy arm at John and Sally. 'They are,' he said.

'You're going to have to be more specific.'

'They bring trouble,' Dewi said. 'Fucking townie, eco-terrorists, trying to tell us how to live.'

Jack glared at him. 'You should watch your mouth, boy. Could get you into trouble.' He looked back at Gwilliam. 'What are you doing here?'

'Showing support for our friend.'

'Who might that be?'

'Gill Baird, local gamekeeper. He just rang me, said you'd accused him of killing that WPC.'

'She was a detective sergeant,' Jack said firmly.

'Doesn't really matter what she was now, does it? What does matter is you trashing a man's reputation, and this bunch, squatting the land and conning an old man into selling it for a pittance. Disgraceful!'

John stepped closer. 'You should go home, Mr Griffiths,' he said. 'If you don't leave, you'll be guilty of trespass. You are relying on assumed consent to be here – which you don't have.'

Gwilliam chuckled, a high-pitched, wheezy sound. 'What does that even mean?'

Jack grinned at the short man. 'It means – get off his land!'

Dewi took a step forward. Ben noticed and stepped forward, relaxing as Jack turned angry eyes on the lad, who instantly stood down.

'On your way then,' Jack said. 'I'm getting wet stuck out here arguing the toss with you. Expect a visit from us in the not-too-distant future, boys.'

Gwilliam hesitated. 'Uh, are you going to give our guns back?'

'Not now. Pick them up from Brecon police station. Make sure you bring your gun licences and suitable carry cases with you.'

Gwilliam's shoulders slumped lower. He knew he was beaten so he turned and, followed by his son, stomped away along the footpath. John laughed and slapped Jack on the shoulder.

'Hope I never piss you off, Sergeant. That glare-thing you've got going on is impressive.'

'Thanks for seeing off those nasty little bullies,' Sally said.

'Do they give you grief like that often?' Ben asked.

'Every now and again,' John said. 'They own the crow-scarer.'

'Do you think they may have damaged the turbine?'

John shrugged. 'Possibly, but they're not the only locals who hate us being here. Could be any of them.'

'Bloody hell,' Jack said. 'Sometimes Mid Wales is like the Wild West. Now, can I please have a cuppa and at least ten minutes out of the rain? I'm soaked.'

* * *

At the end of the day, Ben took his place at the head of the table in the incident room and addressed his team.

'I won't keep you long,' he said, removing two A4-sized photographs from a file and pinning them on the board. 'Two new faces,' he said. 'Father and son, Gwilliam and Dewi Griffiths, neighbours of Dolgarrog and the estate.'

'What have they got to do with this?' Ollie asked.

'Jack and I bumped into them today. They were shouting the odds with John and Sally, and armed with shotguns. They had a lot to say and many grievances. Elsa, first thing tomorrow dig into their backgrounds. Also, take a look at this carbon offsetting thing by planting trees. They also mentioned Mr Lloyd being leaned on to sell the valley. We've heard that more than once and I'd like to know if there's any truth to the chatter.'

'Yes, sir,' she said.

'Did the fingertip search turn up anything?'

'Not really,' Ollie said. 'A handful of shotgun cartridges, a few more .22 shell cases, some cigarette butts, a couple of cigar ends and some rubbish – beer cans, crisp packets, and plastic bottles – left by the shoot perhaps. It's all with the lab.'

'OK, good.'

'There was one thing though. Most of the brass shells we recovered weren't as shiny as the one Heidi picked up, they looked older.'

'That's interesting,' Tegan said. 'There's bound to be some sort of test to tell how long it takes brass to tarnish.'

'Sounds reasonable,' Ben said. 'Have a word with the lab. Any progress with HMP?'

Tegan grinned. 'Heidi rang earlier, seems she's been digging around online, and she gave me a name for the bones. Katrina Randall.'

'Which of the five on your list is she?'

'The one accused and convicted of killing her children, only she didn't. She was released just over two years ago, conviction overturned. No licence issued on release.'

'Christ,' Ben said and took a breath. 'OK, more work on that tomorrow. We need to discover the full circumstances, together with how and why she ended up buried in Badger's Bank.'

'I'll give the prison a ring,' Tegan said, 'talk to the governor. Could be quicker than waiting for the records to turn up.'

'That poor woman,' Jack said. 'She must have had a terrible time inside, labelled as a kiddie-killer.'

'Doesn't bear thinking about,' Tegan said.

'Any news from the hospital?' Ben asked. 'Is Will North still in a coma?'

'Yes, he is. I spoke to his doctor this morning. The lad is now stable and breathing on his own but hasn't woken up yet.'

'Do the medical staff think he will?'

'No way of telling. He's no longer being sedated and the doctor I spoke to has promised to contact me if anything changes. They still can't say whether he has suffered any brain damage, but there's a fair chance he might have. Skulls and lump hammers don't mix.'

Ben sipped from his mug. 'OK then, tomorrow. Jack and I will have another chat with the Lloyds, the rest of you check through the statements and reports we've amassed. Remember, we are not only looking for the vandal and the attacker of Will, but whoever killed Erica. It seems too coincidental to me for these events to be unconnected, so we're also looking for anything that might link them.'

Ben saw nodding heads around the table.

'What about Katrina?' Tegan asked. 'Do you think her death could be connected to everything else?'

Ben groaned and rubbed his face. 'I honestly can't see how, other than because of where she was found, but make the call to the prison governor. Find out as much as you can about Katrina's case, the time she spent inside and the exact circumstances of her release. You could also take a look at the court transcripts, and keep in touch with Heidi in case she discovers anything else useful.' He got to his feet and slipped on his jacket. 'That's it for today. See you in the morning, troops. We must make more progress and soon.'

Ben left the room and walked upstairs to provide CS Warren with an update, then went out to the car park. He sat behind the wheel of his car and tapped Stacey's number on his mobile phone.

'Hi, you,' he said when she answered. 'How are things with you and Heidi?'

'We're hanging in there,' she said.

'What have you been doing?'

'Sorting out the mad library mainly, but today we were wandering around the grounds looking for the best spot to bury Erica – when her body is finally released.'

'Heidi still wants to bury her in the grounds of the pink house then?'

'Yes, she does.'

'I've just been chatting with the chief super,' Ben said. 'She was talking about a police funeral, all the bells and whistles.'

'Heidi won't go for that. I'm utterly convinced she won't.'

'Could you mention it to her?'

'I will, when the time is right. Any closer to finding out who shot Erica?'

'No, not really.'

'Are you making any progress with the rest of the investigation?'

Ben sighed. 'Not much, to be honest. I've discovered the residents of Dolgarrog aren't at all popular with pretty much all the locals, but no definite suspects, and not much in the way of hard evidence either. Will North is still in a coma so he can't tell us who attacked him, and we've found no witnesses.'

'How are you and your team?'

'Shocked sums it up. We haven't lost a serving officer for years and they all knew Erica. She was their friend, mine too.' He took a deep breath. 'I can't imagine how Heidi is feeling.' He paused. 'I wouldn't cope if I lost you.'

'Good to know. I was beginning to think you were fed up with me, worried you'd had enough and we might split up.'

'We'll never do that, *cariad*, not if I have any say in the matter. Sleep well and don't worry.'

Ben cut the call and returned the mobile to his pocket. He started the car, pulled onto the main road and headed towards Llanagethin.

* * *

Stacey went to the kitchen and hunted for something to cook for supper. Her mobile chirped and she picked it up.

'Hello?'

'Stacey? Sally here from Dolgarrog.'

'Hi there. How are you?'

'Not bad thanks. How about you and your friend?'

'Hanging in there. Heidi obviously misses Erica but doesn't seem to want to talk about her death. We're just keeping busy, like women do when they're unhappy.'

'Fancy doing something else tomorrow?'

'I don't see why not. What do you have in mind?'

'Before I tell you, I have to swear you to secrecy.'

'Now I'm interested.'

Sally took a deep breath. 'OK, it's like this, a local climate group is planning an action tomorrow and a tame reporter could be useful. I thought you might be up for it.'

'Definitely.'

'Good. I looked you up online and you're good at what you do.'

'Thanks, but don't waste flattery, I'm in, although…'

'Problem?'

'Might be. I'm not sure about leaving Heidi.'

'You could bring her with you.'

'I'll have a chat over supper and let you know. Shall I come to you?'

'No, meet us at the bus station car park in Abergavenny. Five thirty in the morning and don't be late, we won't wait for you.'

'When you say "we", how many are we talking about?'

Sally giggled. 'A few. I hope you can make it.'

'Me too, thanks for thinking of me.'

'No problem. You'll be doing us a favour if you can get the action in the news.'

'I'll do my best and hope to see you in the morning.'

Stacey hung up as Heidi wandered into the kitchen and plonked herself at the table.

'Who are you hoping to see in the morning?' she asked.

'That was Sally, she invited me to cover some sort of protest – but I'm not supposed to mention it.' Stacey put mincemeat to brown in a cast-iron frying pan and opened a tin of tomatoes. 'I don't have to go,' she said. 'I'm here to look after you.'

'At least you didn't say "keep an eye on you", makes me sound like a toddler.' Heidi helped herself to a glass of wine. 'You go, I don't need looking after.' She fiddled with a small square of paper from an old-fashioned telephone jotter, owned by the previous resident. 'What has your friendly eco-warrior got up her velvet sleeve?' she asked.

'Very secret squirrel. All I know is I need to be in Abergavenny bus station car park at half five in the morning.'

'No idea what she's planned?'

'Nope, not a clue. She wants me there for publicity and documentation, and hinted there might be trouble.'

'How delightfully curious.' Heidi placed a tiny origami lizard on the table. 'I could do with an outing so I'll come with you.'

'Sure you're up for it?'

'Yeah, I reckon.'

Heidi began fiddling with another piece of paper. 'What's for supper?' she asked.

'Lasagne and peas, no salad left.'

'I won't miss salad, it doesn't do anything for me. Do you need a hand?'

'No, thanks. Any further revelations regarding Katrina?'

'Nothing concrete. Still hunting.'

'I must admit I'm looking forward to a day out, I just hope it isn't chucking it down tomorrow. Hours hanging about in the rain won't be much fun.'

Chapter sixteen

The next morning dawned grey, but mild and dry. Nearly half an hour after leaving home, Heidi pulled into a nearly empty car park and immediately spotted three white rental vans, parked at the far end of the tarmac. She drove closer and parked her truck in the row behind. As she turned off the engine, the back doors on one of the vans opened. Sally peered out and beckoned towards them.

Heidi glanced at Stacey. 'Into the unknown then?' she asked.

'I think you might be exaggerating. It's probably just going to be a sit-in.'

'Whatever, let's not keep the warriors waiting.'

They left the truck and walked towards the van.

Sally smiled. 'Hop in. Good to see you both.' She looked at Heidi and rested a hand on her shoulder. 'I'm pleased to meet you and I'm very sorry for your loss.'

'Thanks,' Heidi muttered and climbed in.

Stacey pulled the doors closed. 'Can you tell us where we're going?' she asked.

'Offices in town, we want to get into position while the streets are quiet.'

'What sort of action are you planning?' Heidi asked.

'You'll see. Just make sure you don't get in the way, either of you.'

A few minutes later the vans stopped, the doors opened and disgorged activists of all ages. Stacey recognised Matt and Maxine from Dolgarrog, dressed in climbing gear, ropes and racks of gear looped across their bodies. They approached a glass-fronted building, tall and wide, which reminded Stacey of a department store. Heidi tugged her arm. They moved away, found a doorway opposite and Stacey began taking photographs.

Apart from the activists, the street was deserted except for an elderly man, battered trilby on his head, pipe clamped between his teeth, a small black and tan terrier trotting by his ankles. Stacey watched as the man strolled closer to the young climbers.

'What you young 'uns up to this early?' he asked.

Stacey saw Maxine smile and heard her say, 'Would you believe we're window cleaners?'

The pensioner cackled past his pipe. 'Not for a second, my lovely. Make sure you don't fall off.' He gazed up at the glass wall, then shuffled away around the corner.

Matt and Maxine sorted clips and karabiners, metal clinking in the quiet street. Another young couple stood close by, ready to assist and keep passers-by at a safe distance once the climb began. The remainder of the protestors separated. A group of four – holding what looked like fire extinguishers – wandered slowly along the front of the building and sprayed lime green paint on the plate glass – "Stop Greenwashing". The thin paint dripped down the windows and formed pools on the pavement.

'Bloody hell,' Stacey said, capturing the spectacle on her favourite Nikon, 'I didn't expect this. Isn't that criminal damage?'

'Not if it's poster paint and washes off.' Heidi almost grinned. 'It rains a lot in Wales. They'll be lucky if their message is still there by the end of the day.' She nudged Stacey. 'Isn't that your mate, Sally? By the entrance.'

'I see her.' Stacey snapped some more. 'Looks like she's locking onto the door with her husband, to stop anyone getting inside, I guess. Can you find out who owns or leases this place?'

'Work of a moment,' Heidi said and tapped at her phone.

Stacey pointed her lens up towards the building's facade and was surprised to see the climbers were already above the first storey. She had never been good at heights and experienced the familiar acrophobic flutter in her stomach and the flinch of her bones. She couldn't see what the pair were hanging on to – their sticky rock boots flat against the glass – and swallowed hard.

'Land management company,' Heidi said. 'Carbon offsetters, called Carbon Zero Cymru. Yeah right!'

'What do they do?'

'As far as I can see, they buy up land – whole farms in some cases – to plant trees. It's a scam.'

'How can you possibly know? You've only just heard of them?'

'Because it doesn't work. Everyone knows that.'

Stacey wasn't sure she did but would research the issue later. The street was slowly growing busier. More pedestrians appeared, heading to work, opening shops and cafes in the car-free zone. The remaining activists sat on the pavement in a line across the front of the building. Some held placards which read, "Zero emissions, not Zero crops" and "Food not firs" and "Wales not for sale". A small crowd began to congregate, faces craned upward as they watched the young couple scale the building.

'Are they spidermen?' a young boy asked his mother.

The mood suddenly changed as three men in suits, briefcases clasped in their hands, approached the building. Stacey moved closer, Heidi by her side, mobile held high as she captured the action on video. The tallest man strode up to the protestors.

'What the hell do you think you're doing?' he yelled. 'Get out of the bloody way.' He nudged a middle-aged woman with his foot and she looked up at him.

'Don't do that,' she said. 'I can't move because I've glued my hand to the pavement.'

'You've done what? Why the fuck have you done that?'

'To make a point.' The woman looked away.

The angry man turned. His face changed when he spotted the graffiti, and again when one of his colleagues drew his attention to the climbers, now approaching the third floor.

'Oi!' the man screamed. 'You two! Come down. You're on private property.'

Not receiving a response, he stabbed at his phone and a short while later, half a dozen police officers arrived, bristling with radios, batons and tasers. Stacey moved closer to the action and Heidi continued recording. A large, tubby sergeant, with several chins and a florid complexion, squashed into a stab vest, stomped towards the activists.

'Come on, you lot,' he shouted. 'You've had your fun, made your point, now on your way.'

'Sorry, officer,' a white-haired man said, 'we're glued.' With his free hand he pointed at the message on the windows and then above his head.

The sergeant's face grew even redder and his bushy eyebrows formed a deep frown. He spoke angrily into his radio, then marched back to his constables.

'Right!' he said loudly. 'Listen up. We need to close the street and lose the sightseers. Reinforcements are on the way. As soon as they arrive, send them to me. Meantime, we need to get those two' – he pointed at the climbers – 'back on terra firma, cuff the graffiti artists and peel this lot off the pavement.' The man strode back to the protestors.

Stacey took more photographs anxious to record the event properly. Matt and Maxine had now reached the top of the building and secured themselves with ropes and clips. With their hands free they removed a thick roll of something from a bag strapped to Matt's back. They fiddled with their burden then suddenly unfurled a long banner which dropped down to the top of the first floor. It read, "Hands off Wales". The other protestors cheered at the sight as three Transit vans, crammed with coppers, pulled into the street. Stacey lifted her camera and suddenly felt someone grab her arm and tug roughly.

'Hey!' she said. 'Let go!' She looked into the angry eyes of the sergeant.

'Not a chance, missy,' he snarled. 'You're under arrest.'

'I'm press,' Stacey said.

She tried to remove her press pass from her pocket, but the man grabbed her other arm, pulled both behind her back and she felt the cold metal of handcuffs encircle her wrists.

'No!' she yelled. 'You can't do this. I'm covering the protest. You are not allowed to arrest journalists.'

He didn't answer and began pushing her towards one of the riot vans. Heidi, mobile still in hand, appeared in front of him.

'Uncuff her immediately, you bloody moron,' she snapped. 'She's told you she's press.'

The sergeant stepped closer; he looked dangerous and Heidi pointed the phone at his face. Shockingly, the angry man lost it, he swiped the device from her hand and it shattered on the concrete.

'Bad move,' Heidi said and raised a fist.

'Heidi! No!' Stacey yelled.

Heidi blinked once, lowered her arm and was instantly cuffed. Two constables marched her to the van and shoved her inside. She flopped onto the bench next to Stacey.

'What have things come to when Old Bill nicks journos?' Heidi asked.

'I'm really glad you didn't smack him,' Stacey said.

'I'm still conflicted about my choice, he deserved a slap.'

Stacey peered through the window and watched as teams of officers began the process of unsticking, then nicking the activists. Matt and Maxine abseiled down from the roof and were promptly arrested. The small crowd behind the barriers burst into applause and the young couple, hands cuffed, took a bow and encouraged a few whoops. The banner remained where it was, swinging from side to side in the breeze. A specialist team worked at freeing John and Sally from the entrance doors, while a lone officer rounded up four fire extinguishers. There was no sign of the graffitists.

'What do you think the police will do with us?' Stacey asked.

Heidi snorted. 'Depends on how many cells they have. Might hang on to us for a few hours then probably release us under investigation. They can't charge us with anything.'

Stacey peered through the window again. 'I should be out there reporting this.'

'It's not your fault you ran into a complete arse. Tell you one thing though.'

'What?'

Heidi didn't smile but said, 'I'd hand over a stack of cash to see Ben's face when you tell him you're in the jug.'

Stacey squeezed her friend's arm.

* * *

An hour later, Stacey and Heidi were standing in front of the booking-in desk. Heidi fixed the officer behind it with her pale grey eyes.

'That fat sergeant is out of control,' she said, 'and I'm going to cook his goose for him.'

The grey-haired, moustachioed man was unmoved and glared at her.

'Name?' he demanded.

Heidi frowned. 'You'll get nothing out of me. This is an unlawful arrest. You've seen my friend's credentials so tell me, when did British bobbies start nicking journalists? Bloody morons, the lot of you.'

'You should watch your mouth, young lady.'

'Or what?'

Heidi stared at him and, uncomfortable, he looked away. He picked up a small plastic card, studied it for a couple of seconds and then turned his gaze on Stacey.

'Are you Stacey Logan?' he asked.

'You can see I am from the photo on my press pass. Care to explain what I'm doing here?'

'We want to make sure you are who you say you are.'

'You honestly think my pass is a forgery?'

The grey-haired man grinned. 'Stranger things have happened.'

'We're entitled to phone calls,' Heidi said, 'and we want them right now.'

'You're just gonna have to wait. We're a bit short-staffed having to clear up after you people.' He wagged a finger at her as though chastising a child. 'You can't run around spraying paint on other people's property without there being consequences.'

Heidi, face flushed with anger, turned to Stacey. 'Don't say anything else to this guy, he's an idiot. Nothing until we've been granted access to a phone, OK?' She winked at her friend. 'I really hope I'm in the room when everything crumbles around their hairy ears.'

The sergeant finally lost patience and called for two custody officers to escort his prisoners to the cells. Due to the number of activists arrested, Heidi and Stacey were banged up together. Heidi settled herself on the concrete shelf, backed into the corner, and Stacey perched on a thin, plastic mattress.

'Bloody hell,' Stacey said, 'this has turned into a disaster.'

Heidi shook her head. 'Far from it, this is great. The story you write will make the front page – "Journalist Arrested" – and the action will get much more publicity. Your grumpy editor will be cock-a-hoop.'

'Yeah, I guess, but if I'm honest I don't like being in here.'

Heidi snorted. 'That is sort of the point. Anyway, all that pales into insignificance. I can't wait to watch as Chief Inspector Ben James and the mighty Frederick Holtz tear into this lot. Wish I could sell tickets.'

'Shame about your phone and the footage. The video would have been great.'

'You think I'm an idiot? I live-streamed everything. The footage will be all over the net by now. You're probably already famous.'

Chapter seventeen

Having made sure the team knew what they were doing, Ben got to his feet and was about to head out to the manor estate, when his mobile rang. "Number withheld" flashed on the screen.

'DCI James,' he answered.

'Ben, it's me,' Stacey said.

'Sorry, *cariad*, I'm just on my way out so can't really chat. Where are you? Your number didn't come up.'

'I'm banged up with Heidi in Abergavenny police station.'

'What, in a cell?' Ben asked.

'Yes, a real cell with a concrete bunk.'

'Bloody hell! What's happened?'

'I was covering a climate protest in the town with Heidi and we both got arrested.'

'What were you doing?'

'Standing in the wrong place at the wrong time with cameras in our hands.'

'But you're a journalist. You shouldn't have been nicked. Did Heidi do something she shouldn't?'

Stacey chuckled. 'No – not quite.'

'Have either of you been charged?'

'No, there was some talk about Section 43 but I'm not sure what that is.'

'It's part of the Terrorism Act but is a stop-and-search power only. God, what a mess. Does Freddie know about this?'

'Heidi called him and I don't reckon he's overjoyed.'

'I can imagine. OK, I'm on my way.'

'Why not just ring your opposite number and ask him to release us?'

'Because I want my say and I'll be in the neighbourhood. Won't be long. Sit tight.'

'Funny. See you soon.'

Ben put his phone away. 'Jack?' he called. 'Change of plan. I'm needed in Abergavenny. Heidi and Stacey have been nicked. I need to get them released then read the Riot Act. Back-up would be good.'

'Shit,' Jack said. 'What have they been up to? Don't tell me, Heidi thumped someone.'

'Seems not, which will make things easier. Go and grab a car and I'll see you out front.'

* * *

Ben barged through the main door of Abergavenny police station, Jack close behind, and marched up to the desk, warrant card held in front of his chest. The civilian member of staff blinked.

'What can I do for you, sir?' she asked.

'I need to speak to the officer in charge on an urgent matter,' Ben said.

'Yes, sir. That'll be Inspector Sawyer. I'll give him a call. Take a seat.'

Ben paced and Jack leaned on the counter standing up straight when a short, uniformed man, with two Order of the Bath stars on his epaulettes, entered the office. The man smiled as he introduced himself and held out a hand which Ben ignored.

'DCI James and DS Trent, we need a word, Inspector, somewhere quiet,' Ben said.

'Certainly, we'll go upstairs to my office. I'll arrange some tea.'

'No, thanks.'

Sawyer shrugged and led the officers up two flights of stairs and inside a modern but sparse office, which looked as though it hadn't ever seen a decent day's work.

'How can I help you?' he asked.

'I understand your officers policed a climate protest in town this morning,' Ben said. 'Can you tell me how that went?'

Ben listened as the small man recited details of the protest, its location, and how many arrests had been made.

Ben nodded. 'How many have you charged?'

'None yet, we're still processing them. We'll probably charge a few for criminal damage.'

'You arrested two women,' Ben said. 'Stacey Logan and Heidi Holtz, can you tell me anything about them?'

'Not really. Logan said she was a reporter – we're checking into that – and Holtz… your guess is as good as mine. She isn't being very cooperative. What is your interest in them?'

Ben stepped closer to the desk, rested his hands on the edge and glared at Sawyer.

'Stacey Logan is a reporter and should not have been arrested. In case you are interested, she's also my partner. Heidi Holtz is an ex-DC, and a recently bereaved police widow.' Ben moved back from the desk. 'This is not your finest hour. I want to speak to the sergeant who was in charge of the operation.'

'I… uh… not sure he's in the station,' Sawyer said.

'Then get him here,' Ben said. 'We'll wait.'

He sat on a chair facing the desk, Jack took a seat next to him, and they watched as Sawyer began tapping numbers into his phone.

Within five minutes there was a knock on the door and the sergeant walked in.

'You wanted me, sir?' he asked.

Sawyer introduced his visitors. 'Chief Inspector James would like you to tell him about two arrests you made this morning. Stacey Logan and Heidi Holtz.'

The sergeant grinned. 'Oh, those two,' he said. 'They were waving cameras in my face, making a nuisance of themselves. The little one with white hair verbally abused me so I nicked them both.'

Ben glared at the man. 'Easy collars for you then? A journalist and a police widow? What were you thinking?'

The man frowned. 'I was doing my job, sir,' he snapped.

'Not very well,' Jack muttered. 'Since when do you nick members of the press?'

'When they get in my face.'

'Not an answer,' Ben said. 'As you and Inspector Sawyer are about to find out – even though I am furious and intend to progress this matter – it isn't me you need to worry about.' He took a breath. 'As you will doubtless discover, Mr Frederick Holtz – Heidi's father – is an influential man in Whitehall and not without contacts. The pair of you should be prepared for the shit you threw at the fan to plaster you from head to foot.'

Jack caught Sawyer's eye and grinned. Sawyer looked away.

'So what now?' the inspector asked.

'Release Logan and Holtz immediately. Deal appropriately with him' – Ben waved a hand at the sergeant – 'and pray you survive the resulting fallout.'

Sawyer realised he was in a hole. He ran a hand across his face and nodded. 'OK, I'll release the prisoners. If you wait in the front office, I'll have them brought out to you.'

'Good. Make it quick,' Ben said. 'DS Trent and I need to be elsewhere, investigating the murder of a serving police officer.'

Ben left the office as Sawyer's phone rang and smiled when he heard the man say, 'Ah, Mr Holtz. I was expecting your call.'

Jack followed his boss and frowned at the overweight sergeant. 'With a bit of luck, you'll be offered more than words of advice,' he said. 'My advice to you would be to jump before you're pushed. This is more than likely going to get sticky.'

After a short wait, Stacey and Heidi were delivered to the front office by a female officer, who kept her eyes down and escaped without a single word.

'Ben!' Stacey said. 'Good to see you. Sorry I had to drag you over here, but thanks for rescuing us.'

Ben smiled. 'I wouldn't have left you in the cells. Are you both OK?'

'Pissed off,' Heidi said, 'and pretty bloody angry.'

Jack chuckled. 'Don't worry. As we left the office Sawyer took a call from Freddie. I wouldn't want to upset your pa.'

'Right then,' Ben said, 'let's get you back home. I won't be able to stay I'm afraid, we have an appointment with the Lloyds at the manor estate.'

'No need,' Heidi said. 'My truck is in the car park in town. Drop us there.'

'OK, if you're sure.'

'What about the other protestors?' Stacey asked. 'Can you get them released too?'

Ben shook his head. 'Sorry, they'll have to take their chances, but I'll keep an eye on the situation. Now, look lively, the car is out the front.'

Jack stepped out of the station and opened the vehicle's doors, then he slipped behind the wheel, drove to the bus station and parked next to Heidi's truck. The women transferred vehicles and half an hour later Heidi pulled up outside her large house.

'Well,' Heidi said, 'that was an experience. Not what I'd expected at all.'

'No, nor me,' Stacey said. 'Let's get inside. I'm starving and need coffee. My caffeine monster is growling.'

Stacey toasted cheese sandwiches under the grill while Heidi put the kettle on. They sat at the table to eat and Heidi pulled her sandwich apart, smothered the still-bubbling cheese with brown sauce and took a large bite.

'I was ready for this,' she said.

'Me too,' Stacey said. 'I've got an article to write and can't do that on an empty stomach.'

'Make sure you check out the video footage before you get stuck in.'

'Yeah, I will. Clever of you to live-stream it.'

'I know.'

'What are you going to do?'

'I need some fresh air, get the stink of the cop shop out of my nostrils. I'll have a wander around the grounds while it isn't raining.'

'Are you OK?'

'I'm fine,' Heidi said. 'I'll be back in time to cook supper.'

Heidi cleared the table and left the kitchen. Stacey posted a couple of logs inside the old Aga, collected her laptop from the library, and got to work.

* * *

Ben and Jack stood outside the front door of the manor house and after a short wait it was opened by Joanne Lloyd.

'You're late,' she grumbled.

'Yes, I apologise,' Ben said, 'but we were needed elsewhere.'

'Well, you're here now so come in and we'll get on with it.' She closed the door. 'We've told you everything we know and I have to say, your visits are becoming an irritation.'

'We have a few more questions,' Ben said, 'and still need to speak to your sister, Shirlee. I hope she is feeling better today.'

'Like you care. Go to the drawing room and I'll give Darryl a ring. He gave up waiting for you and went out with Gill.'

Jack led the way into the large room and the detectives took a seat. Ten minutes passed before the door opened and Joanne walked in followed by her sister. Ben saw the younger woman didn't look well. Her hair was tousled as though she had just left bed and her skin was pale; she shuffled slowly to an armchair. Joanne helped Shirlee settle, tucked a cushion behind her back and draped a woollen blanket over her knees.

'Darryl rang and isn't available – he's gone to town,' Joanne said. 'As you can see, my sister is not fully recovered so I would be grateful if you can keep this visit as short as possible.'

'We'll do our best.' Ben glanced at Shirlee. 'Are you happy to speak to us?'

Shirlee nodded, her hands twisting the edge of the blanket.

'Before we start,' Ben said, 'your sister told us you have mental health issues. Is there anything regarding your health we should know about?'

'Not really. I suffer from bouts of extreme anxiety and depression, in between manic episodes. I've been diagnosed as severely bipolar.'

Joanne cut in. 'This grilling isn't helping. Not like any of it has anything to do with us.'

'Hardly a grilling,' Jack said. 'We are making inquiries into the death of a serving police officer.'

'Firstly, can you confirm where you were on the morning of the shoot?' Ben asked.

'In the kitchen with Joanne, preparing lunch for the guns,' Shirlee said.

'How about earlier that day, between midnight and eight in the morning?'

'In bed. I got up at eight and was in the kitchen by nine.'

'So you didn't leave the house for anything?' Jack asked.

'No, I didn't.'

Jack made notes.

'And your sister was with you in the kitchen the whole time?'

'Yes, she was.'

'Where was your brother?'

'I guess he was out with Gill, helping him with the preparations for the shoot. I don't think he left the house in the night either.'

'What can you tell us about the residents of Dolgarrog?' Ben asked. 'How well do you know them?'

'Hardly at all,' Shirlee said. 'I don't go down there and they don't come here. Darryl wouldn't let them in anyway, and I keep away.'

'What about Will North? You know he's been badly injured, don't you?'

'Yes, Joanne told me.' Shirlee's knuckles turned white as she clasped and knotted the rug.

'Do you have any idea who might have attacked him?' Jack asked.

'No, I don't, but I know it wasn't one of us.'

'You know that how?'

'Because we wouldn't do such a thing – never would.' She rubbed her face with the edge of the blanket.

'I think that's enough,' Joanne said. 'My sister tires easily and should really be in bed. We've already answered your questions.'

Ben sighed and got to his feet. 'OK. Just give us the name and contact details of the solicitor who handled the sale of the land, and we'll leave you in peace.'

Joanne crossed the room to a large antique desk in the bay window, flipped through an address book and scribbled on a note pad. She tore off the sheet and handed it to Ben.

'Thank you,' he said and glanced at Shirlee. 'I hope you feel better soon.'

The young woman didn't speak and Joanne showed the officers out. As they got into their car, Ben's mobile chirped. He slipped it from his pocket and peered at the screen.

'Sally,' he said for Jack's benefit. 'All the activists have been released under investigation and are nearly home. Not one has been charged.'

Jack chuckled. 'You really rattled Sawyer. Bet he couldn't wait to get rid of them.'

'Good, he needed rattling. Anyway, Sally has asked if we can pop in for a chat.'

'Did she say why?'

'Didn't give me any clues. Park in the lane and we'll pop in before we head off to speak with the solicitor.' He checked the note Joanne had given him. 'William Williams.'

'Great name. Where's his office?'

'Brecon. Let's get a move on, we've lost too much time already today.'

Chapter eighteen

Stacey worked for nearly two hours on her article, harvesting images from the video Heidi had taken, then got up from the table and stretched. Glancing at her watch, she was surprised Heidi hadn't returned and peered through the kitchen window. Fine misty rain drifted on a breeze, coating everything it touched. She noticed a pair of ring-necked doves huddled together in a birch tree and was glad she was indoors. The only good thing about the miserable weather was it stayed mild – too mild for snow.

Stacey was about to put the kettle on when movement outside caught her attention and she spotted Heidi trudging towards the house. The petite woman huddled inside her hooded top, hands shoved deep into her pockets, and was covered in mud from the knees down. Stacey grabbed a towel, left the kitchen and met her friend in the boot room.

'You've been out for ages, and you're soaked. How did you get so muddy?'

Heidi removed her sodden top, draped the towel around her shoulders and sat on an old monk's seat to drag off her boots. 'It wasn't raining when I started,' she grouched. 'Bloody weather.'

'Started what?' Stacey asked.

'Digging Erica's grave.'

Heidi got to her feet and padded into the kitchen. Stacey followed.

'You don't have to do that,' she said. 'We could hire a mini digger. That would do the job in no time.'

'I know, but I want to do this myself, the old-fashioned way with a shovel.'

Stacey didn't feel she could ask why, so she dragged a dining chair closer to the Aga and topped up the firebox.

'Sit here,' she said, 'and dry out. I'll make a cuppa.'

'That'll be good, thanks. I'll start supper after I've taken a shower and put on clean clothes.'

Stacey handed over a steaming mug and Heidi wrapped her small hands around it, wincing as the heat stung a crop of blisters on her palms. Stacey dug some antiseptic and a pack of plasters out of a drawer and passed them over.

'Here,' she said and watched as Heidi cleaned and covered the wounds. 'How did you get on with the digging?'

'About halfway there.' She sipped from the mug. 'I spoke to Carrie Salmon yesterday and she's arranged the release of Erica's body.' Heidi took a deep breath. 'At least the autopsy proved she probably didn't know anything about it. Single shot to the heart, death was instantaneous.' Heidi got to her feet. 'I'll have that shower now, then come down and cook.'

'I'll do that,' Stacey said. 'I found some steak in the freezer. Do you fancy that with some chips?'

'Sounds good. Thanks.'

After Heidi had left the kitchen, Stacey made a quick call to Freddie, updated him on recent events and assured him all was well. He was grateful for the call and said he'd pop over to Abergavenny in a few days. Stacey knew he wanted to check on Heidi for himself.

* * *

Ben and Jack left the car on the lane and walked down to the hobbit houses, trying not to slip on the wet grass. They carefully navigated the steep stone steps leading into the settlement and tapped on Sally's door. John opened it almost immediately and smiled.

'Thanks for coming,' he said, 'and for whatever you said to the copper who nicked us.' He chuckled. 'They don't usually let us out so fast.'

'The whole thing was ridiculous,' Ben said. 'Glad I could help.'

'Come in and I'll make some tea.'

The detectives ducked their heads and stepped down into the main room. Sally appeared from behind the curtain and smiled.

'Perfect timing,' she said. 'Seren has just gone for a nap. Please, sit by the fire and get warm. How are Heidi and Stacey?'

'Safely back at home after their brief detention. I couldn't believe it when Stacey rang to say they'd been arrested.'

'Good job she had you.' Sally giggled. 'Good job we took her with us.'

John handed out tea and the group sat.

'So,' Ben said, 'you wanted a chat?'

Sally nodded. 'Yes, I did. I don't think it's anything to worry about, but thought you should know that Geraint has left us.'

'Oh?' Ben raised his eyebrows. 'What, for good?'

'I can't really say. I went to let him know we'd made it home, but couldn't find him. The door wasn't locked so I took a peek inside and it looks like he's packed up his stuff. I couldn't find a note, but I did find his mobile. I asked Janet Crabtree if she knew anything – her place is next door – but she says she hasn't seen him for a couple of days and he didn't mention he was going anywhere.'

'Has he done anything like this before?' Jack asked.

'Not since he moved in, but he is a wandering spirit. I'm surprised he stayed as long as he did.'

'Did he ever mention family to you?' Ben asked. 'Anything about where he came from?'

'No, nothing,' John said. 'I know he denied having anything to do with Will getting clobbered, but I'm not so sure.'

'You think he took the chance to leg it?' Jack asked.

'You have to admit it looks bad. He's lived here for over a year and seemed happy. I don't know what other reason would make him up and leave without saying anything to anyone. Rhys is fuming, he's still convinced that it was Geraint who whacked Will.'

'We haven't yet found a reason why he would have done that,' Ben said. 'Would it be OK if we take a look inside his place?'

'No problem. We locked the house up but I have the key.' John got to his feet, rummaged in a kitchen drawer and pulled out a key ring. 'Let's do it now,' he said. 'More rain is on the way and after this morning's escapade I fancy a quiet evening by the fire.'

John climbed the stairs and walked outside followed by the detectives. They strolled past the vegetable garden and made their way towards the end house.

* * *

Ben and Jack found nothing useful in Geraint's place and as it was getting late, made the decision to visit the Lloyds' solicitor the next day. When they walked into the incident room at the station, Tegan looked up from her work and smiled.

'How did you get on, sir?' she asked. 'Did you manage to free Heidi and Stacey?'

Jack chuckled. 'He certainly did. The officer in charge nearly threw them at us once Ben had pointed out the error of their ways.'

'Wish I'd been there,' Tegan said.

'I wish I'd got it on film.'

'Good job you didn't,' Ben said and took a seat at the head of the table. 'Are you making any progress, Tegan?' he asked.

'A little. The hospital has been in touch to say they've seen signs that Will North is regaining consciousness.'

'That's good news. Any idea when we might be able to talk to him?'

'No, sir. From what the doctor said it could be a while yet but the staff are monitoring the situation closely.' Tegan opened a cardboard file. 'Also, I've been chatting to the governor at HMP Drake Hall, the prison in Staffordshire where Katrina spent the last few years of her time inside.'

'Did he have anything useful to tell us?'

'She – Miss Nightingale – knew Katrina well, said the woman had a tough time of it.' Tegan took a deep breath. 'She was able to confirm Katrina's teeth had been removed by the prison's dentist – not uncommon apparently – and also that her wrist and fingers were broken when a couple of inmates in the kitchen where she worked held her hand in the bread mixer and switched it on.'

'Christ. That could have been so much worse, she was lucky.'

Tegan nodded. 'Yes, she was. An officer spotted what was happening and managed to put a rapid stop to it.'

'What did the governor have to say about Katrina's release?'

'That she wasn't surprised the conviction was overturned, only how long it took. She never believed her prisoner was guilty. From what Miss Nightingale said, I think she really liked Katrina – who worked hard as a Listener – an inmate trained by the Samaritans to help other inmates – and was delighted when the conviction was quashed.'

'Does she know who collected Katrina on the day of her release? Where she went after she left prison?'

'No, sir. The governor assumed her husband met her. It seems he visited his wife every two weeks without fail, but no address was left.'

'Do we know where Mr Randall lived while his wife was incarcerated?'

'Yes, sir, he had a place not far away in Talgarth. I've managed to speak to a few of his neighbours. One remembers Katrina coming home but said the couple moved away shortly after and couldn't tell me where.'

Ben nodded. 'OK, keep at it. We really need to talk to the husband. Did you manage to track down any other family?'

'The neighbour I spoke to said the Randalls had a son who went to university, she thinks, but couldn't give us a name. I haven't been able to find him, or anyone else, but I'll keep looking.'

Ben groaned. 'We need to make much more progress. Where are Elsa and Ollie?'

'They went out to talk to the farmers who own land bordering Dolgarrog – Gwilliam and Dewi Griffiths.'

'Better hope they return with something useful.'

The door opened as he finished speaking and Ollie and Elsa entered.

'What a waste of time,' Ollie grumbled.

'No luck with the Griffithses?' Jack asked.

'No sign of them. We hung around for a while in case they were out checking stock, but they didn't return and we couldn't get them on the phone.'

Ben nodded. 'OK, Jack and I will have another go tomorrow. We're planning to chat to the Lloyds' solicitor first thing, so we'll call in at the farm after that.' He stood, slipped into his jacket and addressed his team. 'Tomorrow, paperwork! Read through the statements we've collected, we must be missing something. Tegan, keep on with the search for anyone, or anything, to do with the Randalls. Oh, and Ollie, check all locally issued firearms certificates and specifically look for people who own rifles the same as the one used to kill Erica.'

'Yes, sir,' they said in unison.

Ben glanced at his sergeant. 'Fancy a trip over to Abergavenny? I'd like to check on the girls.'

'Yeah, I'm up for that. Julie's taken the twins to Welshpool for a couple of days.' He grinned. 'My kids make such a racket when they're at home, but when they're away the place is way too quiet.'

'No pleasing some,' Ben said. 'Right then, gang, I'm off. See you in the morning.'

Chapter nineteen

Stacey smiled when she opened the door and saw Ben and Jack standing on the step.

'Hey,' she said. 'This is a nice surprise. Come in.'

'Is Heidi here?' Ben asked.

'Yes she is.'

'How is she?' Jack asked.

Stacey lowered her voice. 'She seems OK but won't discuss losing Erica with me.' Stacey looked over her shoulder into the hall and, seeing it was empty, whispered, 'She was digging the grave today.'

Ben raised his eyebrows. 'Is she in the library?'

'No, kitchen. We've just finished supper.'

Jack grinned at his boss. 'You could have timed that better, guv.'

The group entered the kitchen and found Heidi sitting at the table, laptop open in front of her. She glanced up as the door opened.

'Evening,' she said. 'How is the investigation going? Making any progress?'

Ben took a seat on the opposite side of the table and told Heidi what actions had been taken to try to discover who killed her wife, and what would be done over the coming days. He reluctantly concluded that progress was slow.

'Have you got anything useful to tell me?' Heidi asked when he had finished.

'Well,' Ben said, 'Will North is showing signs of regaining consciousness, and Sally told us a couple of hours ago that Geraint Jones has left Dolgarrog.'

'That's interesting,' Heidi said. 'Any idea why?'

'Not really,' Jack said. 'We took a quick look inside his house. The only personal possession we found was his mobile, sitting on the worktop.'

'Leaving his phone behind proves he doesn't want to be found,' Heidi said, 'which means he planned his disappearance. It won't be easy to track him down, and of course his surname doesn't do us any favours, being that "Jones" is one of the most common names in the UK, probably more so in Wales.'

Stacey put a plate of Welsh cakes on the table next to a large teapot and a block of local butter. The detectives gratefully helped themselves.

'So,' Ben said around a mouthful of sugary crumbs, 'what have you two been up to since you got home?'

'Researching, mainly,' Stacey said. 'I've been looking into greenwashing and the company that was targeted this morning. Heidi thinks Carbon Zero Cymru is a scam.'

'Do you?' Jack asked, eyes on Heidi. 'Why do you think that?'

'Because the concept is wrong from the start. For example,' Heidi said, 'everyone knows flying is bad – catastrophic – for the environment, but companies like CZC will plant trees on your behalf and offset the carbon generated by the flight, which doesn't work.'

'Not an illegal scam then?' Ben asked.

'Give me time,' Heidi muttered.

'Until she finds something,' Stacey said, 'I'm looking at the wider picture.'

'Which means what?' Ben asked.

'It seems to me that offsetting appears to be a licence to keep on polluting. It distracts all of us – especially governments – from the real task which is actually cutting emissions.' Stacey buttered a griddle cake and took a bite.

'I'm going to interview the CEO of CZC tomorrow, one Laurence Fitzherbert.'

Ben laughed. 'And you think he'll welcome you with open arms after your part in the protest this morning?'

'I didn't have a part,' Stacey said, 'until I was unlawfully arrested.'

'Best of luck with that then.' Ben topped up his mug. 'Any chance Jack and I could stay over tonight? Don't fancy another hour on the road and besides' – he blew Stacey a kiss – 'I've been missing company.'

'No problem,' Heidi said. 'The beds in the rooms at the back of the house are made up. Might even get some breakfast if you're up early. I've got a busy day myself tomorrow.'

'Oh?' Ben asked. 'What will you be up to?'

'Digging,' Heidi said. 'I can collect Erica's body on Friday evening and plan to bury her on Saturday morning. Freddie's coming over with my sister, Greta, and Pixie. Obviously you are all welcome to attend, but it isn't compulsory.'

'About that…' Ben took a deep breath. 'CS Warren was hoping for a proper police funeral, dress uniforms, the whole nine yards.'

'No chance. Erica was married to me, not the job.'

'I'm good with a shovel,' Jack said. 'Would you like a hand?'

'No, thanks. I want to do this for Erica – and myself.'

Stacey changed the subject. 'You said Will North is improving?'

'He's in and out,' Ben said, 'but we really need to ask him who wielded the hammer.' He groaned. 'We haven't been able to connect anyone to the attack so the investigation has stalled. No evidence, no witnesses – for anything.'

'Are you linking the attack on Will with Erica's murder?' Heidi asked.

'Not officially but we are keeping open minds and not ruling anything out.'

Heidi nodded. 'Keep at it, OK? I'll stay out of your way, but not forever. I need to know who killed her.' She got to her feet and yawned. 'I'm knackered and off to bed, see you all tomorrow.'

* * *

Just after ten the next morning, the tyres on Jack's car crunched and bumped over frozen mud as he turned into a scruffy farmyard. A group of miserable-looking chickens perched on a broken fence, feathers fluffed up against the cold. He pulled up next to an ancient tractor which had seen much better days. The cab was missing, one rear wheel guard dangled at a peculiar angle, and there was definitely more rust than metal. The farmhouse was in a similar state of repair. A few slates were missing from the roof, a long section of guttering was only attached by a single bracket, and it had probably been well over a decade since a paintbrush had been anywhere near the windowsills.

The detectives stepped out of the car and picked their way towards the door. A noise from the rear of the property reached their ears, a sort of smacking and clinking sound. They changed direction and walked around the end of the house towards the backyard. Ben stopped and held up a hand. With the other, he pointed towards an old stone barn with a corrugated tin roof. Dewi was standing some thirty metres away from the open door and tucked into his shoulder was the wooden stock of a rifle. The officers watched as he peered through a large telescopic sight, checked his aim and pulled the trigger. A pyramid of old beer cans, balanced on a bench next to the barn, clattered to the icy ground.

'Dewi Griffiths,' Ben shouted. 'Police! Put your weapon down.'

Dewi turned and lowered the gun.

'Oh, it's you,' he said. 'Have you brought our shotguns with you?'

'No,' Jack said. 'I told you to pick them up from the station. We don't run a delivery service, and if we'd known you owned a rifle we would have confiscated that too.'

'It's an air rifle,' Dewi muttered. 'Don't need a licence for this.'

'Unless it's overpowered. Hand it over, let me take a look.'

'You can't take it off me,' Dewi said.

'I won't, unless it's been ramped up.'

Reluctantly the lad walked closer, Jack removed the weapon from his hands and checked it out.

'OK for me to have a go?' he asked.

'I suppose.' Dewi held out a few pellets, and Jack loaded the gun, took aim and fired at the fallen cans, making them skitter across the frozen earth.

'Nice gun,' Jack said. 'Looks new, expensive. Have you had it long?'

'A while. I look after my kit.'

'Quite a marksman too.'

Dewi shrugged and stared at his boots.

'Is your da in?' Ben asked. 'We need a word. A couple of officers called yesterday but there was no sign of either of you.'

'We were at the market in town,' Dewi said. 'Da's in the house, follow me.' He reclaimed his air rifle and headed towards the back door.

Inside the kitchen, his father was hunched over the table, a mug of tea and an open newspaper in front of him. He glanced up and groaned when he saw the detectives.

'What do you want?' he grumbled.

'Official statements,' Ben said, 'about where you were and what you were doing the morning of the shooting in the valley.'

'Working on the farm, what do you think I'd be doing? Lot of work a farm, always things to do. This time of year we're out feeding the sheep on the hills most mornings.'

'Is that what you were doing?' Ben asked. 'Your son too?'

'Yes, same as every morning.'

'Dewi is a good shot,' Jack said. 'Just been watching him in the yard. Have you any more weapons in the house? Any rifles other than the air rifle?'

'No reason to have rifles. Shotguns are enough for our purposes. Dewi has the air rifle for a bit of fun, shoots the odd pigeon but nothing more.'

'Would it be OK for us to take a quick look around?' Ben asked.

Gwilliam leapt to his feet. 'Of course it bloody wouldn't,' he huffed. 'No reason for you to search my home and definitely not without a warrant. We have nothing to do with what's been going on in the valley and we stay away from those bloody hippies.'

'You didn't stay away the other day,' Jack pointed out, 'when we found you shouting the odds with John and Sally.'

'That was different,' the man said. 'Gill had been accused of murder and we wanted to set the record straight.'

'By yelling at your neighbours? Waving shotguns around?'

'We were out rabbiting when Gill rang. We didn't take the shotguns purposely, we already had them with us.'

Jack nodded. 'Fair enough I suppose, although I have to say, I don't understand your animosity towards the residents,' he said. 'Now, let's get on with those statements and we'll get out of your way.' He glanced at Dewi. 'Put the kettle on, boy. This will take a little while and I'm parched.'

Chapter twenty

Having parked her car on the edge of Abergavenny, Stacey strolled through the pedestrian area window shopping. The cold, sunny morning had encouraged others out and the streets were busy. A little before half past twelve, she arrived outside the offices of CZC and took a moment to replay the protest in her mind, remembered how the climbers shimmied up the building. She saw Heidi had been right, the wet weather had washed nearly all traces of green paint from the windows. She pushed through the main doors, announced her arrival to the smiling receptionist, and perched on a modern, uncomfortable chair to wait for Laurence Fitzherbert.

Ten minutes passed before a tall man in his late thirties, dressed in an expensive handmade suit, with shoes to match, opened a door next to the desk and strode towards his visitor, hand outstretched.

'Good afternoon,' he said in a plummy English accent, and grabbed Stacey's hand. He blinked and his grip faltered. 'We've met before, haven't we?'

'Yes, briefly,' Stacey said. 'I was covering the protest yesterday.' She offered a business card. 'I work for *The Mid Wales Times.*'

Fitzherbert shook his head. 'No, that can't be right. I saw you arrested and wearing handcuffs. You're one of them.'

'What you saw,' Stacey said, reclaiming her hand, 'was an unlawful arrest. Have you not seen the paper this morning?'

'Who has the time for papers?' He hesitated. 'I don't think it is appropriate for me to provide an interview – given the circumstances.'

'There are no "circumstances". I am a journalist and report the news in an unbiased way. It's my job. I'm here to learn about what your company plans to do for Wales, listen to your side of things.'

Fitzherbert shrugged. 'Go on then. I doubt I'll get rid of you any other way.'

Stacey smiled, anxious to put the CEO at ease. 'I have been called tenacious in the past.'

'Follow me then,' he said and glanced at the receptionist. 'Bring in some tea, Sarah.'

Stacey followed him towards the rear of the building and inside a large office. Through an enormous expanse of plate glass, she gazed at the Bannau Brycheiniog, green and rusty-brown, autumn flanks burnished by the sun, scattered sheep, like small, white, full stops.

'Wow,' she said. 'What an incredible view. If this was my office I probably wouldn't get any work done at all. Just beautiful.'

'One of the reasons I decided CZC should be based here, in this building,' Fitzherbert said. 'We can never forget just what it is we are trying to save.'

He waved a hand at a modern easy chair and Stacey sat. A tap on the door announced the arrival of refreshments. Fitzherbert poured two cups of tea from a glass teapot then sat on a matching chair facing his guest.

'Well then, Ms Logan, what would you like to know?'

Stacey sipped her tea and smiled. 'I have a few questions, but I admit I don't know a lot about the business you are in, how it all works.'

'Not many do,' the CEO said, 'it's fairly complicated. Red tape by the mile and more rules and regs than you could count in your lifetime.'

'Could we begin by you explaining some of the terms used? They are thrown around in the media but I'm not sure my readers know what they mean. For example, what is a carbon credit?'

'Put simply, it is a kind of permit which allows the owner to emit a fixed amount of CO2 or other greenhouse gases. Organisations buy the credits – at today's prices around sixty pounds each – and if they don't use them all they can sell them on in a regulated market.'

'So as long as they buy enough credits, they can continue to pollute?'

'Sort of, but each year the number of credits they can buy is reduced, therefore gradually cutting the overall emissions.'

'OK, thanks.' Stacey scribbled. 'How about carbon capture and removal?'

'That's a lot more complicated. There are new technologies being developed all the time. Essentially, we need to remove CO2 from the air, as well as directly from emissions, then capture it. Disused mines are being considered for storage and more schemes are in the planning stages.'

'But you don't do any of that?'

'No. CZC is a carbon offsetting company. We plant trees which suck up CO2 naturally and reduce our overall carbon footprint.'

'Interesting, thanks for that. Let's concentrate on the trees. Does your company plant them? Do you buy the land first or lease it from the owners?'

Fitzherbert drank from his cup. 'We do all of that,' he said. 'We source suitable land – which we prefer to purchase, but will lease – and plant trees. Offsetting is focussed on trees, but there are some interesting plans involving planting seaweed forests around the coast.'

'Who pays for all that?' Stacey asked. 'Where does the money come from?'

'A range of places, either from large organisations, or from individuals. For example, a nominal fee of five pounds each month would offset your family's carbon emissions, even things up.'

Stacey nodded and scribbled some more. 'I've read that Greenpeace – and others – have stated offsetting is in fact greenwashing. That the trees take twenty years to deliver the results being promoted.'

Fitzherbert shrugged. 'It's difficult to calculate' – he grinned – 'even for experts in the field.'

Stacey consulted her notes. 'On your website,' she said, 'you promise jobs for rural areas.'

'Yes, that's right. We'll be good for Mid Wales.'

'Maybe, but trees are fairly self-sufficient, whereas the farms you are buying need workers. The Farmers' Union of Wales have received reports on a weekly basis of entire farms being snapped up for schemes like yours – agricultural workers losing their jobs, and in some instances their homes. Surely this will have a negative effect on Welsh farming communities?'

'You need to look at the long-term plan, Ms Logan. When the trees are ready for harvesting, that is a very labour-intensive operation.'

Stacey nodded noncommittally and turned a page in her notebook.

'The protestors held up signs yesterday saying, "Food not Firs". They've got a point, haven't they? If you snaffle up agricultural land and plant trees, what are we going to eat? As it is, the UK is less than fifty per cent self-sufficient.'

Fitzherbert chuckled. 'Things aren't that easy. The ground beneath the trees can be used for animals.'

'Only if you plant broad-leaved, open woodland, and don't introduce many animals. The plantations I've seen are conifers, crammed in, ground below devoid of undergrowth; they're like deserts covered in pine needles.'

'Well,' he said, 'you were right. You don't know much about the subject. More research required, Ms Logan.' The man shot a sleeve and peered at a chunky, and no doubt costly, wristwatch.

'I'm sorry,' he said, 'but we've nearly run out of time. I hope I've been able to answer your questions, but please ring if you'd like another chat. I'll fit you in if I can. Ask the receptionist to give you a full information pack on the way out.'

He stood and Stacey looked up at him.

'Just one last question, if you don't mind. Do you really think that injecting trees into capitalism will help us solve the climate crisis we're in?'

'Well,' he said, 'we have to do something, so why not this?'

* * *

A young woman showed Ben and Jack to William Williams' inner sanctum. She rapped on the door and pushed it open.

'DCI James and DS Trent,' she said.

'Thank you, Ruth.'

As the officers entered an old-fashioned office with walls lined with books, a man probably in his late seventies, with white, sparse hair, and dressed in a pinstripe suit, stood to meet his visitors, a wide smile on his lips.

'Please, gentlemen, come in and make yourselves comfortable.'

'Thank you, Mr Williams,' Ben said.

'Call me Bill,' the solicitor said, 'it makes everything much easier.' He laughed. 'What were my parents thinking? Can I get you a cup of tea or coffee?'

'No, thanks, sir. We'd like to talk to you about the sale of some land on the manor estate about eight years ago.'

'Ah, you probably mean the wooded valley.'

'Yes, that's right. What can you tell us about it?'

'Not much to tell. George – Old Mr Lloyd as the locals knew him – asked me to handle the sale. A group of young men and women wanted to build a settlement of off-grid homes.' Bill smiled. 'George was so impressed by their plans and really wanted to help. "To be a part in shaping the future" was what he said.'

'Did you meet anyone from the group?' Jack asked.

'Most of them actually, delightful individuals.' His face crinkled with another smile. 'I remember when Seren was born, the next generation. Well, I can tell you, George was as happy as a milking parlour cat.'

'A few people have told us,' Ben said, 'that Mr Lloyd was leant on, or groomed, to sell the land. That maybe his mental capacity was on the wane.'

'What rubbish!' Bill said. 'Sharp as a knife and certainly knew his own mind – unlike his fairly useless children.'

Ben raised his eyebrows. 'Oh?'

'They all take after their mother; needy, clingy individuals at their best – they got worse since they inherited the estate.'

'What happened to their mother?' Jack asked.

'She died when Darryl was five. She drove too fast on the mountain road once too often, lost control of her car and took off into space.'

'So, her early death affected the children,' Ben said.

'It certainly didn't help. Joanne became very ill and spent six months in a private mental health facility. I guess you'd call it a breakdown. Shirlee is bipolar and has struggled for years.' He sighed. 'George did a great job of caring for them, they didn't want for anything.' He smiled. 'Listen to me rabbiting on.'

'It's useful stuff,' Ben said. 'From our conversations with them, they seem really angry about the sale of the valley. Do you know why?'

'That's not difficult to answer. An offsetting company approached them recently, offered three thousand pounds an acre above the going rate, without realising the land was no longer part of the estate.' He chuckled. 'The gamekeeper was pissed off too. Have you met Gill Baird?'

'We have, yes.'

'Not my cup of tea at all,' the solicitor said. 'I think he influences the children, behaves like an overbearing grandfather.'

'Has he ever been in any sort of trouble?'

'Not really. He never liked people on estate land though, tried blocking the odd footpath in the past.' He chuckled. 'I remember an incident many years ago, long before the settlement was founded. He surprised a courting couple, waved his shotgun about and frightened them off. He did such a good job, they left some of their clothes behind. Kept locals gossiping for months. I'm rambling again, my apologies.'

'No need. Background is exactly what we're after.'

Jack glanced up from his notebook. 'There have been some incidents of vandalism at Dolgarrog, broken generation systems, that sort of thing. One of the settlers was attacked with a hammer, and one of our officers was shot dead. Do you think any of that might be something Gill would be capable of?'

The elderly solicitor nodded sadly. 'I read about it all in the paper. As to whether Gill would be capable? I don't know, Sergeant, I suppose it is possible, but I like to believe that people mellow as they grow older, even overbearing gamekeepers.'

'Any reason you haven't mentioned Darryl?' Ben asked.

'Not really. Being the youngest – and having Joanne as an elder sister – he hasn't had time to develop his own mind.' Bill frowned. 'As you will have worked out, Joanne is very much in control, has been since George died. Darryl, to get away from her, spends too much time with Gill. But that is only an old man's view.'

There was a tap on the door and the receptionist peered in. 'Sorry to disturb, but your two o'clock is here.'

'Thank you, my dear. Please tell Mrs White I'll be right out.'

The detectives stood and Ben held out a hand. 'We'll get out of your way, sir. Thanks again for your time.'

'You know where I am, Chief Inspector, should you have any further questions.'

* * *

Ben and Jack walked into the incident room and found the team up to their necks in the mountain of paperwork the simultaneous investigations had generated. They looked up as he called them together and gathered around the large table.

'Afternoon,' Ben said. 'Are we making any progress? Any sudden insights – regarding anything?'

'Not really, sir,' Tegan said. 'Still no luck tracing Katrina's husband, or her third son – if she even had one. I'm convinced that when Katrina was released, the family changed their names so they could vanish and that's why I've hit a brick wall.'

'Yeah, maybe.' Ben sighed. 'Ollie, anything useful on rifle ownership?'

'Not great news, sir,' he said. 'Over six hundred and twenty thousand firearms certificates were issued in Wales last year, and more than half of those for weapons other than shotguns. Rifles, handguns, stuff like that.'

'You need to scale down the search area,' Jack said. 'County by county.'

'Seems like a lot of hassle,' Ollie grumbled. 'Even if I track down every rifle in the country, we might only end up proving that DS Bevan was shot with an unregistered weapon.'

'What do you suggest we do?' Ben asked. 'We have no witnesses, precious little in the way of evidence, and not a single credible suspect. In the absence of any of that, we have to look elsewhere, so do as I ask.'

'Yes, sir,' Ollie muttered.

Ben turned to look at Elsa. 'Found Geraint Jones yet?' he asked.

'No, sir. No sign. He doesn't own a vehicle so he either uses public transport, walks or hitches maybe.' She opened a folder and ran her finger down a printed list. 'I haven't been able to find a bank account, no driving licence or passport, no details of any previous address, and no mobile contract. The phone he left behind was a burner and held no information.'

'He told us he had been to university,' Jack said, 'but didn't tell us which one. Said he'd dropped out.'

'I had a quick go at looking for him somewhere like that but it's almost impossible with a name like Jones.'

'Bloody hell, we haven't really got anything.' Ben scrubbed at his face. 'OK then, we need to dig deeper into the lives of those involved in this mess. Jack and I have come from speaking to the Lloyds' solicitor. He filled in some of the family's history, but it isn't enough. Then there's the Griffithses. Jack and I saw Dewi shooting a fancy air rifle at his place today, and he's good, more than good. I want to know when he bought it, how much he paid and where the money came from. Heidi told us right at the start that she thought a marksman made the shot that killed Erica.'

'But Dewi doesn't own an actual rifle,' Ollie said, 'only shotguns.'

'Unless he has one of those unregistered weapons you mentioned.'

'Yeah… unless he does.'

'Gill Baird sounds like he was a handful long before the settlement was built,' Ben said. 'Mr Williams mentioned a couple who were chased off the land at the wrong end of a shotgun; it seems that the gamekeeper hated anyone on the estate and in the past blocked footpaths and rights of way. It's weak but the closest thing we have to a motive that I can see. More digging required.' Ben glanced back at Tegan. 'Anything from forensics?' he asked. 'In particular, anything regarding the ageing of the spent shell cases?'

'Not really. Seems it is an imprecise science, too many potential external factors to be useful. Some of the other cases collected during the fingertip search were from both of Gill's rifles, but many more from unidentified weapons. Ballistics checked their records and no match. There is one thing though.'

'Oh?'

'I've taken a quick look at the company that attracted the protestors earlier in the week. The CEO and founder – Laurence Fitzherbert – has been a regular visitor to the manor estate's shoots, together with a couple of guys on the board. Seems he approached the Lloyds offering to buy land. He was also at the shoot the day DS Bevan died.' She sighed. 'I'm not sure it's even relevant, but there is a tenuous link.'

'Yes, you're right. Stacey had an interview planned at his head office. I'll ask what her opinion is of the man. OK then, plans for tomorrow… research, research, research. If Tegan has found one link, there must be others.' Ben waved a hand at the incident board and the table below, piled with files and reports. 'The answer to all of this is here, I'm sure, we just have to find it.' He got to his feet and looked down at the team. 'One more thing,' he said, 'Erica's funeral will take place on Saturday morning at Heidi's house outside Abergavenny at eleven o'clock. Uniforms are not to be worn. You might want to add it to your calendars.' He saw heads nodding around the table. 'That's it then for today. Back here first thing and find me the clue to break the case, or even a decent motive.'

Chapter twenty-one

Ben and Stacey lounged together on the old Chesterfield, while Heidi draped herself in an easy chair next to the fireplace in the library.

'Lovely you found time to pop over this evening,' Stacey said.

'Purely selfish,' Ben said. 'The bed is too big without you.'

'That's sweet,' Heidi said. 'I know what you mean.'

Ben paused. 'I might not be able to get back again until Saturday when…'

'I bury my wife.'

'Yes, for the funeral. CS Warren has asked if she can attend.'

'Of course, but not in uniform.'

'I'll make sure she knows.'

Stacey changed the subject. 'I did manage to interview Laurence Fitzherbert today and I think Heidi is right. This offsetting business doesn't make sense to me. There's a lot of money sloshing around in these schemes and I'm not convinced the benefits they deliver outweigh the other stuff; loss of agricultural land for food production, family farms being swallowed up, and of course the negative impact on communities isn't great either.' She added another splash to her brandy glass. 'Fitzy has spent loads of money, I wonder where he got it from.'

'That's easy,' Heidi said. 'He made his fortune running a social media platform which he sold to the highest bidder.'

'Any clues why he got involved with planting trees?' Ben asked.

'Guess he thinks that's where he can make another load of money – and he's probably right.'

'So you've been digging into his background?'

'Yeah, a bit. Working class roots. Mother was a nurse, dad a bus driver. Seems they worked all hours, scrimped and saved and sent Fitzy to good schools, followed by uni. After graduation, he went to the States, spent some time in Silicon Valley, and returned to the UK, pockets stuffed with cash.'

'Any criminal activity?'

'Beyond a shadow of doubt – he just managed not to get himself officially nicked for anything, here or across the pond.'

'I didn't like him much, he has more than a touch of sleaze about him and spent a good portion of our meeting mansplaining.' Stacey chuckled. 'I didn't think he'd let me in. Said I was "one of them".'

'We took a quick look at him,' Ben said. 'CZC was the company who approached the Lloyds offering to buy the valley, without realising it was no longer part of the estate. Fitzherbert often attends the shoots and was on site when Erica was shot.'

'Do you think he killed her?' Heidi asked.

'We're not ruling anyone out, but I'll be candid, progress is painfully slow.' Ben sighed heavily. 'We're working the investigation hard, no slacking, but no evidence or even a single decent suspect.' He rubbed his eyes. 'The only person we've arrested was Geraint Jones, and now he's gone walkabout. He seems to have lived an off-grid life, no passport, driving licence, not even a bank account that we've found.'

'Not like there's proof he had anything to do with the shooting though,' Heidi said. 'He was nicked on suspicion of walloping Will North and you couldn't prove he'd done that.' She sipped from her glass. 'Have you traced Katrina Randall's husband yet?'

'No, we haven't. Mr Randall lived in Talgarth while his wife was in prison, but a neighbour told us the family moved away within weeks of Katrina's release. The same neighbour mentioned a son but couldn't give us a name. Elsa thinks she can't track them because they changed their names.'

Ben's phone chirped. He didn't recognise the number and answered, 'DCI James.'

A distressed howl hurtled down the line and he moved the phone away from his ear.

'Hello?' he said. 'Who is this?'

'He's dead,' a woman's voice wailed. 'We've just found him and he's dead.'

'Please, madam, take a breath and tell me who is dead.'

'Darryl. Gill found him floating in the pond at the top of Dolgarrog. You must come.'

'OK, Shirlee. I'll be there as quickly as I can. Where are you now?'

'In the house with Joanne. Gill brought Darryl here. He's in the hall. Please,' she whined, 'we need your help.'

'Stay in the house. I'll leave now.'

Ben hung up and dialled Jack's number.

'Yes, guv? It's late,' he said when he picked up.

'Get over to the manor estate. Shirlee Lloyd just rang to say Darryl is dead. He was found in the turbine's header pond. I'll ring round, get the troops there. Will you contact Carrie Salmon for me?'

'No problem.'

'I'll head to the scene. You go to the house and I'll meet you there.' Ben cut the connection.

'Darryl Lloyd is dead?' Stacey asked. 'How?'

'You know as much as I do,' Ben said. He got to his feet and put on his jacket. 'Sorry to cut this so short. I'll ring as soon as I can. Look after each other and stay here.' He fixed Stacey in his gaze. 'Please, don't come out, it'll make things difficult and might not be safe.'

'I won't,' Stacey said, 'but be sure to keep in touch.'

* * *

By the time Ben arrived at the head of the valley there were several vehicles parked in the lane. He recognised the pathologist's truck and was glad she had arrived promptly. After pulling on a pair of wellies, and digging out a large torch from the boot of his car, Ben headed down the sloping, grassy land and soon stood next to the manmade pool. Lights had been erected and a pair of SOCOs were unrolling a tent to place over the crime scene, while Carrie peered at the muddy ground. Ben walked closer.

'Evening, Carrie,' he said. 'Thanks for getting here so quickly.'

'It's more or less on my doorstep,' she said. 'Thought I'd take a quick look at the scene before examining the body. I understand why Darryl was dragged out of the water, but it would have been better to see the body in situ.'

'Find anything?'

'Not really, too dark to conduct a proper search – that will have to wait until daybreak – but this section of the bank is a little chewed up. Signs of a scuffle maybe?'

'As you say, difficult to be sure.' Ben waved Ollie Langdon closer. 'Secure the site,' Ben said, 'and keep people off the banks. No one here but SOCO, OK? I'll go up to the manor with Carrie. If you find anything, phone me immediately.'

'Yes, sir.'

'Come on then, Carrie. Jack should be at the house. Shirlee told me the body is in the hall.'

She nodded and they began the trek up to the lane where Carrie got into her truck and followed Ben's car as he drove on to the manor house. He parked next to Jack's vehicle and they walked across the gravel to the front door which was standing open, yellow light spilling into the darkness.

The hall felt crowded. Darryl lay prone on the carpet, water seeping from his sodden clothes. Standing a couple of meters away from the body were the Lloyd sisters, arms around each other. Shirlee sobbed, torrents of tears streaming from her eyes. Joanne's eyes were dry, glassy and she stared at nothing. Gill wore a deep frown, and her trousers were wet, presumably from dragging Darryl out of the pond. He clasped his hands behind his back and his eyes flicked from the body to the women and back again, unsure what to do, whether to try to comfort them. Jack stood close to the body, scribbling in his notebook. He looked up as Ben and Carrie entered, and took a few steps back.

Carrie pulled on gloves and took a series of photographs before squatting on her heels next to Darryl.

She peered closely at his hands, examined the fingernails, then covered the hands with evidence-protecting plastic bags, held in place by elastic bands. She worked her way up the body, pointed out a button had been torn from Darryl's shirt, several facial abrasions, a bloodied nose and a split lip. Carrie glanced up at Ben, eyebrows raised.

'Jack,' Ben said. 'Take the family to the living room, find out what has happened.'

'No!' Shirlee wailed. 'I want to stay with my brother.'

Joanne held her sister tighter and Ben rested a hand on Shirlee's arm. 'Please, go with DS Trent. I promise we won't take your brother from the house without telling you.'

Shirlee's shoulders dropped and as the hall emptied, Elsa walked in through the front door. Ben held up a hand for her to wait.

'So, Carrie,' he said. 'What can you tell me?'

'First impression suggests he's probably been in a fight – fisticuffs; I can't see any obvious damage caused by a weapon.' She pointed at Darryl's face. 'Punch on the nose, another to his left eye, a third split the lip.' She drew Ben's attention to a scrape on one cheek. 'This might have happened during his tumble into the pond, it looks like a grass burn.'

'Was he killed before he went into the water?' Ben asked.

'I don't think so. Burst blood vessels in the eyes indicate drowning. He might have been unconscious though. I'll be able to tell you more once I get back to base.'

Ben nodded. 'OK, thanks. Let's get him on a trolley so the girls can say their goodbyes.'

Carrie waved a couple of attendants closer. They zipped the body into a bag, lifted it onto a wheeled trolley, and covered the black plastic with a blanket leaving the face uncovered. Ben and Elsa went to the living room and, with Jack's help, escorted Joanne and Shirlee into the hall.

Gill Baird followed behind. Shirlee kissed her brother on his undamaged cheek, Joanne kept her distance. They watched silently as the gurney was wheeled out then the officers coaxed them back into the living room. The women sat side by side, clasping each other's hands as though they themselves were drowning. Joanne was still not crying, but her eyes were wide open and staring into space. Shirlee sobbed steadily, while Gill leant on the tall mantelpiece, eyes downcast, like a depressed lord of the manor. Elsa went in search of the kitchen to make tea. Ben and Jack sat opposite the women.

'So,' Ben said, 'tell me again how Darryl was found.'

Shirlee raised a quivering hand and pointed at the gamekeeper.

'Gill found him,' she said, 'and brought him up to the house.'

'I was on my rounds,' Gill said and rubbed his face. 'Full moon last night, perfect for poachers, so I was out late. I was close to the head of the valley and spotted something in the water.'

'Did you see anyone about? Hear anything?' Ben asked.

'Nothing. Quiet as the–' Gill stopped speaking abruptly. He took a deep breath before continuing. 'Anyway, I ran down the slope, recognised Darryl by his jacket. He was face down in the pond, so I waded in to drag him out.' He closed his eyes reliving the moment. 'I tried CPR, kiss of life – all of it. But nothing was any good. I failed him. I failed the family.'

Joanne glanced up at the older man. 'No, Gill, you haven't. You tried your best to save him, that's what is important.'

'How did you move him up here?' Ben asked.

'I had the quad. Drove it as close as I could to the pond and loaded…' He ran out of words and pinched the bridge of his nose.

'Do any of you know why Darryl was out so late?'

'No,' Joanne said. 'I don't.'

'When did you last see him?' Jack asked.

'We had supper together, so about seven thirty.'

'Did Darryl often walk the estate after dark?' Ben asked.

Joanne shrugged. 'Sometimes – usually when he couldn't sleep.' She sighed. 'He suffers… uh, suffered–' she gulped '–from night terrors. Always had since mum died.'

Shirlee blew her nose loudly. 'Do you think it was an accident?' she asked. 'That he slipped and fell in the water?'

'We'll know more in the morning,' Ben said. 'DS Trent and I will get off now. We need to secure the scene and begin a search of the area. I'll leave Constable Duffin here with you and as I soon as I have any news I will return.' Ben got to his feet and buttoned his jacket. 'I am very sorry for your loss.'

Jack also hauled himself upright. He tucked his notebook in his pocket and opened the door for his boss. They got in their cars and drove back to the lane above Dolgarrog.

Chapter twenty-two

Hours passed before Ben and Jack were able to leave the scene and make their way to the morgue. Carrie was sitting in her office documenting her findings. Her recent client rested on a wheeled gurney and was covered with a sheet. She looked up as they walked in and poured two coffees from a glass jug sitting on a hotplate.

'You look done in,' she said. 'Here.'

She handed the mugs over and cleared files from a couple of chairs. The detectives muttered their thanks and sat.

Ben nodded at the gurney. 'What can you tell us?' he asked.

'Pretty much what I thought. I can confirm he was alive when he went in the pond, the lungs are full of water. The injuries are consistent with someone punching him. His knuckles are scraped and bruised which indicates he fought back. It doesn't look like murder to me, but that's not my call. He might have fallen in the water, or been pushed in, no way of telling for certain. Blood alcohol too high for driving, so he'd probably had a few, but was not incapable of walking. I've sent samples to toxicology.'

'Time of death?'

'A couple of hours before he was discovered. Difficult to be completely sure. Immersion in cold water always messes with the cooling process.'

'Any clues on the body?' Jack asked. 'Like a nice lump of someone else's skin plus their DNA under his fingernails?'

Carrie shook her head. 'Doesn't look like it, just mud and detritus from the pool. I've taken samples but I'm pretty sure there's nothing to find.' She sipped from her own mug. 'How did it go with the family?'

'About what you'd expect. The gamekeeper told us how he'd found the body and taken it to the house. The younger sister is very distressed and Joanne seems badly shocked.' Ben drained his mug. 'Thanks for this, Carrie. We're off to grab a couple of hours of sleep, due back at the scene early tomorrow. All we can hope for is we find something to tell us who Darryl ran into last night, otherwise…' Ben sighed. 'Come on, Jack. We need a breather and the sun will be up in no time.'

* * *

After a couple of hours shut-eye inside a vacant cell in the custody suite, the detectives met in the incident room before seven the next morning. Tegan was already at her workstation, tapping her keyboard and shuffling paper. She looked up as they walked in.

'I didn't expect to see you, sir,' she said, 'but I'm glad you're here.'

'Something up?' Ben asked.

'Yes, sir. I found something odd last night before I knocked off, and came in early to check it out.' She dragged a file out of the heap next to her screen. 'I discovered a batch of DNA results relating to the skeleton, Katrina Randall. It seems as though no one looked at them, presumably because we had managed to identify her.'

'There's bound to be the odd oversight,' Ben said, 'with so much going on. I'll have a word upstairs, maybe there are a couple of uniforms we could use to take up some of the slack.'

'Yes, sir, I agree, but the thing is–' Tegan took a deep breath '–her DNA matches the sample we collected from Geraint Jones.'

'What? Are you sure?'

'Yes, sir. Katrina is the mother of Geraint.'

Ben dropped on a nearby chair and wiped his eyes. 'Bloody hell. That can't be right, surely.'

'I've double-checked and it's a clear match.'

'What the hell does this mean?' he snapped and glanced up at Jack. 'What are the chances?'

'I really can't see it's random, guv,' Jack said. 'Geraint must have known she was here, so the question is, did he kill her? If he did, then he returned to gloat.' He sat next to Ben.

'This is just mad,' Ben said. 'He only moved in just over a year ago. What was he doing here? Where was he when she died?' Ben scrubbed the top of his head.

'We need to find him and ask. Put him on the national watch list. He'll be picked up eventually. Erica really should be our priority.'

'You're right. Unless we find out more about the Randall family, we're flying blind.' Ben looked at Tegan. 'I know it's a big ask, but if you have a minute, could you check to see if the Randalls became the Joneses? Might be why you haven't found Katrina's husband.'

'I'll do my best, sir, but you're right, with a name like Jones it is a big ask.' Tegan smiled. 'Just the sort of thing that comes under the heading of "slack". A couple of extra personnel would make the world of difference.'

'I'll have a word, meantime, keep an eye on things here for us. If anything comes up that I need to know about, get in touch.'

Ben's phone vibrated in his pocket. He dragged it into the light and peered at the screen before answering.

'Ollie,' he said. 'Something to tell me?'

'Yes, sir. SOCO have found a couple of good-quality footprints on the bank, and a few of what they say are air gun pellets, specifically for a rifle.'

'Is the search continuing?'

'It is, but I thought I'd bring the evidence back to base, then pass it to forensics.'

'Good idea, do that. When you have, return to the scene. Any word from Elsa?'

'Not so far,' Ollie said. 'I'll stick my head in at the house on my way back. An FLO might be a good idea though. Elsa's been up all night and could probably do with a break.'

'I'll see to it. Keep in touch. Jack and I have a call to make, but we'll be there as soon as we can. If SOCO don't need you, pop in to Dolgarrog and let the residents know what's going on, then get up to the house and begin taking formal statements.'

'Yes, sir.'

Ben slipped the phone back in his pocket. 'Jack, we need another word with Dewi Griffiths. We need to collect his air rifle and footwear and convince him to come to the station to help us with our enquiries. There's an outside chance he might have been involved but we don't have anything like enough to arrest him.'

'I'll go and find a car,' Jack said and left the room.

Ben picked up the desk phone and spoke to CS Warren. He asked for the extra staff, updated her on the evolving investigation, and told her she was welcome to attend Erica's burial at the weekend. Then he hung up.

'Hold the fort, Tegan,' he said. 'Help is on its way but if you need me for anything, get in touch.'

'Will do, sir.'

Ben ran down the stairs, slipped into the passenger seat of a black Mondeo, and Jack headed towards the home of the Griffiths family.

* * *

Stacey was hunched over her laptop in the library, while Heidi wandered along the bookshelves in search of more duplicates. The weather had turned, heavy monsoon-like rain washed away the autumn sunshine and turned the ground to mud. Stacey hoped her friend had covered the grave, and it didn't fill with water, but didn't feel able to ask. Heidi wandered closer and peered over Stacey's shoulder.

'What are you working on?' she asked.

'The death of Darryl Lloyd, to keep my editor off my back.'

'Are you still planning a feature about CZC and greenwashing?'

'Yes, I've made a start. I have a few interviews with local farmers booked. Those who have sold up, and some who haven't.'

'Good,' Heidi said. 'I've been keeping away from the investigation into Erica's murder – as I promised Freddie I would – but there's a lot of money sloshing around. Money is right up there as a motive for murder.'

'Fancy sharing your research into Fitzy and CZC?'

'Of course, I'll send you the file.'

'Thanks.' Stacey closed her laptop. 'Can I ask, what will happen on Saturday? Is there anything you'd like me to do?'

'No, it's fine.' Heidi flopped on a nearby chair and rubbed her face. 'Saturday will be pretty much what you'd expect, but without all the religious crap. As you know, the grave is under the yew tree in the back garden, so we'll carry Erica from the house, place her in the ground, fill in the hole and it will be done. Then we – I – can move on.'

'Do you have plans? About moving on?'

'I'm working on it. After Saturday is over, you should go home. I'll be fine here, there's masses of work to be done and we've already agreed that keeping busy is the way to go.'

'If you're sure…'

'I'm certain. Thank you for being here, but I need some space soon.'

* * *

Jack parked next to the decrepit tractor outside the farmhouse. The detectives got out of the car and splashed across the yard, collars turned up against the rain. Ben hammered on the door. A dog barked loudly on the far side and after a short wait, Gwilliam Griffiths opened up and peered out into the grey day.

'Christ, not you two again,' he grumbled. 'What do you want now?'

'A word with your son,' Jack said. 'Is he in?'

'He's eating his breakfast, go on through.'

Ben led the way into a small kitchen with a low ceiling. Dewi was sitting at the table, a plate of bacon and eggs in front of him. His fork paused halfway to his mouth when he saw the officers.

'Morning,' Ben said and took a seat.

Jack leaned on the doorframe effectively barring any quick exits.

Dewi looked up at Ben. 'What?' he asked.

'Where were you last night after the sun went down?'

'Here at the farm. Where do you think I was?'

'That's right. He was here with me all night,' Gwilliam said.

Ben looked back at Dewi. 'You didn't go out after your da was in bed?'

'No, I didn't.'

'OK, fair enough.' Ben got to his feet.

'Is that it?' Dewi asked, eyes wide with surprise.

'Pretty much, except we're on our way to the station. Wondered if you wanted a lift to pick up your shotguns.'

'Uh… well… I guess.'

'Could you bring your air rifle with you?' Jack asked.

'Why would I do that?'

'We need to carry out a quick check to properly make sure it isn't overpowered. No biggy, and once we've checked it, no one will bother you again.'

'Might as well, boy. Too wet to do much outside this morning, but I'd be glad to have the shotguns back, keep the vermin down,' Gwilliam said.

Dewi shrugged. He put the last of his breakfast into his mouth, lifted a waterproof coat from a hook on the back of the door, and followed the officers out to their car. As Dewi got into the back seat, Jack caught Ben's eye and winked.

Chapter twenty-three

When Dewi arrived at the station, he was shown inside an interview room and offered tea which he accepted. Jack passed the air rifle to Ollie who took it away for "testing" and handed Jack a cardboard file. Ollie grinned as he passed it over. Jack took a peek inside and saw a black-and-white enlarged photograph and a small evidence bag.

He became aware of a smile blooming on his own face and made his way towards the interview room, looking forward to grilling Dewi. He'd always known the boy had too much anger for his own good. He already felt certain the right man had been detained and that he could have been responsible for killing Erica. He entered the room and took a seat at the table next to Ben.

'How long will he be with my gun?' Dewi asked, eyes on the closed door.

'Not long,' Jack said. 'While you're here, maybe you could help us with something.'

Dewi shrugged. 'I guess.'

Jack removed the plastic evidence bag from the file. It contained three small, lead-coloured pellets.

'We came across these,' he said. 'Can you tell us what gun would fire these?'

Dewi peered at the contents of the bag and a small frown creased his forehead.

'Well,' he said, 'an air rifle.'

'Like yours?'

'Yeah, like mine. Lots of guns take this ammo.'

Jack looked at the young man and smiled. 'Would you mind if I take a look at the soles of your boots?'

'What? Why?'

Jack opened the file. 'To see if they match these.' He held up the photo showing a clear imprint of a boot.

'What's going on here?' Dewi asked. 'Something is. I know it. I reckon you've got me here on false pretences. What are you trying to prove?'

'That you were in fact out and about last night. That you went to the header pond on Dolgarrog's land. Now let's see the bottom of your footwear, boy.'

Dewi reluctantly lifted his foot, and Jack compared the sole to the photograph, and grinned.

'Looks like a perfect match to me,' he said. 'We lifted a really fresh print, before the rain came.' Jack smiled. 'You've been lying to us.'

Dewi chuckled. 'Don't be daft. There are boots like that all over the place, everyone wears them. Bog-standard work boots.' He got to his feet. 'Now, I want my guns and a lift back home. Da needs me on the farm.'

'Sit down,' Ben said, 'and hold out your hands so I can see the backs.'

Dewi blinked and stuffed both hands inside his pockets.

Ben glared at him. 'The easy way or the hard way – your choice.'

Dewi slowly removed his hands and held them out for inspection. Both sets of knuckles were grazed and the injuries were recent.

Ben peered at the damaged hands. 'How did you do that?' he asked.

'I dunno. Farm work is hard on hands, I'm always cutting myself on wire and stuff.'

'But those aren't cuts,' Jack said. 'Looks to me as though you've been fighting. Who did you fall out with?'

'No one.' Dewi got to his feet. 'I've had enough of this. I need to get back to the farm.' He grinned at the detectives. 'You haven't arrested me, so you can't have any real evidence of anything. I'm off.'

Jack returned the lad's smile and took a breath. 'Dewi Griffiths, I am arresting you on suspicion of murder. You do not have to say anything, but it may harm your defence if you do not mention, when questioned, something you later rely on in court. Anything you do say may be given in evidence. Now – sit down!'

'I haven't killed anyone,' Dewi yelled. 'This is bloody mental. You can't do this. I haven't done anything wrong. Like I said, you haven't got any evidence.'

'We will have,' Jack said. 'Now give me your boots so the lab can test them. I bet you a tenner your boots match the impressions from the murder scene.'

Ben leaned in close. 'Why don't you come clean?' he asked. 'For all I know there might be a perfectly reasonable explanation of why we found your footprints by the pond. You might have been out with your fancy rifle looking to nab a couple pheasants for you and your da.'

'I wasn't there.'

'We're not interested in a bit of poaching,' Ben continued. 'All we want to do is clear up the death of Darryl Lloyd. If you were there, you might have seen something, a witness rather than a suspect, but keeping quiet makes us suspicious. You can understand why, can't you?'

Dewi folded his arms and scowled at his inquisitors. 'I want a solicitor before I say another word to you, bastards.'

'Fine,' Jack said, got to his feet and towered over the lad, 'but we still want your boots. Take them off, now.' Jack stuck his head out of the room and called to the custody sergeant.

Dewi tried to front it out. 'You've got nothing on me,' he muttered.

Jack leaned across the table and got in Dewi's face. 'But – as I said – we will have,' he growled.

'Then get on with it, copper, the clock is ticking. You can't hold me for long.'

Ben smiled. 'Obtaining an extension won't be a problem. You better get comfy because it'll be a while before you see the farm again.'

The detectives swept from the room, leaving the custody sergeant to process and house his newest guest. Upstairs, Ben was pleased to see the promised extra staff were already ensconced in the incident room and Tegan was bringing them up to date on the investigation that was growing into a hydra-like monster. She looked up as they entered.

'Carrie's been on the phone, sir,' she said.

'Good news?' Ben asked.

'Pretty much as good as it gets.' She smiled. 'Carrie said to tell Jack she found nothing under the victim's fingernails.'

'How is that good news?' Jack asked.

'Because she did find something stuck between Darryl's front teeth.'

'What did she find?'

'A tiny fragment of skin, more than likely torn from the knuckle that connected with Darryl's mouth. Carrie said it was an incredibly lucky find. It hadn't washed away because the victim's mouth was closed.'

'Did she give any idea how long it will take to get the DNA details?' Ben asked.

'Hopefully not as long as it usually does. Carrie has delivered the sample to the labs herself and will be leaning on them, I'm sure.'

'Marvellous! Let me know the second the results are in. Jack, get the boots to the lab and have ballistics take a look at the air rifle and recovered pellets.'

'Yes, guv, I'm on it,' Jack said and left the room.

Ben took a seat in front of the incident board and stared up at the information displayed there. The many-headed case had been divided into three main sections. Top and centre, a photograph of Erica Bevan dominated. To the right a picture of Will North, shots of the damage caused to the water turbine – and his skull – beneath his image. On the left hung a study of Darryl Lloyd, leaning on the ornate fireplace in the manor house. Lists of names, facts and locations were scrawled below the photographs of the victims. In some cases, arrows linked the notes to each other, but nothing jumped out at Ben. He couldn't see how Dewi could be connected to the other incidents, but was certain he was guilty of causing Darryl's death. He felt the truth in his belly. Maybe it wasn't such a stretch that the rest of it was down to Dewi as well.

He sighed and picked up the phone. He spoke briefly with Stacey, told her he would be busy for some time to come, and asked Heidi for her help in tracing Geraint Jones. Sounding more like her usual self, Heidi said she would get on it and ring as soon as she had something to tell. Ben also confirmed a contingent of Erica's friends and colleagues would be attending the funeral on Saturday, and that he and Jack would arrive Friday evening and stay the night.

Jack returned and poured two mugs from the coffee pot, carried them to the head of the table and put one in front of his boss.

'What now, guv?' he asked and took a seat.

'We need to get back to the Lloyds. I've been onto Heidi and asked her to help looking for Geraint Jones. Nothing is gonna happen on that aspect of this mess without us finding him, or Katrina's husband coming forward, and I can't see that happening.'

'Nor me. Do you think Geraint is involved with Katrina's death?'

Ben sighed. 'Who the hell knows, but he's a loose end, and the son of the woman whose skeleton we found. We have a duty to track him down and ask him what he knows about his mother's death.'

∗ ∗ ∗

The detectives travelled over the ranges to the manor house, windscreen wipers working overtime as they tried to cope with the gallons of water that gushed from heavy grey clouds. Jack steered carefully around huge puddles, his eyes fixed on the narrow road; visibility was not great. He eventually pulled up next to a couple of cars parked in front of the property. They left the shelter of the car and dashed inside. A young constable met them in the hall and introduced himself as the FLO on duty, PC Martin Grimes.

'How are things, Constable?' Ben said.

'Quiet, sir. Shirlee has taken to her bed. Joanne is in the kitchen with the gamekeeper.'

'Is DC Langdon here?'

'No, sir, he's down at Dolgarrog. He's taken statements from the family and left when I arrived.' The man shrugged. 'I feel a bit like a spare part. Mr Baird has tried to send me away a couple of times now.'

'You did the right thing staying. In situations like this, things can change suddenly. Grief does funny things to people. You said Gill and Joanne are in the kitchen?'

'Yes, sir.'

Ben nodded and, with Jack by his side, walked to the rear of the house, tapped briefly on the kitchen door and entered. Joanne sat at the table, Gill perched on a stool next to a long counter. Both nursed mugs of tea.

'Afternoon,' Ben said. 'How are you both? Can I do anything to help?'

Joanne raised angry eyes and glared at Ben. 'Yes, you can help,' she snapped, 'by catching whoever killed my brother. That's what you can do.'

Ben took a seat at the table. 'We haven't confirmed he was murdered yet. It's too early in the investigation.'

'What bollocks! Of course he was murdered. You saw his poor face, someone had battered him, then more than likely threw him in the water and held him under until he drowned. It's not bloody rocket science.'

'Who would do that to your brother?'

'How am I supposed to know? That's your job, to find out.'

'It is important we don't jump to conclusions,' Ben said. 'We need to gather evidence and it is the evidence that will show us what actually happened. Tell me, did your brother have any enemies? Had he upset someone recently?'

'You shouldn't be here,' Joanne said. 'You should be down at the squatter camp, talking to them. One of them did this, I know they did. They beat him and drowned him.'

Ben took a breath. 'We have found evidence that Darryl had been involved in a fight and that he fought back. He wasn't hit with anything other than someone else's fists. Has anything like this ever happened before?'

'Of course not! Darryl? Fighting? No, never happened. He was attacked and it's your fault. My sweet, gentle brother is dead because of you.'

'Why do you say that?' Ben asked.

'You're the ones who drive around with "protect and serve" on the side of your cars. Didn't protect us, did you?' She suddenly surged to her feet and strode from the room.

Gill slipped off the stool, filled a kettle and put it to boil on the top of an old, black range. He glanced at the officers. 'Tea?' he asked.

'Please,' Ben said, 'we could do with a cuppa.'

Gill nodded and removed three mugs from an overhead cupboard.

'Have you any thoughts, sir?' Ben asked.

'Plenty, Chief Inspector, but nothing remotely useful.'

'Care to share?' Jack asked as he took a seat at the table and removed a notebook from his breast pocket.

'Not sure I should.' Gill sighed deeply. 'They all revolve around what I'd like to do to the individual who carried out this monstrous act. If I could get my hands on…' He stopped speaking, poured boiling water into the teapot and carried it to the table. 'Do you really think Darryl had been involved in a fight?' he asked.

'It looks that way,' Ben said. 'An early report from the pathologist has documented several blows to Darryl's face, but also damage to his hands, which indicates he hit back.'

'There was definitely a scuffle,' Jack said. 'Darryl drowned but there's no indication he was drowned deliberately.' He added sugar to his tea and stirred. 'Think back to when you discovered the body. Are you sure you didn't see anyone about? No lights or anything?'

'No. I've already told you the moon was full, the sky clear.' Gill joined the detectives at the table. 'A beautiful poacher's moon. I've had a problem with some of those buggers over the last month or so. I found some snares on our land too. Nasty self-locking devices which were banned. That's why I was out so late.'

'"Our" land?' Jack asked.

'Turn of phrase. I've lived here all my life so I do sometimes look on the land as partly mine. It is certainly my home.'

'But you don't actually own any of it? You're not on the deeds or anything?'

'Not really.' Gill sighed. 'Old Mr Lloyd left me Keeper's Cottage in his will, plus the acre of land around the place, but that's it.' Gill removed a handkerchief from his pocket and wiped his eyes. 'Remarkably generous of him. There's not a day passes he doesn't cross my mind. Although, I have to say, I'm grateful he isn't here to see this. He had no idea what would happen allowing those people to set up home in the valley. I warned him but he was convinced he was doing the right thing. Helping to save the planet.'

'Do you really think Darryl's death was caused by someone from Dolgarrog?'

Gill snorted. 'Who the hell else would it have been? We've never had trouble like this before. We shouldn't have let strangers move onto estate land. I'm sure they are responsible for this tragedy.'

Chapter twenty-four

Ben arrived in the incident room early the next morning. The team were already at their desks and looked up from their work as he entered. Jack poured his boss a coffee and handed it over together with an internal envelope.

'What's this?' Ben asked.

Jack grinned. 'Seems Carrie has her pestering down to a fine art. DNA results from the lab.'

Ben removed his jacket, sat at the head of the table, took a sip from his mug and slit open the envelope. A bright orange Post-it note was stuck to the front of the documents. The pathologist had written a single word in large black letters – "RESULT!" Ben chuckled. He peeled the orange scrap from the report and held it high so his colleagues could read the word.

'Right then,' he said and got to his feet. 'Dewi is in for an interesting morning. Jack, is the duty solicitor attending today?'

'Said he would be, guv.'

'Then let's get the main players in the right place and have another crack at the lad. Interview room in an hour, OK?'

'Do my best,' Jack said and strode from the room, banging the door behind him.

Ben addressed the team. 'Anything I need to be aware of before I go downstairs?'

'Yes, sir,' Tegan said. 'Hereford Hospital have been on. Will North is now fully conscious and well enough to be interviewed.'

'That's good news. Elsa?'

'Yes, sir.'

'When Ollie arrives, go to the hospital and speak with Will. With a bit of luck he'll be able to tell us who attacked him.'

'More or less bound to be Dewi Griffiths,' Elsa said.

Ben smiled. 'Yes, you'd think so, but we can't jump to conclusions.' He took a deep breath. 'I'm really glad Will made it. Nice lad, clever.' Ben slipped on his jacket. 'All this good news! It seems like the tide is on the turn. If you need me, you know where I am. Could one of you update CS Warren for me?'

'I'll do it,' Tegan said. 'Good luck, sir. Hopefully Dewi will be in court tomorrow.'

Ben nodded, drained the last of his coffee and walked downstairs to the custody suite. The uniformed sergeant looked up as Ben entered.

'Morning, sir,' he said.

'Morning. Has Dewi Griffiths been fed and watered?'

'Yes, sir. No problems overnight.'

'Good to know. Dick Nyle – the duty solicitor – should be on his way, so we'll start the interview as soon as possible.'

The sergeant grinned. 'You've had good news,' he said, 'I can tell by the smile.'

'You're right. I have.' Ben patted his colleague on the shoulder. 'I'll be in room one. As soon as DS Trent and Mr Nyle arrive, bring the lad in, would you?'

'Yes, sir.'

Ben walked along the corridor and pushed inside room one. He checked the recording machine, then settled on one of the plastic chairs. He took several deep breaths, tried to calm himself but found it difficult. He knew that barring any monumental cock-ups, Dewi was banged to rights. With a list of circumstantial evidence nearly as long as his arm, and a very conclusive piece of hard evidence, there wasn't a chance the prisoner would walk away.

Ben rubbed his face and let his mind wander. Was it possible that Dewi Griffiths had also shot Erica Bevan? Was the young man sitting in a cell a few metres away responsible for all the crimes that had occurred in the valley? He had certainly fought with Darryl – the DNA evidence was clear and beyond doubt. Ben smiled. Juries loved DNA even though they didn't – in the main – understand it. They didn't need to. If the prosecution told them there was one in a billion chance of an exact match, they never took long to return a guilty verdict. Muffled voices in the corridor outside encouraged him to his feet as Jack and Dick Nyle entered.

'Morning, Dick,' Ben said and shook hands with the solicitor. 'Are you ready to go? Need more time with your client?'

'No, thanks. I spent an hour with him yesterday evening and I'm fully abreast of the situation.'

'Marvellous. Jack, gee up the custody sergeant, let's have Dewi in here.'

Jack slipped out of the room and reappeared a few minutes later with the prisoner walking in front of him. Jack removed the handcuffs and Dewi flopped on a chair next to his solicitor. Ben switched on the recording device and stated date, time and those present in the room. He looked at Dewi.

'Before we begin,' Ben said, 'I want to confirm that you understand you are being interviewed under caution and were arrested yesterday on suspicion of the murder of Darryl Lloyd.'

'Yeah, I get it,' Dewi muttered.

'Is there anything you would like to tell us regarding Darryl's death?'

'Only that I had nothing to do with it. Told you yesterday, I wasn't there.'

Jack smirked. 'Yeah,' he said, 'we heard you. We just don't believe you.'

Dewi shrugged. 'Can't help that, can I?'

Ben cleared his throat. 'I know we covered some of this yesterday, but I need to revisit much of the same ground for the benefit of the tape.'

'Knock yourself out.'

'OK. You told us that you hadn't been on Dolgarrog's land the night Darryl died, said you hadn't left the house after dark.'

'Yeah, that's what I said.' Dewi leaned back in his chair, hands behind his head as though he was lounging in a deckchair on a beach, not inside an interview room of the local police station.

'So, you didn't see or speak to Darryl in the immediate hours before he was discovered.'

'No, I didn't.'

Dewi actually yawned and Jack covered a grin with his hand. Ben opened the file in front of him, and removed the photograph of the boot mark in the mud on the bank of the header pond.

'The lab has confirmed,' Ben said, 'that this impression was made by your left boot. Perfect match, beyond any shadow of doubt.'

Dewi shrugged. 'So what? I walk all over the valley. A footprint doesn't prove I had anything to do with the Lloyd boy's death.'

Ben removed the small bag of pellets. 'The lab also confirms this ammunition is used by an air rifle like the one you own. That the brand is the same as those found in your rifle case.'

'Heaps of people use those. They're sold everywhere.'

Jack folded his arms and glared at Dewi, hardly blinking, searching the young man's face for the tell.

Ben opened the file again and slid a report across the table. Dick Nyle cast a careful eye across it.

Dewi asked, 'What's this?'

'Your DNA record,' Ben said.

'So? One of your guys took a sample yesterday when I was arrested. Stuck a cotton bud in my mouth.'

'Thing is,' Ben said, 'this sample came from a fragment of your skin, discovered wedged between Darryl's lower front teeth.'

Jack winked at Dewi. 'We've got you, boy,' he said. 'This is where you stop lying and start confessing.'

'My sergeant is right,' Ben said. 'This is your only chance to set the record straight. If you don't, bad things are going to happen – I promise you.'

'Yeah?' Dewi said. 'Like what?'

Ben leaned across the table. 'I can prove you were involved with Darryl's death, conviction is a dead cert.

When that happens, it shouldn't take much to convince the CPS you had a hand in the attack on Will North.'

'Don't forget the cold-blooded murder of a serving police officer, guv,' Jack said.

Dewi chuckled nervously. 'Now you're having a laugh. Kill a cop? Me? Yeah right.'

'I'm glad you find this funny,' Ben said, 'because I am taking this very seriously. Once you've been sentenced for killing Darryl Lloyd, and are tucked up safe and sound in a prison cell, I intend to prove you murdered a police officer.' Ben took a deep breath. 'And when I do, I will bury you so far underground that you'll never be able to crawl back to the surface. If I have my way, you will die in prison.' Ben glanced at the solicitor. 'Talk to your client. Inform him there's only one way this is going.' Ben checked the time on the clock above the door. 'Interview suspended at 10.52.'

* * *

Elsa peered into a side ward on the upper floor of the hospital and saw Will North, head heavily bandaged, propped up in bed. He looked up warily.

'Hello,' he said. 'Who are you?'

Elsa held up her warrant card. 'I'm DC Elsa Duffin, this is DC Oliver Langdon. Can we come in?'

'Yeah, if you like.' Will turned his attention away from his visitors and back to the large window and the view of Hereford. 'The doctor told me some cops were coming. Have I met you before?'

'Briefly,' Elsa said, 'the day after the bones were discovered at Dolgarrog. Do you remember John and Rhys digging them up?'

'Yeah, vaguely. Everything is a bit hazy. Some's missing and some's mixed up, not in the right order.' He cradled his bandaged head in his hands. 'My head really hurts but I don't like taking the pills, they stop me thinking.'

'Do you mind if we stay a while?' Elsa asked. 'We need to take a statement.'

'Fine by me, it'd be good to have someone to talk to. Would you ask John and Sally to come, if they have the time?'

Ollie nodded. 'No problem, mate. Apart from your headache, how do you feel?'

'Not sure, I feel different. It's hard to explain but it feels like I'm thinking a different way round, it's all mangled up.'

'What does that mean?' Ollie asked.

'There's chunks I can't remember, like I've got holes in my head.' Will took a deep breath and his face dropped. 'What if I can't build stuff because I can't remember how? If I can't fix stuff, keep things running, John and Sally won't want me. They only moved me onto the land because I was useful, and now I'll have to move and I don't…'

Elsa placed a gentle hand on the young man's arm.

'I'm sure they won't ask you to leave and it's early days yet. I spoke to the doctor on the way in and he said that memories often return, you just need more time to heal.'

Will didn't seem convinced and looked back out of the window.

Elsa pulled a chair closer to the bed and opened her notebook.

'Let's start with the day you were attacked. Can you remember anything about that? Can you tell us why you were in the turbine shed after dark?'

'To stop the vandals,' Will said. 'The turbine always got wrecked at night, so I'd been kipping in the shed to make sure it didn't happen again.'

'How long had you been doing that?'

'Since the last attack when the pipes were smashed. Repairs always cost money and time to fix.'

'Did anyone know you were sleeping in the shed?'

'I didn't tell anyone.'

'So the night you were attacked, what can you remember about that?'

Will groaned. 'Not much, really. It was cold and I should have taken more than one blanket. I heard the foxes screaming at each other, then… nothing. Not a bloody thing. Waking up here in hospital was a real shock.' He rubbed his eyes. 'I need to go home. I don't like it in here.'

'You should stay, just for a while. The doctors will tell you when you're well enough to go home.'

'I don't fit in here,' Will said. 'I need to be back with the trees. Living in the green where I can breathe. All this concrete' – he waved a hand at the view – 'it does my head in.'

'I know what you mean,' Ollie said, 'I've always preferred the countryside. Do you know of anyone who would attack you so violently? Did you upset anyone recently?'

'Can't think of anyone, other than the bloody locals. They don't like us living in the valley.' He took a deep breath. 'Why can't people keep their snouts out of other people's business? It's not like we're hurting anyone.'

Elsa nodded. 'When you were discovered, Geraint Jones was in the shed with you… He'd found a lump hammer, that's what was used to hit you with. Do you think Geraint could do something like that?'

Will laughed. 'Geraint? Not a chance. Him and me are mates and he doesn't hurt anything or eat meat. No way he did this to me, I don't believe it.'

Chapter twenty-five

Stacey pulled into the yard of Brynmelyn Farm, home of the Griffiths. One of the other local farmers she had spoken to earlier in the day told her the owners of

Brynmelyn had been approached by CZC, who had offered to buy the entire farm. Rain pounded on the roof of her car and she took a few moments to wriggle inside a long, waxed cotton coat; she pulled up the hood, then left her vehicle and scurried towards the front door, dodging large muddy puddles. As she drew near, the door opened and Gwilliam Griffiths peered out into the murky weather.

'Who are you?' he asked.

'Stacey Logan. I'm a reporter.' She walked closer. 'I've just been speaking to one of your neighbours who told me you might be able to help with a story I'm writing.'

'What's it about?'

'Land being bought up for tree-planting to offset carbon. Do you have a few minutes to spare?'

The man nodded. 'Can't do much outside in this bloody weather.'

He pulled the door open wider and Stacey slipped inside. He led her to the kitchen.

'Here,' he said, 'give me your coat, I'll hang it near the fire. Cuppa?'

'Yes, please.'

Gwilliam busied himself rounding up mugs and filling an elderly kettle.

'You said you're a reporter. Is that true?' he asked.

'It is, yes. I work for *The Mid Wales Times* in Brecon.'

'Well,' Gwilliam said, and dropped on a wooden chair near the old range, 'I have a better story for you than trees. My only son, Dewi, was dragged out of here yesterday. The police took him to the station, some rubbish about collecting our shotguns. Next thing I know, he's on the phone saying he's been charged with killing a lad. Darryl Lloyd from the manor estate.'

'Wow,' Stacey said, 'that is a story. What did your son tell you?'

'That the cops had charged him and that he'd be in court in the morning. He's been told he won't get bail.' Gwilliam rubbed his face. 'How the hell am I going to run the farm without him? I'm an old man and it's too much work for one – especially with my worn-out hip. I'm on a waiting list but I'll probably die before I get to the top.'

'I'm very sorry. Did Dewi say why he had been charged? I mean, the police must have some evidence or they would have let him go.'

'Some rubbish about DNA. Dewi wasn't making much sense, to be honest; this has really shocked him. Unlawful arrest, that's what you should write about. Police abusing their powers, bullying us hill farmers. It's not right.'

The sound of a vehicle in the yard encouraged Gwilliam to his feet so he could peer out of the window.

'My good God,' he said, 'now I've got a police car on my front step.'

He hauled himself upright and limped from the kitchen. Stacey followed, camera in her hand in case the opportunity presented itself. Gwilliam opened the door. Two uniformed officers stood in the rain.

'Come for me now, have you?' the farmer snapped. 'Not content with my son, you want me too?'

'No, sir,' one of the officers said. 'We just need a look inside your son's room.'

'What, like a search? Don't you have to have a warrant?'

'Only if we were searching the house, but we're not. It's just your son's room and he's under arrest, so we don't need a warrant for that.'

'Guess I haven't got a choice then. Upstairs, first on the left.'

As the officers walked up the stairs, Stacey snatched a photo, then pointed her camera out to the yard and took a couple of the squad car. Gwilliam returned to the kitchen and poured boiling water into the teapot. Stacey hesitated in the doorway.

'Do you want me to keep an eye on them?' she asked.

'Yeah, I guess someone ought to. Stairs are a struggle for me these days.'

Stacey smiled to herself, left the kitchen and quietly followed the officers upstairs. She hovered unnoticed on the small landing and watched as they began the search. Within minutes, a brown envelope had been found tucked in a tatty bedside cabinet. The officer who found it peeled open the flap and inside was a stack of twenty-pound notes. Showing the find to his colleague, he finally spotted Stacey in the doorway.

'Hey,' he said. 'Who the hell are you? You can't be here.'

'I'm fairly sure I can,' Stacey said. 'Mr Griffiths has given me permission to observe the search. How much cash is in that envelope?'

'No idea,' the man said, 'I haven't counted it.'

'Maybe you should. I can be a witness.' She grinned. 'That way no one can accuse you of dipping.'

'How dare you suggest–'

'Don't, mate,' the second officer said. 'She's within her rights.' He glared at Stacey. 'No pictures though.'

Stacey shrugged and slipped the small camera into her pocket. Mr Griffiths called up the stairs.

'What's going on up there?' he asked. 'How long does it take to search a room?'

'Won't be long, sir, but we have our orders.'

Gwilliam snorted loudly. 'So did the bloody Nazis.'

'Don't panic,' Stacey said, anxious the situation wouldn't escalate. 'They aren't wrecking the place.'

Half an hour later, the officers left, clutching several evidence bags. After they had pulled out of the yard, Stacey shared a second cup of tea with the elderly farmer. When his rant ran out of steam, she went out to her car and drove back towards Abergavenny, with a great story to write.

* * *

At eight o'clock the next morning, Dewi Griffiths was removed from the cell in the custody suite at the police station and driven to the local magistrates' court. After spending two nights in a cell the prisoner looked tired and unkempt. He sat hunched on the back seat of the car, hands cuffed. The journey was conducted in silence. Arriving at the court, Jack opened the back door, took hold of Dewi's arm and escorted him inside the building. Ben hadn't been surprised to see Stacey loitering near the front steps of the court building and smiled to himself. For once he was pleased she was in attendance and looked forward to reading the next edition of *The Mid Wales Times*.

At exactly ten o'clock, the magistrate took the bench and Dewi was brought to the dock by two officers who stood on either side of him. Dick Nyle prepared to represent his client, documents spread on the desk in front of him, his battered briefcase on the floor next to his ankles. The charges against Dewi were read out, who stood to confirm his name and address, then sat as the legal arguments began. Dick Nyle got to his feet and addressed the bench.

'Sir, I wish to make an application for bail,' he said. 'My client is of previous good character and lives with his elderly father at Brynmelyn Farm. His father, Gwilliam Griffiths, is not in the best of health and will struggle without his son to help him run the farm and care for him.' The solicitor flipped over a couple of pages in a slim file. 'I do not consider my client to be a flight risk, therefore I ask the court to release him on conditional bail.' He nodded at the magistrate and sat.

The solicitor representing the CPS stood, smiled at her opponent and addressed the court.

'You won't be surprised, sir, that we wish to contest the application,' the young woman said. 'Mr Griffiths has been charged with aggravated manslaughter – a serious crime which can carry a life sentence. Due to the circumstances leading to the death of a blameless young man, we request the defendant is remanded.'

The magistrate removed his glasses and smiled at the woman.

'Is anyone "blameless", Miss Reynolds?' he said.

The solicitor shrugged, knowing an answer wasn't expected.

The magistrate continued. 'It is my understanding that further – possibly more serious charges – could well be brought against Mr Griffiths. Can you tell me anything relating to these charges?'

'No, sir,' Miss Reynolds said, 'not at this point, but a large investigation is underway as we speak. In light of this, we do consider the defendant to be a flight risk and repeat our request that he be held on remand.'

The magistrate replaced his glasses, examined his notes and eventually nodded.

'I agree,' he said. 'The defendant will be remanded in custody. A date will be set for the plea and case management hearing at the earliest opportunity.'

Dewi surged to his feet catching his guards unawares, and they scrambled to their own feet.

'What about my da?' Dewi yelled. 'No way he can manage the farm on his own, he can hardly walk most of the time. I need to be at home with him.'

The magistrate glared from the bench. 'You will have plenty of opportunity to state your case, Mr Griffiths,' he said, 'but this is not the time.'

'But this is a bloody fit up! The cops have got the wrong man. I didn't kill anyone. You must let me go home to help my da.'

'I have made my decision.'

The magistrate glanced at the dock officers who took hold of Dewi's arms. They led him from the dock and down to the cells below the court, to await transport to prison. Dick stuffed papers inside his briefcase and headed for the custody suite, while the representative from the CPS gathered her belongings and left the court. The second case of the day – a twelve-year-old boy accused of joyriding – was led to the dock. Stacey met the detectives in the corridor outside.

'I won't ask how you found out about this,' Ben said.

Stacey smiled. 'I was drinking tea with Gwilliam Griffiths when Dewi's room was searched and he gave me chapter and verse. Any chance you can tell me anything about the "possible further charges"?'

'No, I can't. Too early to say.'

'Oh my God! Do you think Dewi was responsible for killing Erica?'

'Keep your voice down,' Ben hissed. 'We can't talk in here, but we're coming over to Heidi's place this evening, so we'll talk then.'

Jack asked, 'Do you know what's going to happen tomorrow, when Heidi buries Erica? I mean, do we bring flowers, dress in black? What?'

'I don't really know,' Stacey and took a deep breath. 'Just do what you feel is right. Heidi has dug the grave beneath an enormous yew tree at the back of the house. I've tried asking but she hasn't said much, only that Erica's friends will attend and there will be no religious element.' She paused and rubbed her eyes. 'She was going to the morgue today to collect Erica – who will spend the night in the library – then she will be placed in the ground tomorrow morning. Freddie Holtz will be coming over with Heidi's sister, Greta, and Pixie, the young woman Erica rescued from the cult a while back.'

'Ah, well,' Ben said. 'I guess we'll find out tomorrow.' He brushed a kiss on Stacey's cheek. 'Jack and I should be with you around seven this evening. If I don't hear from you, we'll bring a takeaway with us to save anyone having to cook. See you later, Pumpkin.'

* * *

At eleven the next morning, after the guests had assembled, the men, together with Heidi, Stacey and CS Warren, hoisted a wicker coffin on their shoulders and carried it slowly to the grave beneath the ancient tree. A colourful display of orchids and delicate ferns sat on the top. Greta had placed straps across the deep hole, together with a couple of planks to rest the casket on before it was lowered. Four of the pallbearers took hold of the straps, the planks were removed, and gently Erica's body was lowered into the dark, Welsh earth. A large group of local officers who had worked with Erica congregated at the graveside, none of them wearing a uniform. Heidi stood at the head of the grave, and when the lowering had been completed, she began to speak.

'Here lies Erica,' she said, 'my first and only love, my friend, my supporter, my wife. I have been very fortunate to have known such an outstanding individual. She was a very special woman, a one-off.' She smiled briefly at the others surrounding the grave. 'Must have been, to put up with me. Even after all the grief I brought to her door, she never gave up on me and never let me down, like I'm ashamed to say I did to her – once or twice. Living without her will take some getting used to, but that's what we all have to do, go on living.' Heidi held up a small black device. 'This is a mini recorder,' she said. 'Please feel free to speak your truth, but no hour-long eulogies.'

The guests shuffled their feet awkwardly. Ben was the first to speak.

'Erica was a good friend and a great copper, fair, brave. I will miss her always,' he said.

'She saved me,' Pixie said, tears running down her face. 'She gave me back my life.'

'Me too,' Greta said. 'She was clever, kind and beautiful, fearless.'

CS Warren cleared her throat. 'DS Erica Bevan was a valued member of Dyfed-Powys Police. Her death leaves a hole which will be difficult – if not impossible – to fill.'

'She brought joy,' Freddie said, 'to my daughter, my family and everyone who knew her. I shall always be in her debt.'

'One of the best friends I have ever had,' Stacey said. 'She made me laugh and cry in equal measure. I will never forget her.'

Jack swiped a hand across his eyes. 'Erica was a truly remarkable woman and I for one will not rest until her killer is caught and incarcerated in the deepest, darkest cell on the prison estate. I promise I will catch that individual and make them pay.'

'Hear, hear,' Ben, CS Warren and the other officers muttered.

Heidi turned off the micro recorder, then, together with a handful of damp earth, threw it on top of the coffin, the others copied her actions, then she took a couple of steps towards the yew, picked up a shovel and glanced at the mourners.

'If anyone fancies giving me a hand, there are more shovels behind the tree. Let's get this done before it rains again, then we'll go inside, drink a toast, and it will be done. Thank you for coming, it means a lot.'

Chapter twenty-six

As Stacey drove away from her friend's house early the next morning, she glanced in her rear-view mirror and her throat tightened painfully. She saw Heidi standing outside the house, looking small and very lonely. Stacey gulped, swallowed hard and her foot hovered over the brake. Should she turn around? She shook her head. Heidi had been clear. She hadn't wanted any of the mourners to stay overnight, didn't want a houseful of guests to consider. Reluctantly, Stacey put her foot back on the accelerator, and waved a hand from the open window. Her friend had said she needed some peace and her own company, and surely she would ring if she changed her mind.

The morning was dry and very cold. Damp-looking road surfaces shone with ice when weak, yellow sunshine brushed across them and Stacey drove slowly. Even the main roads were dangerous and occasionally she felt the tyres shimmy a little. The dashboard display warned her there was ice about and recorded the outside temperature at minus five. The hedges and fields next to the side of the road sparkled with frost and hungry buzzards were plodding about on the grass hoping they might find some worms to supplement their winter diet.

Following a quick dash into Brecon to hand over her latest work to Sam at *The Mid Wales Times* offices, and grab supplies from the supermarket, she drove out of town, turned right at Llywel, and crawled up the steep, narrow lane to the top of the ranges. Just after the cattle grid was an area of hard standing. Stacey pulled over and angled the car so she could look across the wild land to Pen-y-Fan looming in the distance. She turned off the engine, left the car and leaned against the warm bonnet, in air so cold it felt sharp, as though it would shatter.

The mountain was quiet – no traffic, no crackle of small arms fire from the ranges, or large explosions from artillery practising their aim. The occasional cry of a bird of prey travelled on the breeze, and somewhere – probably miles away – Stacey heard the whine of a chainsaw and a barking dog. She took a deep breath and when she let it go was surprised to realise she was crying. Wiping her cheeks with the back of her hand didn't help, and more tears flowed and dripped off her chin onto her fleecy top. The deep-rooted grief had been held in for too long and now it flooded from her. She pulled a tissue from her pocket, dabbed her face and blew her nose. Gazing at the landscape, with the loss of Erica in her heart, encouraged more tears and she gave in, allowed them to fall, and gradually the pressure eased.

Half an hour passed and Stacey began to shiver, so she got back in the car, started the engine, navigated the twisty, narrow road across the tops, and then dropped down towards Llanagethin and her cottage. As it was early she didn't expect to see Ben's car parked outside, yet she experienced a pang of regret not to find it there. Heidi craved peace and solitude, Stacey craved a strong arm around her shoulders and someone to comfort her. She pulled the car into the drive, walked up the front path to unlock the door, then dragged her belongings and shopping bags from the boot and dumped the lot in an untidy heap in the hall. The cottage was chilly so she headed to the kitchen, put the kettle on, and went out to the woodshed for a bag of logs. Even though the old Aga could be temperamental, within an hour the supplies had been tucked away and she was drinking fresh coffee, feet resting against the bottom of the rapidly heating stove. The house phone rang. She stretched out an arm and snagged the handset from the table.

'Hello, Stacey Logan.'

'Morning, Pumpkin,' Ben said. 'Wasn't sure you'd be home yet. Are you OK?'

'I guess, just very tired. Everything's been a bit… intense lately. You?'

'Don't worry about me. I'm fine, just busy.'

'On a Sunday?'

'Gotta keep at it. The investigation has been catching some breaks and I don't want to disrupt the momentum.'

'So what are you doing?'

'Jack and I are going to take a trip over to the remand centre. Have another chat with Dewi Griffiths. Maybe he'll be more talkative now he's had a couple of nights inside. Jack is sure he's the lynchpin of the entire case, we just have to get him to admit his part.'

'Well, good luck.'

'Afterwards,' Ben said, 'I'm knocking off for the day. While I'm in town shall I pick up a pizza from that restaurant you like?'

'I'd definitely be up for that, thanks.'

'No problem. Have a rest today, a hot bath, and be gentle on yourself. Supporting Heidi is bound to have taken it out of you. How was she when you left?'

Stacey sighed. 'Oh, you know. I think she's OK, but I've always found it difficult to know what she's feeling – even after all the years I've known her.'

'A fitting ceremony yesterday I thought,' Ben said quietly.

'Yes, I agree, very moving.' Stacey sniffed and wiped away a rogue tear.

'Right then,' Ben said. 'Must get on. Jack's downstairs waiting for me. I'll send you a text when I'm on my way home. See you later, *cariad*.'

* * *

The laborious booking-in process at Newport Remand Centre never got any easier, even for coppers. The detectives handed in their phones and wallets, and endured two pat-down searches by overzealous, cop-hating screws, before finally making it to the visits room. Dewi Griffiths was already seated in a corner at the back and Jack led the way through many low tables with chairs clustered around. Dewi glanced up as his visitors drew near.

'I'm not sure I want you here,' he said, 'without my solicitor.'

The officers sat.

'You don't have to talk to us,' Ben said. 'You can ask a prison officer to take you back to your cell.'

'Might be a good idea to stay though,' Jack said, 'being that we're here to try to help you.'

'How's that then?' Dewi asked and folded his arms.

'To give you the chance to come clean,' Ben said. 'Tell us what really happened the night Darryl died. Do that and we'll make sure the CPS knows you have been cooperative.'

'So you're here to do a deal?'

'No, we can't make deals, but judges shorten sentences for cooperation and guilty pleas. You'd be out quicker.' Ben frowned at the prisoner. 'If this whole thing was a horrible accident, then tell us. Keeping quiet is not doing you any good at all.'

'It looks bad,' Jack muttered darkly. 'Juries don't like it either, think you've got something to hide.'

'Let's just see how we go, OK, Dewi?' Ben asked.

Dewi shrugged and cast his eyes around the room as though he was bored.

'When your room at the farm was searched,' Ben said, 'fifteen hundred pounds was recovered from a bedside cabinet. Where did the cash come from? Is it yours?'

The prisoner shrugged again. 'The screws told me I don't have to talk to you.' He grinned. 'They don't seem to like coppers. Why is that, do you think? Cos they know what you're like, that you stitch people up?'

Ben shook his head. 'Do yourself a favour and tell us where the money came from.'

Jack leaned a little closer. 'We've checked your bank account. You've never had money like that, so where did it come from?'

'I won it,' Dewi muttered.

'Be more specific, boy.'

'At the trotting races, Beulah way, in the summer.'

'Good at picking a winner then? Bought the gun out of your winnings, did you?'

'Yeah, that's right.'

'How much did it set you back?' Ben asked.

Dewi shifted his gaze. 'Just under fourteen hundred with the scope.'

'What was the name of the horse?' Jack asked suddenly.

'What?'

'The horse that won you nearly three grand. What was it called?'

'Uh... I... don't remember.'

'What rubbish!' Jack said. 'Many years ago I put money on Ben Nevis to win the Grand National.' Jack grinned reliving the moment. 'A tenner to win, half my wages, and it came in at twenty to one.' He slapped the top of the table and made Dewi jump. 'How can you not know? You're a liar.'

'I've never had a good memory, not since I was a kid. Can't help that, can I? Da said I had something wrong with me.'

Jack laughed loudly, which encouraged a hostile glance from the screw on duty.

'This is ridiculous,' Ben said. 'You've got yourself in a real mess. You battered Darryl – we can prove that – then more than likely drowned him, and – bearing in mind the hard evidence we've collected – the jury will more than likely believe that too.' Ben got to his feet. 'Let's go, Sergeant.' He looked back at Dewi. 'That's you done, boy, and when we prove you're guilty of shooting a police officer you'll be over and out, and your old da will die a lonely death in the wreck of that house.'

The detectives buttoned their jackets and took a few steps away.

'Wait!' Dewi said and took a deep breath. 'You're right. It was an accident. He shouldn't have died.'

Jack caught the eye of his boss and grinned. The officers walked back to the table and sat. Jack removed his notebook from an inside pocket and looked expectantly at the young man.

* * *

Ben arrived at the cottage before dark. He parked tight to the verge, snagged the large pizza box from the back seat and headed up the path to the front door. Stacey was standing on the step. Ben wrapped his free arm around her and hugged her close.

'Good to see you, *cariad*,' he said and kissed the top of her head.

'You too, Sherlock. Come inside so we can shut the cold out.'

They went to the kitchen. Ben slid the pizza into the Aga to reheat, while Stacey took a bottle of wine from the larder, pulled out the cork and poured a couple of glasses.

'How did it go at the remand centre?' she asked.

Ben smiled. 'Dewi told us Darryl's death was an accident.'

'What did he actually say?'

Ben took a sip of wine. 'Something along the lines of he was out with his air rifle, hoping to bag a couple of pheasants for the pot, when Darryl approached him out of the dark, shouting the odds and shoving Dewi about. Very quickly the situation escalated and they were soon trading punches.'

'How did Darryl end up in the water?'

'That's where the word "accident" comes in. Dewi said he punched Darryl hard in the face. Darryl missed his footing on the slippery bank and went in. Dewi took his chance and legged it back home without looking back.'

'Do you believe what he told you?'

'It is possible things went that way, but Jack is far from convinced. Dewi went on to say he thought he'd tangled with one of the Dolgarrog residents, said he was shocked when he heard about Darryl's demise.'

'Did you ask him about the vandalism, the attack on Will and Erica's murder?'

'Of course. He flatly denied having anything to do with any of that. Jack likes him for the lot and in truth, we don't have evidence against anyone else. No witnesses, so no suspects.'

'What did Dewi say about the cash found in his room at the farm?'

'He said he'd won it at a trotting race in the summer. Jack pushed him hard, but he stuck to his story and maintained he couldn't remember the name of the horse that earned him so much money.'

'Maybe someone paid him,' Stacey said, 'to make life difficult for the residents in the valley.'

Ben nodded. 'We wondered the same thing. The team will work on it tomorrow, but a cash payment? Not much chance of discovering or proving where it came from.' Ben opened the oven door and removed the pizza. 'I'll be at Darryl's funeral tomorrow.' He groaned. 'Two in a week.'

'Where is that happening?' Stacey asked, as she transferred slices of pizza from the baking sheet onto plates.

'St David's Church at the bottom of the valley. Kick off at noon.'

'I'll see you there. Sam wants me to cover the event and John and Sally have invited me for lunch as a thank you for getting their climate action on the front page.'

The couple ate in silence for a few moments and Ben poured more wine. He smiled across the table at his partner.

'Really good to have you home,' he said. 'I've missed you.'

'That's sweet, it's good to be here.' Stacey took a deep breath. 'My heart really goes out to Heidi. I know she lived alone before she met Erica, but it must be very hard for her to adjust.' She stretched an arm across the table and brushed Ben's cheek with her fingers. 'In similar circumstances I think I'd struggle. Promise me you'll be careful at work and always come home safely to me.'

Ben snagged her hand and kissed it. 'I promise to do my very best.'

Chapter twenty-seven

Ben and Jack left the incident room an hour before the funeral, having first made sure the team knew what they were doing. Most of the outstanding tasks involved dealing with and checking through the enormous amount of paperwork the large investigation had generated. No one had discovered any trace of Geraint Jones, and now they'd been handed the nearly impossible job of trying to discover where Dewi's wad of cash had come from. Privately, Ben didn't think they had much chance of solving either mystery. He considered ringing Heidi to ask if she'd had any luck finding Geraint, but decided to leave it a couple more days before bothering her.

High pressure had seemingly taken root over Mid Wales. The bright sunshine was welcome, but mountain dwellers shivered in the low temperatures and hard night frosts. Council gritters had been out overnight spreading salt on the main roads, but all side roads were treacherous in places and Ben was pleased Jack drove steadily with the correct amount of caution. Just over an hour after leaving the station, Jack turned into a small car park in front of a picturesque church, built by previous generations of the Lloyd family.

A few vehicles were already parked up, and mourners stood around in sad little groups. Ben recognised Gill's Land Rover. William Williams, the family solicitor was standing next to the Lloyd sisters and looked uncomfortable as Shirlee sobbed loudly, Joanne unable to console her. A silver Bentley swished in and pulled up next to the detectives' car. They watched as the driver stepped out and opened one of the back doors for a tall man in a handmade suit to exit.

'Is that the owner of CZC?' Ben asked.

'Yeah, that's him,' Jack said. 'Laurence Fitzherbert.'

'Why would he be here?'

Jack shrugged. 'Knew the family, attended the shoots.'

Fitzherbert strode across the gravel and shook hands with the women and the gamekeeper. A second Land Rover pulled in through the gate. The vehicle was decades old, plastered with mud, one headlight was missing its glass, and a side window was badly cracked. Gwilliam

Griffiths slid out of the driver's seat and limped towards the small group. Joanne spotted his approach and turned her back. She draped an arm around her sister's shoulders and firmly guided her inside the church. Gill shuffled his feet, unsure how to behave, then eventually walked over to his old friend and they entered the church together.

'I'm surprised to see Griffiths here,' Ben said, keeping his voice low, 'bearing in mind his son has been charged with causing Darryl's death.'

'Doesn't look as though he's very welcome,' Jack said. 'Got more neck than a giraffe, that one. Let's get inside, the hearse has arrived in the lane and the press is on its tail.'

The officers left the car and entered the building. The small space had been decorated with large sprays of white lilies. Sunshine poured through delicate stained-glass windows and cast rainbows onto the petals of the flowers. Ben and Jack sat in a pew at the back – Stacey took a seat on the opposite side of the church – and a few minutes later, black-clad undertakers carried the coffin down the aisle. The vestry door opened, a vicar stepped out, took his place next to the coffin and the service began. Jack leaned close to his boss.

'Not much of a turnout, guv,' he said. 'You'd think Darryl had some mates from uni but there isn't anyone here of his own age, no other family present either.'

'Maybe there isn't any,' Ben said.

He surreptitiously checked out the handful of mourners who had attended. He fidgeted on the hard wooden pew and tuned out as the minister delivered a lacklustre eulogy, a sentimental sermon, and a series of prayers. Heidi had been right to avoid a funeral like this for Erica. After nearly an hour, the pallbearers took hold of the coffin and carried it out to the waiting grave. The mourners gathered to watch as the casket was lowered into the ground, while the vicar intoned yet more prayers.

Ben whispered to Jack, 'I want a chat with Fitzherbert. Make sure he doesn't leave.'

Jack nodded, then he turned away and returned to the car park and Ben followed shortly after.

'Afternoon,' Ben said. 'If you have a moment, Mr Fitzherbert, I'd like a quick word.'

'It will have to be quick,' the man said, glancing at his watch. 'I have a busy afternoon ahead of me.'

'I'm surprised to see you here,' Ben said. 'Do you know the Lloyds well?'

Fitzherbert shrugged. 'We met not long after I moved my company to Wales. For a while I was considering buying some of the estate land and have attended the shoots regularly. Seemed the right thing to do – be here for the girls.'

'Were you angry when you discovered the land you were interested in had already been sold?' Jack asked.

'Disappointed rather than angry. There are many other opportunities in Wales for CZC.' He swept a hand across his hair.

'It seems as though you also know Mr Griffiths,' Ben said. 'Have you met his son, Dewi?'

'The lad charged with killing Darryl? Yes, briefly. I made an offer for the farm but his father wasn't interested in selling.'

'Have you met Dewi since?' Jack asked.

Fitzherbert snorted. 'I've no time to waste on lost causes.'

'"Lost causes"?' Ben asked.

'As I said, his father wasn't interested in selling so I moved on. Can't stand still in this business. Now, as I've said, I have things to do. Good day, gentlemen.'

The chauffeur stepped forward, opened the back door of the Bentley and his boss got in. The door was slammed shut, the driver reversed the car out of the car park and drove away. Stacey walked closer to the officers, took a couple more shots of the church and graveyard, then tucked her camera away.

'That wasn't up to much,' she said. 'I hate funerals.'

'Can't say I'm keen either,' Ben said. 'Are you off to Dolgarrog now?'

'Yes, looking forward to lunch.'

'While you're there, see what you can find out about Geraint Jones. We haven't been able to trace him so anything John and Sally tell you could be useful.'

Stacey smiled. 'So you do want my help after all?'

Ben pecked her on the cheek and watched as she got in her car and after some manoeuvring, pulled into the lane and drove away.

'What's next, guv?' Jack asked.

'Back to base. I hope the team have made some progress. CS Warren is leaning on me to catch Erica's killer and we're no further forward.'

'I reckon we've already got the guilty party in custody.'

'I know you do, but we have no evidence to link him to the crime, no motive, and I don't think he's likely to confess. We have to look harder.'

* * *

Stacey parked in the lane at the top of the valley. She slipped on a warm, hooded top, dragged her kitbag from the back seat, locked the car and began the walk down to the settlement. The sun had nearly banished the frost, but large white patches hung on in the shadowy hollows and tucked beneath hedges. Halfway down the grassy slope she took a moment to gaze at the view stretching away from the bottom of the wooded valley and took a deep breath. She detected the scent of wood smoke and the clean tang of the forthcoming winter. Casting her eyes lower, she spotted Sally in the herb garden and waved.

'Hey, Sally,' she called.

Sally returned the wave. 'Hey, you. Good timing, lunch is nearly ready. How was Darryl's funeral?'

'Pretty grim, hardly anyone there. Have the Lloyds got any family?'

Sally walked closer then turned towards her home. 'Don't think so. Old Mr Lloyd used to grumble about not having anyone else to leave his money to. He didn't think his kids would handle the estate well. He had an older brother who never married and died in the war when he was young. George said he had an unlucky family, members tended to die young. He lost his wife early on too.' Sally pushed open her round front door. 'Come on in and I'll get the kettle on.'

'It's lovely and warm in here,' Stacey said and removed her boots.

'You don't tend to get drafts in underground houses.' Sally put the kettle on the wood burner. 'How is Heidi?'

While Sally added fresh herbs to a large pot of vegetable soup, Stacey told her about Erica's funeral, how simple and moving it had been, and about Dewi's arrest and appearance at court. The front door opened and John clumped down the wooden steps.

'Hi, Stacey,' he said. 'Good to see you.'

'You too. Where's Seren?'

'Over with Janet and her girls, making rag rugs.'

'I'd like to have a go at that one day.'

John smiled. 'Have a chat with Janet, she'll be happy to show you how.'

Sally filled soup bowls, carried them to the table together with a large plate of crusty bread, and the meal began.

'Heard anything from Geraint?' Stacey asked.

'Nothing,' John said. 'I'm a bit pissed off with him, just up and leaving like that. We welcomed him into the community and he walks away without even saying goodbye.'

'Why do you think he did that?'

'I have no idea, but it's bloody rude.'

Stacey nodded and wiped her bowl with a bread crust. 'That soup was just perfect, thank you.'

'I'll let you have the recipe,' Sally said, cleared the bowls and replaced them with small plates and a sponge cake. 'Help yourselves,' she said.

'Thanks.' Stacey cut a slice. 'So tell me about Geraint. Do you know anything about his background?'

'Not much,' Sally said. 'He told me he'd been born in Wales, dropped out of university, then spent a couple of years travelling the UK on foot. He'd been in Pembrokeshire for a few months before arriving here. He was a nice guy. I liked him.'

'How did he finance his wandering?'

'Worked odd jobs, cash in hand mainly, and as soon as he had enough money to move on, that's what he did. A restless soul. I'm not sure he'll ever settle anywhere.'

'What a way to live,' Stacey said. 'I wouldn't mind a bit of tramping but I'd need a camper van at least.'

'Geraint had a tent, a nylon nightmare he called it,' John said. 'He walked out of the wood and into Dolgarrog summer before last. We invited him to camp here as long as he wanted and he ended up moving into the end house as a caretaker.'

'Did he seem happy?'

'He loved it here,' Sally said. 'He often said Dolgarrog was the perfect place for him and couldn't believe how lucky he had been to be able to live in the house.'

'So why on earth would he walk away?'

'Nobody knows. It's pretty much all we talk about since he left. We all liked him and miss his presence.' She took a deep breath. 'Anyway, we have some good news.'

'Do you?'

'Yes. Tomorrow morning, John and I are off to collect Will from hospital. The doctors have passed him fit enough to come home.'

'That is good news. Has his memory returned?'

Sally smiled. 'I hope so, but I'll let you know. You'll have to visit again when he's had a day or two to settle back in.'

Chapter twenty-eight

Back at the station, Ben and Jack made their way upstairs to the incident room. Team members were all present, heads down, working through the mass of statements and other documents, or staring glassy-eyed at screens as they searched cyberspace for possible clues. Once the detectives had settled at the table with mugs of coffee, Ollie walked closer to Ben.

'Sir,' he said. 'I think we have a problem.'

Ben raised his eyebrows. 'Oh?'

'Mr and Mrs Bevan – Erica's parents – are on their way in. They've just found out that their daughter was the officer who was shot. They're not happy.'

'I'm not surprised.' Ben rubbed his face. 'OK, I'll have a word with CS Warren. Probably best if we talk to them in her office, although nothing we can say will help.'

'Better they talk to you than Heidi,' Ollie said.

'Have you spoken to her?'

'No, sir.'

Ben got to his feet and walked down to the end of the room where Elsa and Tegan worked side by side.

'Any worthwhile results, ladies?' he asked.

'Not really,' Tegan said.

'Well, keep on with it, as well as trying to discover where Dewi's cash came from.'

Elsa looked up. 'I've been able to have a bit more of a rummage around in Fitzherbert's past.'

'Anything useful?' Ben asked.

'Not sure. We already know he owned a social media platform which he sold for a very large sum. Prior to that, it seems he dabbled at being an influencer. His LinkedIn page labels him as such.'

'I've heard the term, but I'm not sure what it actually means.'

Elsa laughed. 'It doesn't mean much, as far as I can see. There are loads of them around telling their followers how to apply make-up, be a successful businessman, get the girl, invest in digital currency, what to buy… Do I need to go on?'

Ben shook his head. 'Is that it?'

'Well' – Elsa flipped through a pile of printed pages – 'his accounts have large holes in them. CZC isn't his only company. He shifts money between them, awards himself very large interest-free loans, and bends UK tax law to breaking point.' She smiled up at her boss. 'As far as I can see, he's broke.'

'So how is he managing to buy up so much land?'

'Loans, dodgy offsetting schemes sold to the public, and some hefty grants from the Welsh government. Other people's money, basically.'

'Anything we can nick him for?' Jack asked.

'Not so far, but plenty you could ask him about. He isn't on our records, but that only really means we haven't caught him doing something he shouldn't.'

'OK. Put all this in a report for me and I'll have a word with CS Warren. She might have some idea where we go from here.'

The phone rang and Ben picked it up.

'DCI James.'

'Front desk here, sir. Mr and Mrs Bevan have arrived.'

Ben took a deep breath. 'Hold on to them while I speak with CS Warren. We'll ring down when we're ready.'

'I'll do my best, sir.' The desk sergeant lowered his voice. 'Be aware though, they are proper tamping.'

* * *

Stacey arrived home mid-afternoon and began preparing supper. She had decided on a roast and was halfway through stuffing a chicken, when the landline rang. She washed her hands under the tap and, recognising Heidi's number, snatched up the handset.

'Hello, you,' Stacey said. 'How are things? Are you OK?'

'I'm fine,' Heidi said. 'I've spent most of the morning with the lawyers, working through the details of the trust Fliss wanted me to run from the house.'

'How is that going?'

'Mind-numbingly boring, but we're making progress. What have you been up to?'

'Covered Darryl's funeral, then lunch with Sally and John. Ben wanted me to ask them about Geraint. The police haven't been able to trace him.'

'Did the hobbits tell you anything significant?'

'Not much. Sally described him as a restless soul. Said he travelled the UK on foot mainly and slept in a tent. Apparently he spent some time in Pembrokeshire before arriving at Dolgarrog.'

'You're right, that's not much. I'll keep looking at my end.'

'Thanks, Ben will be grateful.'

'I know. Got some time to help me with something?'

'Of course, what can I do?'

'I want to visit Dewi Griffiths in the remand centre, but he is unlikely to accept my visitor's request, mainly because he hasn't a clue who I am. You've met his dad though. You could ask for a visit in your role as a journalist, and I'll do that bloody "researcher" thing so I can come with you.'

'Yeah, I can try. Why do you want to see him?'

'To find out if Jack is right and Dewi did murder my wife.'

'Do you think he'll just tell you?'

'Maybe, if I ask in the right way. Will you set it up?'

'I'll do my best. Uh…'

'What?'

'Roast chicken at my place in a couple of hours. Are you interested?'

'No, but thanks. Stuff to do here. Let me know if we get a visit.'

'I will,' Stacey said. 'I wonder if–' but Heidi had already hung up.

* * *

Ben left the cottage early the next morning as the house phone rang.

'Hello,' Stacey said.

'It's me again,' Heidi said. 'Fancy a trip to the seaside today? Fresh air, icy wind and sunshine? Maybe fish and chips somewhere?'

'Sounds way better than mucking out my office. What's brought this on?'

'I might have tracked down a relative of the Randalls, a guy who lives above a tiny village called Nolton Haven on the west coast. I could do with some fresh air, and sunshine is better for travelling in than Welsh rain any day.'

'How did you find this man?'

'It's complicated, but if you insist, I'll be happy to relate every keystroke on the way over. Have you arranged a visit with Dewi yet?'

'Next on my list.'

'Well, you do that, and I'll see you in about an hour.'

Stacey hung up the phone, switched on the computer and looked up the contact details of Newport Remand Centre. She sent a message requesting a visit then went to the kitchen and packed a small bag of provisions for the road trip. When she heard the toot of a horn from the lane, she pulled on a warm hooded top, grabbed the bags and went outside to meet her friend. She climbed in the truck, Heidi pulled away from the kerb and began the drive through the system of lanes towards Llandovery.

'So,' Stacey said, 'is this chap really related to the Randalls?'

'Won't know until we speak to him, but there is only one Randall in Pembrokeshire. I took a peek at the council's records after you told me Geraint had spent some time there. I'm wondering if Edwin Randall knew Geraint's mother, Katrina.'

'Hang on a minute, I'm missing something here. What are you talking about?'

Heidi chuckled. 'Ben obviously didn't tell you that Katrina is the mother of Geraint Jones.'

'No, he didn't. How do you know?'

'Wriggled around in the investigation. The DNA recovered from the skeleton matched the sample taken from Geraint when he was arrested.'

'Wow! That changes things.'

'Yeah, a little bit.' Heidi turned onto the A40 and put her foot down. 'Of course, Edwin might not be related but as I said, I fancied a smidgen of sea air to blow away the cobwebs.'

Heidi drove through Haverfordwest, picked up the A487 and a couple of miles further turned left onto a narrow lane, and dropped down a steep hill leading to the coast. Stacey cracked open her window. A salty tang slipped inside the vehicle and she took a deep breath. The screams and cries of raucous seagulls entered with the frigid air – such a different environment from the mountains and the scent of conifers. Heidi slowed, then turned left and rattled over a cattle grid. She pulled to a halt outside a newish bungalow perched on a headland, overlooking the wide sweep of St Brides' Bay.

'What a great place to live,' Stacey said. 'Just look at that view.'

'I agree,' Heidi said, 'stunning. Ireland is out there somewhere.'

A movement in front of the truck caught their attention and a very large, dark brindle dog padded closer, ears and tail erect as it scented the air and peered suspiciously at the visitors.

'Bloody hell,' Stacey said, 'that is a huge dog. Do you think it's friendly?'

Heidi shrugged, buzzed down her window and clicked her tongue. The dog turned its head and walked across to the driver's side. Heidi dangled a delicate hand towards it, ready to pull away if the animal displayed any signs of aggression. It wagged its tail, sniffed at the offered hand and tasted her skin with a long, sticky tongue.

'Hey, boy,' she said. 'Are you going to eat us or have you had breakfast today?' The dog licked some more. 'I think we're safe,' Heidi said. 'Appears he's a softie but no sudden moves, OK?'

Stacey nodded, carefully cracked open the door and as the dog trotted towards her, a man in his late seventies appeared at the end of the building.

'Shadow!' he called. 'Come here.' His pet obediently trotted to his side and sat. 'Morning,' the man said. 'Can I help you?'

'Hope so,' Heidi said as she slid out of the truck. 'Are you Edwin Randall?'

'Yes, that's me. Who are you?'

Stacey introduced herself as a journalist, told him she was working on a story and asked if he had a moment or two to spare. The man smiled.

'I've all the time in the world,' he said. 'Would you like a cuppa?'

'Yes, please,' Heidi said.

'Come inside then and we'll see if I can help you. Take no notice of Shadow. He looks like a monster but he's a gentle creature. Enjoys company as much as I do.'

Chapter twenty-nine

The women followed the man and his dog inside the compact bungalow and Edwin shut the door behind them.

'Take a seat, ladies. Tea or coffee?'

'Coffee please,' Stacey said, having spotted an elaborate Italian coffee machine on the counter.

'No problem. Cappuccino? Americano?'

'Espresso would be marvellous,' Heidi said.

While the coffee machine gurgled and whirred, Stacey looked around the neat, modern room. An enormous glass vase stood on the low windowsill, filled with sea glass fragments, and reflected a gentle blue and green light into the room as though lit from inside. Next to the vase a spiky cactus, the size of a basketball, squatted in a ceramic pot, a large scarlet flower tucked between long spines.

'You have a lovely home, Mr Randall,' she said. 'Have you lived here long?'

'I moved in after I'd finally retired, not quite ten years. I was lucky to find such a perfect place. I'm a birdwatcher and photographer,' he explained and offered two small cups to his guests. 'Now, tell me about this story you're writing.' He settled himself in an easy chair and Shadow stretched out on the floor by his side.

Stacey was careful what she said and without giving too much away, steered the conversation to the Randall family, how she had wondered if Edwin was related, and kept well away from skeletons and the hunt for Geraint.

'Oh dear,' he said when she had finished, and rubbed his eyes. 'I had thought that dreadful business was behind us. Poor Peter. He is my nephew and was so very unhappy for so many years.' Edwin sipped his coffee. 'I'm assuming you are here because you've discovered that his wife,

Katrina, spent a long time in prison. Oh dear,' he said again.

'Yes, that's right but I promise you, we're not here to cause trouble,' Stacey said. 'I also discovered that Katrina had her conviction overturned and was released a couple of years or so back.'

Edwin nodded. 'An appalling miscarriage of justice, convicted of killing her children.' A noise like a sob escaped his lips. 'Peter stood by her, never missed a single visit; difficult, as he had a baby to care for.' He took a couple of deep breaths. 'Poor little mite, Rowan he's called. When Katrina was arrested, she was pregnant. Rowan was born in Holloway and removed from his mother when he was two weeks old. Peter cared for him, did an amazing job and still managed to visit his wife.'

'Did Peter take his son with him on visits?' Heidi asked.

'No. He made the decision to wait until Rowan was older. Prison was not the place for a vulnerable child.'

'I agree with him. How old was Rowan when he met his mother?'

Edwin groaned. 'He never met her.'

'Not once?' Stacey asked. 'Do you know why not?'

'Because–' Edwin faltered and removed a handkerchief from his pocket '–when Rowan was six, the kids at school found out about Katrina and bullied him. Peter removed the boy from school and home-educated him.' Edwin wiped his eyes and the dog rested its snout on his knee. 'He made a good job of it, and a couple of years later Rowan came across some scrapbooks his father had kept, full of newspaper clippings about Katrina.' The elderly man got to his feet and gazed through the window at the wide bay where the black hulk of an oil tanker rested at anchor.

'What happened?' Stacey prompted gently.

'Rowan was too young to make rational judgements about his mother. From that point on, he believed she was guilty and had murdered his brothers. Peter couldn't convince him otherwise.' Edwin dabbed at his eyes. 'That poor, poor woman. I have no idea how she survived. Wrongly convicted of killing her boys and having a third removed soon after birth, whom she never saw again.' He turned away from the view. 'Did you know Katrina died within a year of being released?'

Stacey nodded. 'We did know, but not the circumstances of her death.' She held her breath, hoping Edwin would fill in the gaps.

'About seven months after her release, Peter came to see me, sat in this chair and wept. He told how he had woken one morning and found his wife dead next to him. He was sure her heart had been broken.'

'Did you go to the funeral?' Heidi asked.

'There wasn't one. Peter said he wasn't having a service and that Katrina would be laid to rest in a green burial ground. He told me he was planning to travel abroad afterwards and I haven't seen or heard from him since.'

'Why didn't Rowan see his mum after her release?' Stacey asked.

'I really shouldn't speak for him, but I think when the conviction was overturned, Rowan was so ashamed he hadn't believed her that he couldn't face her.' Edwin went to the kitchen and opened a drawer. He took out a bundle of postcards held together by an elastic band and offered them to Stacey. 'Take a look. He sends these occasionally and he's called in a couple of times. The first visit was soon after Katrina's death. He came to collect a letter his father had left here for him.'

'What did the letter say?' Stacey asked.

'I'm afraid I don't know. He didn't open it here. On his next visit, he refused to discuss it and I was in no position to insist.'

'Do you have any contact details for him?'

'No, sorry I don't.' Edwin sighed sadly. 'My small family has slipped away from me.' He patted his dog on the head. 'Good job I've got Shadow. Eh, boy?'

* * *

Jack parked in the lane at the bottom of the wooded valley. The detectives left the car and walked along the footpath through the trees towards Will North's cabin. Fallen leaves thick with frost crunched beneath their boots and a fluffed-up robin kept them company, flitting from branch to branch only a few feet away. As they drew closer, they caught the scent of wood smoke and entering the clearing, they spotted Will perched on a sunny bench outside his home. He looked up as they approached and raised a hand. The young man looked pale and tired, head still sporting a bandage, but he smiled broadly.

'Hiya,' he called. 'John told me you were coming over. Lovely day.' He stuck a rollie in his mouth, flicked a lighter and sucked in a lungful of blue smoke.

'I must say you're looking much better,' Ben said.

'The trees help. Being surrounded by them is much healthier than all that concrete. I can breathe here in the wood.' He got to his feet. 'Fancy a cuppa? I was just about to get the kettle on.'

'That would be great, thanks.'

'Wait here and soak up some sun, winter's coming. I won't be long.'

He disappeared inside his cabin and the officers sat on the bench. Jack took a deep breath of clean air, stretched out his long legs and chuckled.

'What's tickled you?' Ben asked.

'Just remembering how pissed off I was when my masters at the Met sent me here. Never thought I'd get used to all the open space – or the bloody sheep.'

'Yeah, I remember, they really freaked you out. I was surprised when you asked for a permanent transfer.'

'Me too if I'm honest.' He took another deep breath. 'I know how Will feels, I reckon I've developed an allergy to concrete too.'

Will walked out of the cabin with three mugs in his hands, plonked them on a tree stump and perched on the end of the bench.

'I've got milk this time,' he said. 'Sugar's already in.'

'Thanks,' Ben said. 'So tell us how you really feel?'

'Still got a headache most of the time, not as bad as it was though.'

'That's good news.'

Will nodded. 'Yeah. Gotta go back to hospital in a couple of weeks to get checked over, the stitches might come out then.'

'How's the memory?' Jack asked.

'Better I guess.'

'You don't sound convinced.'

'Still missing lumps. The doc said to give it time.' Will slurped from his mug. 'I'm going up to the turbine shed in a bit. Check the repairs are holding up.'

'Any memories about who clobbered you?'

'Nothing, but it doesn't matter. They didn't kill me and I'm back on my feet, back home.'

'It does matter though,' Ben said. 'We need to catch whoever did this to you.'

'Even if you do, it won't change much. I'll still have a hole in my head.' He laughed. 'Glad I don't go on airplanes. With this amount of metal in my skull, they'd think I was a bomber or something.'

'If we caught your attacker, they wouldn't be able to do anything like it to anyone else.'

'Yeah, there is that.' Will drained his mug. 'Right, I'd better get up top or Sally will be down here fussing.'

'We'll walk up with you,' Ben said and took the mugs indoors.

The men strolled along the path beneath the trees, slowing as they neared the spot where Erica had died. Bunches of autumn flowers, foliage and some dried teasels had been placed in vases surrounded by small quartz stones. Jack spotted a jam jar with the lid screwed on and bent closer to take a proper look. Squashed inside was a small toy bear, nose scrunched against the glass. There was a label tied around the neck; the message, in child's writing, read, "To keep you company". Jack looked away and rubbed his eyes, moved by the poignancy of the simple shrine. Will noticed and patted the large man on his shoulder.

'No one's gonna forget your mate,' he said. 'Sally is going to plant a tree here, apple I think, maybe cherry. Growing stuff isn't really my thing.'

'Nice idea,' Jack muttered. He took a quick snap of the scene on his phone, then turned away and continued the trudge up to the settlement.

The bright sunshine had encouraged the residents to come out of their homes. A bonfire of weeds and other garden rubbish burned gently. John and Rhys split logs while Matt and Maxine moved the results of their efforts to the wood store. Janet and Sally were covering empty patches in the vegetable garden while the girls collected bamboo canes. Seren glanced up and shrieked loudly.

'It's Will! Look, Will's coming!'

The others stopped what they were doing and began to run down the slope.

'Be careful, kids,' Sally shouted. 'Will has only just come home, don't knock him over.'

Will stopped walking. He crouched low, held his arms wide and wrapped the children up, a huge smile on his face.

'Bloody hell,' he said. 'You haven't missed me at all, have you?'

'Yes, we did!' Seren said. 'We missed you every day. Are you all better now?'

'Not quite but I'm getting there.'

'We wanted to come down to see you before,' the eldest girl said, 'but we weren't allowed. The grown-ups said we could only go as far as Erica's Place.'

'Was it you who left the flowers?' Ben asked.

All three nodded.

'That was very kind, thank you. A lovely thing to do.'

Sally walked closer. 'Morning, guys,' she said. 'What are you doing here, Will? You should be resting.'

'A bit of walking won't hurt, I don't like being cooped up. Just want to check on the turbine, make sure you lot have been looking after it properly.'

'Take it steady though, OK?'

Will grinned and said, 'Yes, Mum.'

The girls giggled.

The group made their way past the vegetable plots and along the path to the shed. Will smiled, took a couple of steps inside and stopped abruptly. He looked around the room with wide eyes and shook his head, breathing heavily.

'What is it, Will?' Sally asked.

'No,' Will said. 'I don't believe it.'

'What?'

'I remember who hit me.'

Chapter thirty

The detectives marched determinedly back through the wood to their car at the base of the valley. Ben made a call to Ollie Langdon and asked him to drive over to Dolgarrog and take a statement as soon as possible – just in case Will's memory wobbled. They got in the car, Jack fired up the engine and ten minutes later, skidded to a halt outside the front of the manor house. They strode up to the door and Jack swung on the iron bell pull.

'Come on, come on,' he grouched and swung on it some more.

There was a voice from inside. 'OK, I'm coming.'

The door opened and Gill stood in the hall, dressed in his tweed suit, a deep frown furrowing his forehead.

'For God's sake,' he said. 'You'd think the place was on fire.'

'Where are the Lloyd sisters?' Ben asked.

'In the kitchen, why?'

Ben didn't answer and followed his sergeant towards the back of the house. Jack straight-armed the door and the women looked up in surprise. Joanne surged to her feet.

'What the hell?' she spluttered. 'How dare you burst in here? Who the hell do you think you are?'

'Police officers,' Jack said, 'and we're here to make an arrest.' He glanced down at Shirlee. 'Shirlee Lloyd, I am arresting you on suspicion of GBH with intent. You do not–'

Shirlee's mouth flew open and a wail of anguish filled the room. Joanne moved to her sister's side and wrapped her arms protectively around her.

'Are you bloody mad?' she yelled. 'Arrest my sister? Yeah right. Go away, both of you. Get the fuck out of our home. We're in mourning.'

'We can't do that,' Ben said. 'We need to take Shirlee to the station on suspicion of the attack on Will North.'

'On what evidence?'

'Eyewitness,' Jack said and delivered the rest of the caution. 'Come on, Shirlee, on your feet.'

'You're not taking her,' Joanne said. 'I won't allow it. You know she's ill.'

The kitchen door swung open and Elsa dashed in.

'Maybe I can help,' she said and moved closer to the young women.

Disturbingly, Shirlee began beating her chest. Elsa caught hold of her wrists.

'Hey, hey,' she said. 'Don't do that, sweetheart. You'll do yourself some damage. Calm down, deep breaths now, you can do it.'

At first Shirlee struggled, then the fight suddenly went out of her.

'I didn't do anything wrong, really I didn't,' she sobbed.

'Then what we'll do is go to the station and clear this mess up.'

'I don't want to.'

'I know, but we don't have much choice. Come with me now and I'll look after you, I promise.'

Shirlee stood and wobbled on unsteady legs then she allowed Elsa Duffin to lead her from the kitchen. Jack followed and Joanne dropped on a chair, her head in her hands. Gill stepped closer to Ben.

'I don't understand this, Chief Inspector,' he said. 'You can't drag Shirlee away from us, she isn't well.'

'Don't concern yourself, sir. We won't interview her until she's been assessed by a doctor and a mental health professional.'

Gill shook his head. 'You said you have a witness. Who is it? Not one of the eco-terrorists in the valley surely?'

'I can't discuss the case with you, sir. I can promise you will both be informed as soon as there is anything to tell you.'

'I want to go with her,' Joanne said.

'Not possible, I'm afraid. Stay here with Mr Baird.'

Ben turned on his heel, strode along the hall and blinked as he stepped into bright sunshine. There was little conversation as Jack drove to the station, other than Elsa's quiet platitudes from the back seat and the sound of Shirlee sobbing. Less than an hour, Elsa shepherded the weeping woman into an examination room and, together with a uniformed female officer, waited until the doctor arrived to conduct the medical assessment.

As soon as she escaped from the room, Elsa rested her forehead on the cool tiled wall and took a moment for some deep breathing. She hated to see those with mental problems find themselves in trouble; in most cases they struggled badly with their situation and often ended up in prison.

Ben rested a hand on her shoulder. 'Are you OK?' he asked.

'I hate these cases. Prisoners with mental health issues rarely get the help they need.' She moaned. 'It's a stretch for me to believe that girl walloped Will. Whatever could her motive have been? She's too timid for something like this – not so sure about Joanne though.'

'I know what you mean, but we'll only find out during interview, and we can't do that until Shirlee has been assessed, fed and watered and given a rest period.' He rubbed his tired eyes. 'Maybe she had an episode of some sort. I confess I don't much about bipolar disorder, or how the condition affects people.'

'You should get on home, sir. You've had a great result and you need to be rested for the interview tomorrow.'

'About that. You have obviously bonded with Shirlee, so I want you to take the lead in the morning, with Jack sitting in. You did really well today, DC Duffin.'

'Thanks, sir. I won't let you down.'

'Have a word with the custody sergeant. We need to monitor Shirlee carefully and make sure she has access to any relevant medications. Put her on suicide watch – no mistakes, OK?'

'Yes, sir, I'll see to it and be ready to interview her in the morning.'

Ben nodded, went in search of Jack, and sent Stacey a text warning her to expect two guests for supper.

* * *

Arriving at Noddfa, Ben was pleased to see Heidi's truck parked in the lane next to the verge. The officers left the car, walked around the end of the cottage and in through the back door. The kitchen was warm and fragrant, the smell of saffron rising from a curry simmering on the Aga.

'Evening, ladies,' Ben said. 'How are you both?'

'Good, thanks,' Stacey said as she put a pan of rice on to cook. 'Nice to see you, Jack.'

'Likewise,' he said and settled on a chair next to the table. He smiled at Heidi. 'How are you doing?' he asked.

'I'm fine. I wish everyone would stop asking.'

'That's only cos we care.'

'Yeah, I know. It's just a bit much sometimes.'

Ben sat in the old carver and folded his arms.

'You both look pleased with yourselves,' Heidi said. 'Got any good news?'

'Some,' Ben said and recounted the visit to Dolgarrog to check on Will, and the unexpected arrest.

'Bloody hell,' Stacey said. 'You've nicked Shirlee? Do you really think she attacked Will? I wouldn't have thought she had it in her to do something like that.'

'Me neither, but Will was certain. Strange how his memory returned like that, almost as soon as he stepped inside the turbine shed.'

'Brains are amazing,' Heidi said. 'Large lumps of fat basically, stuffed full of neurons and electrical pulses. I'm not surprised the location gave his hippocampus a nudge so he was able to recall his episodic memory.'

'Your brain has always amazed me,' Jack said. 'How do you know all this stuff?'

Heidi shrugged. 'I read a lot and never forget anything.'

Jack pulled his mobile out of his pocket and swiped the screen.

'Got something to show you,' he said and passed the device across the table.

Heidi stared at the small screen and blinked. 'What's this?' she asked.

'The kids at Dolgarrog built it in the wood. They've named it Erica's Place and a tree-planting is planned.'

'Oh,' Heidi said. 'I must get out there soon to thank them.' She glanced at Ben. 'Any suspects yet?'

'Only Dewi, but I'm not convinced. At least the investigation has some momentum behind it now.'

Heidi nodded, sent the image to her own phone and returned Jack's mobile. Stacey dished out supper, Ben poured wine and the meal began. After a few minutes Ben looked up from his food.

'Have you girls been busy today?'

'We have,' Stacey said. 'Took a trip to the seaside, little place called Nolton Haven, right on the coast of Pembrokeshire.'

'Long way to go for some sea air, any particular reason?'

Stacey grinned and shared details of their visit with Edwin Randall, and the story he had told them.

'Oh, my,' Ben said and put down his fork. 'So Geraint Jones is really Rowan Randall. No wonder we couldn't trace him.'

'Not sure it'll be much easier now,' Heidi mumbled around a mouthful of rice. 'He's been off-grid for a couple of years at least and obviously doesn't want to be found.'

'We still need to talk to him,' Ben said.

'Best of luck with that then.' Heidi wiped her bowl with a piece of naan, rounded up the dirty dishes and headed for the freezer in search of ice cream.

'It's a tragic story,' Jack said. 'Fancy being born in prison and to have never met your mother. What does something like that do to a person?'

'Turns you into a restless soul,' Heidi said. 'Rootless, a constant traveller, just like Rowan has been all his life. That's why you won't find him if he doesn't want you to.' She dumped a frosty tub on the table and filled glass dishes with scoops of honey and ginger dessert. 'At least you know Katrina didn't meet a grisly end at the hands of a murderer.'

'If Edwin was telling the truth.'

'Take a drive over yourself and ask him, but trust me, he wasn't lying.' Heidi licked the scoop and dropped it in the washing-up bowl.

'Are any of you planning to stay over?' Stacey asked.

'I'll have to leave you,' Jack said. 'Got some chores around the house I've been promising to do for longer than I care to admit.'

'I'm planning to stop,' Heidi said, 'if that's OK.'

'Of course it is,' Stacey said.

Ben grinned. 'I'm not going anywhere.'

'Good. You can wash up.'

Jack scraped his dish clean and got to his feet.

'Better get off then,' he said. 'We made progress today, guv. Feels good.'

'Yeah, it does. I'll see you at work in the morning, first thing, OK?'

Jack nodded, left the kitchen and let himself out of the front door.

Chapter thirty-one

At half past nine the next morning, Ben settled himself in an office next to interview room one in the custody suite. He sat opposite a live-feed screen and watched as a uniformed officer escorted Shirlee Lloyd inside. A smartly dressed, older woman followed her client and took a seat at the table. Jack and Elsa sat on the other side and the recording device was set in motion.

Jack stated the date and time and said, 'Present in the room are Shirlee Lloyd, her solicitor Ruth Beck, DS Trent and DC Duffin.'

Elsa cleared her throat and began the questioning. She reminded Shirlee she was being interviewed under caution and the prisoner nodded.

'Can I get you anything before we start?' Elsa asked.

'No, thanks,' Shirlee mumbled, hunched over, arms hugging her midriff, eyes on the surface of the table.

'You'll have to speak up for the tape.'

'I'm fine.'

'Maybe you wouldn't mind telling us a little about your mental health, how you're affected?'

'I'm bipolar,' Shirlee said, 'which means I'm either too depressed to get out of bed, or completely manic. It's... difficult.'

'Thanks,' Elsa said. She flipped through a file, closed it and looked across the table. 'Can you start by telling me where you were the night before Will North was discovered injured in the turbine shed?'

'In bed,' Shirlee said, voice gravelly. 'I already told you.'

'Yes, you did, but a witness has come forward who says they saw you on Dolgarrog's land sometime after midnight.'

'Then they're lying. I was in bed.'

Elsa nodded. 'The problem is you were alone and therefore don't have an alibi.'

'I can't help that, can I? Who is the witness?'

Elsa scribbled some notes and changed the subject.

'How often do you go to the settlement? Once a week, a month?'

'Never. Why would I go there?'

'Not friendly with any of the residents?'

Shirlee snorted. 'No.'

'You know them though?'

'Yeah, what of it?'

'So you know Will North?'

Shirlee nodded. 'I know him.'

'Were you friends with Will?'

'Where are you going with this, officer?' Ms Beck answered. 'You can see my client is not in the best of health.'

Shirlee muttered something under her breath and covered her face with her hands.

'Sorry, what did you say?' Elsa asked quietly.

'I... I said I wanted to be,' Shirlee said.

'Wanted to be what?'

'Will's friend.' Shirlee looked across the table. 'I haven't got any friends and Will was nice, different to everyone else. I met him not long after he arrived, I was home from uni for the holidays.' She picked at a small bobble of wool on the sleeve of her jumper. 'He didn't want to be, though.'

'Be your friend, you mean?'

Shirlee nodded and blew her nose on a tissue.

'Did he say why?'

'No.' Shirlee sighed heavily. 'I just wanted someone to talk to. Joanne and Darryl ignored me most of the time. The rest of the time they were horrid, bullied me all my life. It got worse after Dad died, and I couldn't get away from them. I had nowhere to go.'

'I understand,' Elsa said. 'Must have been very difficult for you without your mum.'

'Yes, it was. I still miss her.'

'I'm sure you do. Tell me, when did you last speak to Will?'

Shirlee lowered her head and a flood of new tears dripped onto the surface of the table between her clenched fists.

'I think we could do with a break,' Ms Beck said.

'We only just got started,' Jack said. 'As you know, our doctor and a member of your client's mental health team have passed her fit for interview. Best if we keep going, get it over with.' He glanced at Shirlee. 'Why were you at the settlement the night Will was attacked?'

Shirlee blew her nose again. 'I was walking, that's all,' she said.

'So you weren't in bed like you told us?'

'Not all night, no. I was lonely and wanted someone to talk to. No law against it, is there?'

'Did you go out to look for Will?' Elsa asked.

'No… I mean yes…'

'Which is it?' Jack asked.

'Sergeant,' Ms Beck said, 'I will not allow you to badger my client.'

'It's a simple question.'

'As I've already stated, she is not in the best of health, I–'

'Just shut up,' Shirlee yelled. 'All of you, shut up. I can't think and I want to go home.'

'I'm sorry, but we're not done yet,' Elsa said. 'Will was nearly killed. The doctors had to fit a metal plate in his skull. He's lucky to be alive, and we need to find out who attacked him.'

'Is he… you know… is he OK?' Shirlee asked.

'He's doing well but it's too soon to know whether there is any lasting damage. He's back at home though and Sally is keeping an eye on him.'

Shirlee nodded. 'That's good, I never meant…'

'Never meant what?' Elsa asked.

'To hurt him,' Shirlee wailed and her head dropped to the table and rested on her arms.

Ms Beck placed a hand on her client's back.

'I'm advising you not to say anything further,' she said.

Shirlee shook her hand away. 'I want to,' she said, 'then I can go home. I don't like it in here.'

'Did you hurt Will?' Elsa asked gently.

'Yes, I think I did but I didn't mean to.'

'Just tell us what happened. It'll make things easier for you if you do.'

Shirlee sat upright and scrubbed at her face with a soggy tissue. She took a large, shuddering gulp of air.

'Take your time,' Elsa said. 'There's no rush.'

'I've been really down for months,' Shirlee said. 'Really struggling, worse than usual. Been staying in my room – when the other two left me alone.' She took another deep breath. 'Not sleeping well either. That night, when Will got hurt, I couldn't get off so I got dressed and went out for a walk.'

'And you went to Dolgarrog?'

'I didn't plan to. I was walking along the lane and spotted a light in the valley. It was coming from the turbine shed and I guessed Will might be in there, keeping an eye on the equipment.'

'So you walked down to see him.'

'Yes.' Shirlee closed her eyes. 'I startled him. I think he thought I was a vandal.' She chuckled but the sound was mirthless. 'Anyway, I told him I needed some company. He said he was busy and I should leave, but I didn't want to. I moved closer. I wanted him to give me a hug and I…'

'What did you do?' Elsa prompted.

Shirlee lowered her head. 'I tried to kiss him, just a peck, you know, but he backed off so fast, looked as though I'd slapped him and turned away, and I felt angry.' She rubbed her face. 'I remember the anger and the hurt, it felt hot, like a lump of coal in my heart.' She scrubbed at her face again, cheeks turning red. 'I'm not sure what happened next, but I had a hammer in my hand and there was blood on my glove. I dropped the hammer and ran home. I didn't mean… I never meant…'

'It's OK,' Elsa said. 'Well done. We'll take a break now and bring you some tea. Talk to Ms Beck, Shirlee, she'll advise you where we go from here.'

* * *

Confirmation of a visiting order dropped into Stacey's inbox while she was eating breakfast with Heidi.

'Oh, that's well timed,' she said.

'What is?' Heidi asked, spreading honey on a thick slice of toast.

'Dewi's agreed to a visit. We can go in today.'

'Good. What time are we due at the remand centre?'

'Eleven.'

'OK. I'll take a quick shower and we'll get off.'

A couple of hours later, after a straightforward journey, they stepped inside the reception area of the jail. They handed over their belongings, endured a quick pat-down and were pointed in the direction of the visiting hall. The place was busy. Small children squalled and fidgeted on plastic chairs, while their harassed mothers tried to calm them and snatch a conversation with their imprisoned partners. Stacey and Heidi were shown to a table in the middle of the room and after a few minutes, Dewi Griffiths shuffled towards them. He plonked himself on the orange chair and gazed at his visitors.

'Hello, Dewi,' Stacey said. 'Thank you for agreeing to see us.'

'I wouldn't have done,' he said, 'but I rang Da. He said you're a reporter and might be able to help get me out of here.' He glanced at Heidi. 'Who are you?'

'Ms Logan's researcher,' Heidi said.

Dewi shrugged and refocused his gaze. 'So,' he said, 'can you help me? Get me out of here? I shouldn't be locked up.'

'Why do you say that?' Stacey asked and opened her notebook.

'Because I'm not a killer.'

'Darryl Lloyd died,' Stacey pointed out.

'Yeah, but it was an accident. He fell in the pond and drowned. That wasn't my fault.'

'You did hit him though.'

'And he hit me, but I didn't end up in the water.' He glanced around the room. 'I ended up in this bloody hole. Honest to God, I'm sorry Darryl died, really sorry. It was a horrible accident and I feel bad. I dream about it at night and can't stop thinking about it when I'm awake.' He looked up at his visitors. 'I know I can be a mouthy little gobshite, but I'm not a murderer.'

Stacey nodded and made notes. 'Do you know anything about the police officer who was shot in the valley?'

'What? No, of course not. I've already told you I'm not a killer. Why would I shoot a copper?'

Heidi leaned forward in her chair. 'You'd have been capable. I hear tell you're an excellent shot.'

'Who have you been talking to?'

'Word gets around. You know how it is, small community–'

'I did not shoot the copper! The only reason I'm here is because I bumped into Darryl in the middle of the night. We traded punches and he fell in the pond. I didn't know he was going to drown. How could I have known that?'

'What were you doing there?' Stacey asked. 'Planning to have another go at wrecking the turbine? It was you who vandalised it in the past, wasn't it?'

Heidi smiled at the prisoner. 'You may as well own up, but probably won't admit someone paid you to make things difficult for the residents in Dolgarrog, will you?'

Dewi's mouth dropped open and stayed that way, making his answer superfluous.

Heidi frowned. 'You shouldn't have left all that cash in your room. It made it obvious you'd taken a bung. Vandalism is considered a gateway crime, leads on to other things, and you were responsible for Darryl's death. Why should we believe you when you say you didn't shoot DS Bevan?'

'Cos I bloody didn't, that's why. What is this anyway? It doesn't feel like you're helping me.'

'But we could,' Heidi said. 'Tell us who paid you and exactly what they wanted you to do for them.'

'Then what?'

'We'll have a word in the right ear. It's bound to help your case. Just give us a name.'

'I don't know,' Dewi groaned.

'You have a lot to lose,' Stacey said. 'If you're convicted of manslaughter you'll spend time in prison. If the court knows you've been helpful, assisted with the investigation…' Stacey shrugged. 'Who knows?'

'Just spit it out,' Heidi said, 'it'll make you feel better.'

'It bloody won't if he finds out I've grassed him up,' Dewi muttered.

'We'll be discreet,' Stacey said. 'Promise.'

Dewi rubbed his face. 'Whatever.' He gulped a shuddering breath. 'It was Fitzherbert, the tree-planting bloke. He asked me to let him know what was going on in the valley, then to make things difficult for them.' He fixed Stacey in his gaze. 'It was just a bit of mischief, no one was supposed to die. Please, help me to get home. Da won't survive the winter on the farm if I'm not there to help him.'

Chapter thirty-two

Ben was in the incident room, discussing the interview of Shirlee Lloyd with Jack and Elsa, when his mobile rang.

'Sorry,' he said, glanced at the screen and answered the call.

'Hi, Pumpkin,' he said. 'You OK?'

'Fine, thanks. Heidi and I have just been chatting with Dewi Griffiths. He doesn't like being held on remand and was anxious to talk.'

'Did he say anything interesting?'

'Oh, yes. He told us Fitzherbert paid him to spy on Dolgarrog and damage the turbine.'

'Bloody hell. Did Dewi say why?'

'Only that he thought Fitzherbert still had designs on the valley, but Dewi said he didn't ask much, he was just grateful for the money.'

'OK, thanks. We'll pull him in and have a word.'

'How did the interview go this morning?'

'We'll have to talk later.'

'Of course, but presumably you're convinced Dewi didn't clobber Will? I really don't think he's a bad 'un, just a young man who's had a tough life, never much money around, no mother on the scene, and a dad going rapidly downhill. Atrocious judgement is a given, but I'm convinced he's genuinely upset about what happened to Darryl.'

'OK, I'll take it on board. Gotta go. Jack and I need to visit Fitzherbert, hear his side of things.'

'Will I see you later tonight?'

'Hopefully, but I'll text if I can't make it.'

Ben hung up the phone. 'Tegan,' he called, 'can you assemble a file of documents that relate to CZC's financial irregularities? I don't need everything, just enough to rattle the owner. Jack and I are going to pay him a visit.'

'What did Stacey tell you, guv?' Jack asked.

'She said Fitzherbert bribed Dewi Griffiths to spy on Dolgarrog and smash the turbine.'

Jack snorted. 'I didn't like him from the start. Typical sleazy businessman, with too much money and not enough brains to do anything sensible with it.'

Tegan walked closer, handed Ben a cardboard file and caught Jack's eye.

'I don't reckon he's got so much money these days,' she said. 'A few weeks ago a UK investment agency rated CZC stock as pretty much junk.'

'Any sign why his luck has changed?' Ben asked.

'One of his other companies has–'

'Hang on,' Jack said. 'He has more than one?'

Tegan nodded. 'All variations on a theme, saving the planet, offsetting carbon, that sort of stuff. A couple of the smaller ones went bust spectacularly over the last two years. Shook Fitzherbert up, I reckon, cos since then, he's been making some pretty dodgy transfers from the remaining businesses into his personal accounts.'

'Is he allowed to do that?'

'Not without talking to HMRC and paying the appropriate tax. Have a chat with the forensic accountant if you're interested, he knows more than I do.' She chuckled. 'When Fitzherbert worked as an "influencer", he talked up the benefit of buying digital currency, and a lot of his followers lost money.'

'Was he questioned about the losses?' Ben asked.

'There were lots of online grumbles but not much could be done. He wasn't a registered financial adviser, nor did he claim to be one. He was just a bloke with a blog, who influenced others by bigging himself up, bragging about his wealth and lifestyle, posting pictures of fast cars and massive houses.' She shook her head. 'In the good old days, con artists were clever people and fronted up their marks before ripping them off. These days, they can sit in their bedrooms, spouting rubbish to anyone in the world with internet access who are prepared to listen.'

'Thanks for doing the research,' Ben said, 'very useful.'

'No problem. There's a page of notes covering all this stuff. Read it on the way over.'

Ben nodded and headed downstairs to the parking area at the rear of the station. Jack unlocked a blue Mondeo and the detectives got in. As Jack pulled onto the main road, Ben opened the file and began reading the crib-sheet. By the time they pulled up in Abergavenny, he had a much better idea of what made Laurence Fitzherbert tick – money. Ben and Jack strolled from the car park, through the pedestrian shopping area of town, and before long were standing outside the offices of CZC. Jack gazed up at the roof.

'How on earth did those kids climb up that expanse of glass?' he asked.

'Dunno,' Ben said. 'I wasn't sure I believed it, even when Stacey showed me the photos she took. Right, let's get inside and see what he has to say for himself.'

They pushed in through the main door and reported to reception. The young man behind the desk asked if they had an appointment.

'No,' Jack said and displayed his warrant card. 'I'm pretty sure we don't need one.'

'I'll ring upstairs and ask if Mr Fitzherbert can see you,' the man said.

'Don't bother,' Jack said. 'Just give us directions. We'd like to surprise him.'

The receptionist shrugged. 'Top floor, left-hand corner office. Lift is through there.' He waved a hand and Ben and Jack set off in the indicated direction.

A lift was waiting and took them to the upper floor. The doors swished open and Jack led the way, strode past a secretary sitting at a desk outside their quarry's lair, shoved open the door and marched inside. Fitzherbert looked up, eyes wide with shock. He recovered quickly.

'Don't they teach coppers to knock these days?' he snapped. 'You can't just storm in here unannounced.'

Jack grinned. 'I think we just did.' He sat opposite the large desk and Ben took a seat by his side.

Fitzherbert glared at them, slapped a ring binder closed and slipped it into a drawer.

'Well,' he said, 'one of you better tell me what this is all about, and apologise for the intrusion.'

Jack said nothing but pulled a notebook and pen from his inside pocket.

Ben opened the file Tegan had given him, flipped through a few pages and pulled out a sheet which detailed transfers of large amounts of money between companies held by Fitzherbert.

'During the course of our investigation,' he said, 'we have examined your financial situation.'

'What? You can't rummage around in my private affairs. I have no part in your investigation. I suggest you leave and direct any further questions you have to my solicitor. I'll give you his card.'

Ben ignored the bluster. 'You do have a part in the case,' he said. 'You knew the Lloyds, one of whom is now dead. You wanted their land, didn't you? Wormed your way in with the family and the gamekeeper by regularly attending shoots.'

'I was new to the area, I wanted to involve myself with the local community, especially as I now consider Wales to be my home.'

'I've heard,' Ben continued, 'that when you found out the wooded valley had already been sold, you weren't best pleased.'

'We've already discussed this and I'm not prepared to go through it all again.'

Ben smiled. 'Anyway, during our investigations, some financial irregularities came to light.'

'Then you should be talking to the company's accountant. I pay him to deal with the finances.'

'I'm not sure he'll know anything about the large, inter-business transfers you've made over the last couple of years.'

Ben slid the sheet across the desk and Fitzherbert stared at it suspiciously.

'These transfers were authorised by you,' Ben continued. 'This could look like creative accounting, or the awarding of large, interest-free loans to yourself. Both of these activities are frowned on by HMRC.' Ben took a breath. 'What I frown on is the paying of bribes.'

'Bribes? I'm not sure I follow you.'

'We have evidence,' Ben said, 'that you paid a third party to vandalise the water turbine system in Dolgarrog, and I'm still not convinced you don't know anything about the shooting of my officer.'

Fitzherbert threw back his head and laughed. 'Now I know you're winding me up. You can't come in here throwing wild accusations around. I've told you, I don't know anything about the death of your officer.'

'And in light of what we've discovered,' Jack said, 'we don't believe you.' He glanced at Ben. 'I think this would go better at the station, sir. Let's just nick him. He might be chattier after a night in the cells.'

Fitzherbert suddenly realised the situation was serious and Jack wasn't kidding. His upper lip took on a damp sheen, his cheeks flushed and his forehead was creased by a deep frown.

'Look,' Ben said, 'I'm only really interested in what has been going on in the valley. Being candid, I don't have the manpower to deal with the irregularities of the company accounts. All I'd do with what I've discovered is send everything to the tax office and let them investigate. Our own forensic accountant has taken a look and, well…'

'So, where do we go from here?' Fitzherbert asked.

'Come clean about your part, tell us why you bribed a local, and what you know about the death of DS Bevan. Do that and maybe we won't speak to the tax man.'

'I can't tell you what I don't know.'

'Then start with what you do know,' Jack said. 'Tell us about the money you paid to Dewi Griffiths. What exactly did you pay for?'

Fitzherbert rubbed his eyes and took a deep breath. 'All I asked him to do was keep an eye on the settlement, nothing more.'

'Why?' Jack asked. 'What do you think he could tell you that you'd be interested in hearing?'

'As you've already mentioned, I did want to secure the manor estate land for CZC. The valley and its occupants split up the available acreage. As the situation stands, the amount we would offer for the land would be based on the number of residents. If that number increased, if more… dwellings were built, the amount would need to increase. That's why I wanted to know what was going on there.'

'What about the repeated damage to the infrastructure?' Ben asked.

Fitzherbert chuckled nervously. 'I didn't ask the boy to do anything like that. My guess is he was freelancing. As far as I can see, I've done nothing wrong, certainly nothing you can arrest me for.' He leaned back in his chair.

'You think?' Jack growled. 'We have enough evidence of your unconventional way of doing business to make an arrest.'

'So far,' Ben said, 'you haven't told us anything we didn't already know. Let's focus on the morning my officer was shot and killed. You were on the land that day, taking part in the manor estate's pheasant shoot.'

Fitzherbert shrugged. 'I told you I was, what of it?'

'You were the first away though after the event was halted. We had to track you down. You didn't stay on site as you were asked to. Why was that?'

'Because I have a business to run.'

'I don't think that was the reason,' Jack muttered. 'I think you left so quickly because you had something to do with the murder.'

Fitzherbert flinched at the word. 'I guess I can't control random thoughts in your head, but nothing could be further from the truth.'

Jack got to his feet. 'I've had enough of this, guv. Nick him on the bribery charge then we can toss his office and residence. If we find a rifle, we may be able to add further charges.'

Ben stood and nodded. Jack recited the caution, and a shocked Laurence Fitzherbert was taken from his office, much to the surprise of his young secretary. Once he was locked in the back of the car, Jack started the engine and headed for the station.

'There's no need for this,' Fitzherbert grumbled. 'Take me back to the office and I'll tell you what I know.'

'Too late for that now,' Ben said. 'Anything you say from this point on will be under caution and for the benefit of the tape.'

'Come on, this is ridiculous.'

Neither detective commented and the prisoner slipped lower in his seat. Ben took out his mobile phone and sent Stacey a short text.

Sorry, busy this evening. See you tomorrow Bx

* * *

Stacey received Ben's text as Heidi's truck neared Abergavenny.

'Looks like Ben has arrested Fitzherbert,' she said. 'He says he won't be home tonight.'

'Stay at my place then,' Heidi said. 'Plenty of food in and there are always books to sort.'

'That's a good idea. All I've got waiting for me at the cottage is housework. Thanks.'

Heidi nodded, turned off the main road and drove slowly along the narrow lane leading to her house. As soon as she'd parked, she hustled up the path and opened the front door.

'You go and get some coffee on,' she said, 'and I'll warm up the library.'

Twenty minutes later, the women were sitting on the rug in front of the fire, fluffy throws around their shoulders.

'I don't know how Fliss managed to keep herself warm in here,' Heidi said. 'I can't achieve that and don't do well in the cold.' She grinned. 'No spare fat.'

Stacey laughed. 'None at all.'

'I need to take a leaf out of the hobbits' book, make this place more self-sufficient, fit solar panels and take a look at ground source heat pumps.'

'You should have a chat with Will North. You'd get on well with him. Someone else with an extraordinary brain.' Stacey threw a couple more logs on the growing fire. 'You said you'd spent time with the trust's lawyers. Have you worked out what you're going to do with this place?'

'Pretty sure I have and I think Fliss would approve. I just need to get the place fit for residents.'

'So, tell me,' Stacey said.

'I want to open something along the lines of a children's home for kids who need somewhere safe. Not the ghastly places you hear about in the news, but a properly run establishment that turns out individuals with a future, not damaged ones.'

'Wow,' Stacey said. 'That sounds like a massive undertaking.'

Heidi snorted. 'I won't be trying to do it all on my own, I'll have staff to help me.'

'Not taking in any more refugees then, like Fliss used to?'

'I didn't say that?'

Stacey chuckled. 'No, you didn't.' She dragged herself up from the floor. 'I put some stew on to heat, should be ready by now. Would you like to eat in here?'

'Please, I'm just beginning to thaw out. Want a hand?'

'I can manage. Keep my blanket warm for me.'

Stacey left the library, returning twenty minutes later carrying a large tray. Heidi unwrapped herself long enough to help unload the food and cutlery. Stacey perched on a footstool and reclaimed her blanket.

'I was more than ready for this,' Stacey said. 'Breakfast was a very long time ago. Now, tell me more about your plans for the trust.'

Chapter thirty-three

Stacey slept well and it wasn't until after nine the next morning that she wandered downstairs and into the kitchen, swathed in an oversized towelling robe she had found on the back of the door in her room. Heidi was at the table, laptop open in front of her, fingers dancing across the keys. Stacey helped herself to a coffee and took a seat.

'Good night?' Heidi asked, without taking her eyes from the screen.

'Yes, thanks. This is such a lovely old house, I've always felt at home here.'

'Me too. I'm considering renting out the flat in Brecon and moving in here full time, fresh start. Not only that, but there's lots to do before I can open the place up.'

'How will you fund it?'

'The lawyers say that won't be a problem. Fliss left a chunk of money to carry out the refurbishment and run things for maybe a year. After that, the trustees can apply for grants from local government. I'm not worried about the money.'

Heidi drained her mug and got up for a refill, when a tap on the kitchen window startled her. She looked up and a young man peered through the glass at her.

'That's Geraint!' Stacey said. 'What is he doing here?'

'We won't know until I let him in.' Heidi walked to the kitchen door, turned the key in the lock and pulled it open. 'Hello,' she said. 'Where have you sprung from?'

'I'm looking for Stacey Logan and Heidi Holtz,' he said.

'It's your lucky day. You've found us both. Come in and I can shut the door and keep the place warm.'

He walked inside, slipped a large rucksack from his back, dropped it on the flagstones, and gazed around the large room.

'Sorry to disturb you,' he said, 'but I've spoken with Edwin Randall and he said you were looking for me. I wasn't sure I should come, but he told me about your visit. He said you were good people and didn't think you'd cause us any trouble.'

'He was right on both counts,' Heidi said. 'Coffee?'

'Yes please, that would be great. It was bloody cold last night.'

'Where did you stay?'

'Wild camped a couple of miles from here.'

'You're sleeping in a tent in sub-zero temperatures?' Stacey asked. 'I wouldn't be able to cope with that.'

Geraint smiled. 'I'm used to it and have a bloody good sleeping bag.'

'Must have,' Heidi said and plonked a mug of coffee in front of the visitor. 'So what are you doing here?'

The young man gulped from his mug and wrapped his hands around the warm pottery.

'As I said, I spoke to Edwin – my great uncle – and he told me you'd popped in to see him a couple of days ago. He also said that the police are looking for me. Obviously I will have to speak to them in the not-too-distant future, but don't fancy walking into a police station without some back-up.'

'You could take a solicitor with you,' Stacey said.

'I don't need one. Any crimes mixed up with this affair were committed by the authorities, and against my family.'

'Edwin told us what happened and, I agree, it was an awful miscarriage of justice.'

Geraint nodded. 'Yes, dreadful.' He took a deep breath. 'I'm guessing the police want to talk to me because my poor mother's remains were found on Dolgarrog land.'

'That's a big part of it. Did you know she was there?'

'Yes, I did.'

'Do you know how she ended up in the valley?' Heidi asked.

'My dad buried her there.' He scrubbed at his face. 'Soon after Mum died, he went to see Edwin and left a letter for me. He wrote how he had discovered her dead in bed next to him a few months after her release. He said he wanted to bury her himself, not hand her back to the authorities because they had stolen her life. He used the words "kidnapped by the state".' Geraint sighed. 'I know he shouldn't have done what he did, but I understand why.'

'I have a difficult question to ask,' Stacey said, 'and you don't have to answer. When your mother's remains were examined by the pathologist, she discovered that–' Stacey swallowed '–that only her bones had been buried. Do you know why?'

Geraint nodded. 'Yes, I know. Dad gave her a sky burial. They were both Buddhists – like me – and had travelled extensively in Nepal before they married. Dad wrote in his letter that he took mum up into the mountains, stayed with her while the kites cleaned her bones – doesn't take long, twenty-four hours maybe – then took her to the valley and interred her in Badger's Bank.' He smiled sadly. 'Dad said that's where they'd courted as teenagers – until an overzealous, young gamekeeper chased them off with a shotgun.'

'Goodness,' Stacey said, 'that is certainly some story.'

'Is that why you ended up in Dolgarrog?' Heidi asked.

'Yeah. I'd ignored my mum all her life, wrongly convinced she'd killed my brothers, when they had died due to sudden infant death syndrome.' He stopped speaking and wiped overflowing eyes. 'I know it sounds odd, but when I found out where she was I wanted to be near her, protect her – something like that. Being offered a home to live in, and to be part of the group there, convinced me I was doing the right thing.'

'Then why did you walk away?' Stacey asked.

Geraint shrugged. 'The main reason was because Mum had been taken away from me – again. I wasn't in a good place. I did think about staying on, Dolgarrog is such a fantastic community, but it had changed. Will was attacked and I got pulled in for that.'

'Yes, I know,' Stacey said. 'The DNA swab taken from you proved Katrina was your mother. That's when the police became interested in finding you.'

'Yeah, I guessed as much.' He took a sip of coffee. 'Then the female police officer was killed,' he said, 'and everything changed. The place didn't feel the same and with no reason to stay, I packed my bags and went back to tramping.' He drained his mug and Heidi refilled it.

'Where is your dad?' she asked.

'More than likely in the mountains of Nepal, but realistically he could be anywhere. Apart from the letter he left, I haven't heard from him since Mum died, and neither has Edwin.' He sighed heavily. 'For all I know he might have been given his own sky burial when his own heart broke. He loved Mum with a deep and passionate devotion. Dad and I grew apart because I couldn't believe his truth, and after Mum was finally released, I couldn't…' He ran out of words and covered his face with his hands, unable to staunch a flow of tears. 'I let him down. I let everyone down.'

'You poor man,' Stacey said and rested a hand on his arm. 'None of this is your fault. Such an awful tale. I am so sorry for you and your family.'

'Thanks,' he mumbled and looked across the table. 'Uncle Edwin was right, you're easy to talk to. I've never told anyone all of it before.' He wiped his face. 'So, will you help me? Come to the police station and see fair play?'

'Of course, but not today, OK? Stay here today, spend some time being easy on yourself. We'll all go tomorrow. Safety in numbers.'

'Sounds like a decent plan,' Heidi said. 'Go upstairs and get a hot shower and when you come down, breakfast will be waiting. You do eat meat?'

Geraint smiled. 'When I'm offered it, but then, I'm a very poor Buddhist. Thank you both for hearing me out and making me welcome.'

* * *

Following a sleepless night in a cell in the basement of the police station, Laurence Fitzherbert had lost most of his arrogant bluster, and all of his shine. His expensive solicitor was out of the country, and he'd refused the legal adviser on duty, so he sat alone in the interview room, glowering at the detectives facing him. Jack set the recording machine in motion and verbally noted date, time and names of those present in the room, then took a seat next to his boss.

Ben looked up at the prisoner. 'Right then, let's get on with it.'

'Get on with what?' Fitzherbert snapped. 'I am an innocent man, a business leader, and I should not have been treated in this manner. When I leave here, I intend to sue for unlawful arrest.'

Jack chuckled. 'Knock yourself out,' he said.

'You should take me seriously. I'll make both of you pay for the indignities I've suffered at your hands.'

Jack didn't appear to be bothered. 'Of course you will,' he said.

Ben opened a file and slid four sheets of paper towards Fitzherbert.

'These documents,' he said, 'prove you are far from innocent. Our forensic accountant has highlighted many serious financial issues, both in your business and private accounts.' He smiled. 'And all that on top of the matter of bribing a young man to do your dirty work for you.'

'You can't prove that,' Fitzherbert said and folded his arms.

Jack folded his own arms. 'That's what you think, is it?' He leaned closer to the table. 'I know, that you know, something about the murder of a serving police officer. I know this because I can always tell when someone lies to my face, and also because each time we ask you about it, you avoid giving us an answer.'

'What reason would I have to lie?'

'Because you have something to hide. Not this,' he said pointing at the documents, 'something else. Spill the beans, matey, give yourself a fighting chance in court. This will be your first offence.' Jack shrugged. 'You might get off with an ankle tag, no jail time – unless you are a killer.'

'He's right,' Ben said, 'but you should know that this is the last time we will have this conversation. When we leave this room, you will be taken back to your cell to await the arrival of investigators from HMRC. The government takes a very dim view of tax dodging, especially on this scale.'

Fitzherbert didn't respond. The quietness of the room was only broken by the muffled tick of a utilitarian clock above the door, and the soft whirr of the recording machine. The prisoner stared into space, then rubbed his chin thoughtfully and looked across the table at Ben.

'Earlier today, you told me you weren't interested in the… uh… financial irregularities, not if I helped you solve the murder of your policewoman.'

'Yes,' Ben agreed, 'I did say that.'

'Well…' Fitzherbert took a deep breath. 'I do have some information, but I need your assurance you'll stop digging around in my affairs. CZC is a relatively new company. If you cause trouble local people will lose their jobs, and investors will lose their money. The possible repercussions would be serious.'

'For crying out loud,' Jack snapped. 'Stop all this pissing about and tell us what you know.'

Fitzherbert leaned back in his chair. 'I saw the killer shoot your officer.'

For a few seconds, neither detective said anything and it felt as though even the room was holding its breath.

'Give us the name,' Ben said eventually.

'Gill Baird, the gamekeeper at the estate.'

Jack terminated the interview, slapped off the machine, stuck his head into the corridor and yelled for the custody sergeant. As soon as he arrived, Jack instructed him to return the prisoner to his cell.

'Hey,' Fitzherbert protested, 'that's not right. I've told you what you wanted to know, so now you must let me go.'

'No chance, matey,' Jack growled. 'First of all, we need to confirm what you've told us. If it does turn out to be the truth, I intend to charge you with obstructing the police.' He moved closer to the businessman, invading his personal space. 'You've known the name of the killer all along and not a word to us. I don't care who you are, or how important you think you are; withholding information during a murder investigation is not acceptable.' Jack took a step back. 'Get him out of my sight, Sergeant, and bang him up. We'll need to talk to him again.'

Chapter thirty-four

As the detectives ran upstairs, Ben called Ollie Langdon.

'Yes, sir,' Ollie said when he answered.

'Where are you?'

'A40, just outside Brecon.'

'Who's with you?'

'Elsa Duffin. Why? What's going on?'

'A witness has just told us he saw the shooting of DS Bevan. He named Gill Baird. Get yourself over to the manor house and confirm whether he's there or at the cottage.'

'Yes, sir. Do we arrest him?'

'No, watching brief. If he is guilty of shooting Erica, I'm sure he wouldn't hesitate putting a bullet in either of you.'

'Yes, sir. I'll keep in touch.'

Ben put his phone away. 'Jack, we need more bodies. Round up a vanload of uniforms, and a couple of firearms officers wouldn't go amiss.'

'Do you really think Gill did this?' Jack asked.

'We've enough circumstantial evidence that says it is highly possible, and now we have the witness statement.' He rubbed his face. 'I reckon it's him. What I really want to know is why. I'll meet you out back. I just need to let Tegan know what's going on so she can update CS Warren. You've got ten minutes, Jack.'

Ben turned away and headed upstairs while Jack went in search of the requested manpower. Twelve minutes passed before Ben left the back door of the station and got in the car with Jack, who pulled away before Ben had even got his seatbelt on. His mobile rang and he fumbled it from his pocket.

'Ollie,' he said, 'what can you tell me?'

'Gill's in his cottage,' Ollie said. 'Alone, as far as we can tell, apart from a couple of small dogs.'

'Does he know you're outside?'

'Oh yes, sir, he knows. We were about fifteen yards away when the door flew open and Gill was standing there with a shotgun in his hands.'

'Christ. Are you and Elsa OK?'

'Yes, sir. We backed off rapidly and have tucked ourselves into the undergrowth.'

'What's the suspect doing now?'

'Standing guard at a downstairs window still holding the gun.'

'OK. Stay where you are and keep your bloody heads down.'

'We intend to, sir.'

Ben contacted the officer in the following van and updated him on the situation. 'Pull up outside the manor,' he said. 'No one goes anywhere without my say-so.' He slipped his mobile away.

'Sounds as though it has got lively,' Jack said while overtaking a lorry too close to a blind bend.

Ben blinked and his right foot stamped on an imaginary brake. 'Just get us there in one piece.'

Ben removed his phone again and dialled Sally's number, tapping a finger impatiently as he waited for her to pick up.

'Hello?' she said.

'Sally, it's Ben James.'

'Oh, hi,' she said. 'Everything OK? You sound stressed.'

'We've got a situation above the valley on the manor estate.'

'What sort of situation?'

'All I can say is a potentially dangerous one. I want you, all of you, to put some distance between yourselves and what's happening. It's important, OK? Take the kids and the residents down to Will's cabin. I'd be happier if I knew you were safe.'

'OK, we'll do what you ask. We'll be away from the houses in five minutes. Take care, whatever it is you're doing.'

'Thanks. I'll be in touch. Stay with Will until you hear from me.'

* * *

After a large breakfast, and too many cups of coffee, Heidi took her guests to the library. The room wasn't as cold as Stacey had expected; a large fire burned in the grate.

'Blimey,' Geraint said as he walked inside. 'I've never seen so many books outside of a library.'

'They came with the house,' Heidi said. 'Stacey and I have been trying to sort them out for a couple of weeks. We have made progress, not that it's obvious.'

'Can I help? I'm not good at inactivity, so tell me what to do and I'm your man.'

'Just what I was hoping you'd say. Follow me.'

Stacey's mobile rang. Peering at the screen she recognised Sally's number and answered the call.

'Hi, you. How are things?'

'Bit hectic, to be honest. Ben just rang me and asked all of us to go down the wood and stay in Will's cabin.'

'Gosh. Did he say why?'

'Something about a potentially dangerous situation on estate land. I've only called you in case you were planning a visit. I'll ring again when I know more.'

'Yes, please do and be careful.'

'We will. Talk later.'

Stacey disconnected the call and stared at her phone.

'What's up?' Heidi asked from the far end of the room.

'A possible story,' Stacey said. 'Can I borrow your truck?'

Heidi chuckled. 'Must be a good story. Just remember how much bigger the truck is than your car and bring it back in one piece.'

'Will you two be OK?'

'Of course. We'll spend a couple of hours playing pairs.'

'Playing what?' Geraint asked.

'I'll show you.'

Stacey left them to it. She took a few moments to familiarise herself with the controls in Heidi's truck before firing up the engine. By the time she reached the main road she felt confident enough to speed up, and headed towards Dolgarrog.

* * *

The detectives were still a few miles away from the manor estate when Ben's mobile rang. He yanked it from his pocket and tapped the screen.

'What's up, Ollie?' he asked.

'Where are you, sir?'

'On our way, why?'

'We have a problem – a big one.'

'Tell me what's happening.'

'The gamekeeper has just discharged his weapon through the window into the trees above our heads.'

'Christ! Are you and Elsa safe?'

'Yes, sir, but I don't reckon he's planning on coming out any time soon. A couple of armed officers would be useful.'

'We have some in tow. Keep your heads down and I'll be there in fifteen minutes.'

Ben disconnected the call. 'Put your foot down, Jack,' he said.

Jack nodded, flicked on the blues and twos and sped up. Ben checked his seatbelt then clung to the passenger rail above the door. Luckily, the roads were reasonably quiet and a short while later, Jack turned onto the lane leading to the manor house. Ben wanted to shut his eyes as the car hurtled along the narrow road and he prayed they wouldn't meet a tractor coming the other way. A couple of miles further on, Jack arrived at the gravelled parking area, twisted the steering wheel sharply and the vehicle slid sideways to a stop next to Ollie's car. The Transit van pulled in behind.

Ben opened his door. 'Come on, let's go and find the others.'

'Wait a sec,' Jack said. 'Fools rush in and all that.' He made a quick phone call, then glanced at his boss. 'Elsa and Ollie are close to the far end of the path leading towards the cottage. Let's do this slowly. Gill's shotgun is obviously loaded and we don't want to spook him into doing anything stupid.'

Ben nodded and with Jack at his shoulder, the squad following on behind, walked steadily but quietly towards Keeper's Cottage.

⁎ ⁎ ⁎

Stacey parked the truck in the lane above the valley, grabbed her kitbag from the passenger seat and dangled her favourite Nikon from her neck. She locked the doors and walked past the small electric vehicle owned by the residents. She squeezed through a narrow gate and was about to creep down towards the settlement when the blast of a shotgun seared the air and sent a skein of jackdaws flapping out of the treetops. She paused, calculated where the sound had come from and changed direction.

She kept low, using hedges and the odd ditch to remain concealed, and slowly made her way past the front of the manor house. A group of vehicles were parked on the gravel. A lone uniformed officer leant on the bonnet of a Transit van and smoked a cigarette. Undetected, Stacey slunk by and slipped inside the patch of woodland which surrounded Keeper's Cottage. She stopped walking, adjusted the strap of her weighty kitbag and listened hard. She thought she could hear voices a short distance away and walked even slower. Through the trees she spotted a trickle of smoke threading its way between bare branches and knew she was close. She was about to move forward when a strong hand grabbed her arm and pulled her back, as a second hand clamped over her mouth. She struggled and a voice hissed in her ear.

'Stop wriggling and keep quiet.'

The hand pulled away and she twisted her head and saw Ben glaring at her.

'What the hell are you doing?' he asked. 'We're in the middle of an armed siege and you turn up. It's bloody dangerous and you shouldn't be here.'

'Should I go back to the manor house?' she asked.

'Too late for that,' Ben snapped. 'Just get down and don't move.'

'I heard a shot, has anyone been hurt?'

'Not so far and I want to keep it that way. Elsa is trying to negotiate with Gill.' Ben waved a uniformed female officer closer. 'Stay with Ms Logan,' he ordered. 'She's press so don't let her out of your sight.'

'Yes, sir.'

Stacey made herself as comfortable as possible on a layer of fallen leaves and peered through the lens of her camera, zooming in on the clearing where the cottage stood. About twenty feet away from the building, she saw Elsa Duffin, wearing a bulletproof vest, standing on the icy ground, an open window, and Gill Baird holding a shotgun, barrel aimed at the young officer. Stacey snatched a few pictures earning herself a frown from her minder, so she lowered the camera and strained to hear what Elsa was saying.

'Why don't you put the gun down?' Elsa called. 'Don't make a bad situation worse. No one has been hurt and we need to keep it that way or things will get silly. There are armed officers on site, there's a possibility you might be shot. Help me here, Mr Baird.'

'Why should I?' the gamekeeper yelled. 'Not like I've got anything to live for anyway.'

'That's not true,' Elsa said.

Gill laughed. 'Yes, it is. You don't walk in my shoes, don't know what my life is like. Everything has fallen to pieces and there's nothing left for me.'

'I don't understand. Tell me what this is all about.'

'What do you think? The Lloyd family has been decimated and the estate is crawling with hippies and incomers from England trying to take the land from under our feet.' He took a deep breath. 'I'm on my own now, being bullied for being old, a different generation with different values.'

'Tell me who is bullying you,' Elsa said and bravely took a step closer to the cottage. Gill didn't appear to have noticed, but a movement in the trees to the right caught her eye. A snatched glance informed her an armed officer wasn't far away and she took a calming breath.

Gill snorted. 'Not like it matters now, does it. Only two ways out for me, death at the hands of one of your officers, or prison. Can't say I'm keen on either.'

'It does matter, I'd like to know. Tell me who was giving you grief.'

Gill took one hand from the gun and dabbed his brow with a dirty handkerchief. The barrel wobbled alarmingly and Elsa gritted her teeth, determined not to flinch.

'Why don't you put the gun down, Gill?' Elsa asked. 'There isn't any need for anyone to get hurt. It'd be easier to talk to you without that thing in my face.'

Gill tucked his handkerchief away and pointed the gun back out through the window. Elsa persisted.

'If someone is treating you badly they should be punished, but that can't happen if you don't give me a name.'

Another movement twenty yards inside the trees flicked past Elsa's peripheral vision, but she kept her eyes front and centre.

'You can't stay in there forever,' she said. 'I'm worried about you. Let's put an end to this before things get completely out of control. I'm trying to help you, but you need to help me too. Who has been tormenting you, Gill?'

The gamekeeper rested the barrel of the shotgun on the windowsill and the handkerchief made a repeat performance. When he looked up, he fixed the young officer in his gaze.

'Laurence Fitzherbert,' he said clearly.

'What has he done?' Elsa asked. 'Tell me. Let me help you.'

Gill's shoulders seemed to sag and Elsa took another couple of small steps closer.

'The bastard saw me shoot that woman.' Gill rubbed his eyes. 'I didn't know she was a policewoman,' he said as though the excuse absolved him, 'of course I didn't. I just thought she was another bloody trespasser, someone else with designs on estate land, and I'd had enough, so I… shot her.'

Elsa was shocked by his confession but didn't let him see it. 'How do you know Fitzherbert saw you?'

'He called at the cottage the next day, walked straight in, bold as brass, didn't even knock, like he owned the place.'

'What did he say?'

'That he had seen what I did and wanted hush money.'

'He tried to blackmail you?'

'Yes, and when he found out I was broke he said he would take the cottage and the acre it sat on.' He levelled the gun at Elsa. 'I think it's time for you to leave,' he said.

'What did you tell him you'd do?' Elsa asked, anxious to keep the conversation going. 'Were you thinking of signing the place over?'

'Of course not, where would I go?'

'Well,' Elsa said, 'you shouldn't worry. That won't happen. DCI James arrested Fitzherbert yesterday, got him locked up in a cell.' She took another half a step closer. 'Come on, Gill, put the gun down and we can sort this out.'

Gill tucked the stock into his shoulder and glared at Elsa.

'Stop moving,' he said. 'Come any nearer and I will shoot you.' He laughed a chilling sound. 'You can only put me in prison once. One dead copper or two makes no difference from where I'm standing.'

A sharp clatter at the far end of the cottage snatched his attention. He leaned a little further out of the window and looked in that direction, as an armed officer emerged from a bramble thicket at the opposite end. The officer dashed across the few yards of open ground, handgun held in a double grip. He stuck his weapon through the open window and aimed it at Gill's head. The old gamekeeper was startled, his grip on the shotgun momentarily loosened and, in an act of bravery, the armed officer grabbed hold of the barrel and shoved it upwards to point at the sky. Gill's finger tightened on the trigger and a deafening explosion filled the clearing before the gun was wrenched from his hands.

The armed officer yelled, 'Clear!'

Officers burst out of the trees, Ben and Jack leading the charge. Elsa, exhausted by her efforts to talk Gill down, dropped to her knees. A uniformed officer crouched next to her on the frozen mud and gently coaxed her back to her feet. Stacey realised her minder had also legged it towards the clearing and followed, capturing shot after shot as the situation was brought under control. Moments later, Jack dragged the gamekeeper from the cottage, his hands cuffed in front of him.

Ben emerged with the shotgun in his grasp. He handed the weapon to one of the armed officers, arranged for Ollie to organise and oversee a search of the prisoner's home, then set off along the footpath back to the waiting vehicles. He arrived in time to see Jack shove Gill in the back of a car and lock him in. Stacey walked closer. Ben spotted her approach and frowned.

She held up her hands. 'I know, I know,' she said, 'but this is my job.'

Ben shook his head. 'You should find another one. You won't keep on getting away with it. How did you know we were here?'

Stacey ignored the question. 'I know you're going to be busy for the next few hours, but you and Jack really should try to make it to Heidi's place this evening. You'll need supper, and there's someone there you should meet. Trust me, it's very important.'

'Can you give me a clue?' Ben asked.

'Better if I don't. We'll eat around eight. If you can't make it, send a text. Hope to see you later.'

Not wanting to get into a lengthy discussion, Stacey turned away and began to walk back to Heidi's truck parked on the lane.

Chapter thirty-five

At a quarter to eight, Heidi pushed open the door of the large kitchen and shepherded the detectives inside the warm room. She poured them wine as they took their seats, and Stacey removed a roast chicken from the old, black range. She glanced up and smiled.

'Really pleased you could make it,' she said. 'You both look done in.'

Ben flopped on a wooden chair and rubbed his tired eyes. 'We are,' he said. 'It's been one hell of a day.'

'Have you charged Gill Baird?' Heidi asked, handing out glasses of wine.

'Yes, we have. During the siege, he told Elsa he killed Erica. After his arrest, he made a full confession on tape at the station.'

'Did he tell you why he murdered my wife?'

'Not really,' Jack said. 'He told us he was trying to keep "incomers" off the land and didn't know Erica was a copper. I reckon he's lost the plot.' He sighed. 'Don't worry, none of that holds water. In court tomorrow, he'll be remanded, convicted and locked away for the rest of his miserable life. He has no wriggle room at all.'

Heidi nodded. 'Knowing that should make me feel better, but it doesn't really change anything, does it?'

Stacey ferried bowls of vegetables to the table as Ben took hold of a large carving knife and started work on the roast. The kitchen door opened and Ben glanced over his shoulder and nearly dropped the knife as he recognised Geraint Jones.

'Bloody hell,' Ben said. 'Where did you spring from?'

Geraint smiled. 'Around. I heard you were looking for me so thought I should get in touch, fill you in on recent history regarding my mother.'

'We do have some questions,' Ben said.

'Yes,' Stacey said, 'we know, but let's eat first.'

Ben loaded a platter with roast meat and the others helped themselves to vegetables. Heidi kept the wine glasses topped up which ensured no one would be driving home. When the meal had been finished, the dishes piled in the sink, and – glasses of brandy poured – the group decamped to the warm library. They settled themselves around the fire and Geraint told them the story of his mother's life, his birth, her death and her burial.

'You said your father left a letter with your great uncle?' Ben asked.

Geraint nodded. 'Yes, he did. That's how I knew where my mum had been buried.'

'Do you still have the letter?'

'Of course.' Geraint removed an envelope from his pocket and passed it over.

Ben slipped out two sheets of writing paper, switched on a lamp close to his chair and began to read. The room was quiet apart from the odd crack and spit of a lively log in the grate. Stacey gave it a poke and added a couple more. When Ben finished reading he looked up at Geraint.

'My goodness,' he said and passed the letter to Jack, who peered at the spidery writing. 'Have you heard from your father since you received his letter?'

'No, not a word. As I told Heidi and Stacey, I'm sure he'll have travelled back to Nepal. He and Mum spent a gap year there before they married, they always referred to it as their second home and had ideas of retiring there after a long and happy life.' Geraint sighed heavily. 'Best laid plans of mice and men and all that. You know why that didn't happen, and now you know how Mum died and how she ended up in Badger's Bank. If Dad went anywhere, Nepal is where he'll be.' Geraint smiled. 'If you do manage to find him, tell me where he is so I can go to visit.'

'Bloody hell,' Jack said when he finished reading. 'What a tragic story.'

Geraint nodded. 'Once you've completed your enquiries, I'd like it if Mum's remains are returned to me so she can be laid to rest again.'

'Of course,' Ben said. 'We will need you to come to the station though and make a formal statement.'

'I guessed you'd want me to do that, it's why I hung around.'

'Where will you bury her?' Jack asked.

'I'd like to take her back to Badger's Bank but I'll have to speak with the residents at Dolgarrog. I'm not sure they are my biggest fans since I walked away without a word.'

'I'm sure they will understand once you've had a chance to explain things,' Stacey said. 'Now, Ben, tell us, what charges have been handed to Laurence Fitzherbert and how long do you think he'll get?'

The Mid Wales Times
POLICE KILLER CAPTURED *by Stacey Logan*

In dramatic scenes, Gill Baird, 78, of the Manor Estate, Brecon, was arrested by armed police following a siege at his home, and charged with the murder of DS Erica Bevan, a serving police officer.

An intense investigation had stalled due to lack of evidence, until an eyewitness to the shooting came forward. Baird had lived on the estate all his life and worked as a gamekeeper, as had his father and grandfather before him, and was a well-known local figure.

When police officers arrived outside his cottage, Baird fired his shotgun, barricaded himself inside his home and warned officers not to approach. A siege situation quickly developed and armed police were requested. Despite the best efforts of the officers in attendance, Baird refused to leave his home. An armed officer finally managed to disarm the man who was swiftly arrested. Baird made a full confession while in custody and will appear in court before the end of the month, charged with the murder of a police officer.

DCI Ben James said, "My officers showed great courage in an extremely dangerous situation. I have made a recommendation to the chief constable that two of those officers should be considered for official commendations. I for one am proud to call them my colleagues."

Epilogue

On the winter solstice, the shortest day of the year, a pale, yellow sun rose low into the clear skies above Dolgarrog valley and sparkled on vegetation coated with frost. A small group had gathered outside the round front doors and were bundled in heavy coats against the bitter cold. A large dog sat next to a sturdy picnic table in the middle of the clearing. On the table was a dark wooden box, its sides smooth and polished, the top heavily embellished. A curling mass of leaves and flowers had been carved into the wood and twisted around a single name – Katrina. The box wasn't large nor heavy. A young man stepped forward and with the help of a much older man, they lifted the box between them and walked slowly away from the houses, the black dog padding at their side.

The residents followed, heads low, ice crystals coating the toes of their boots, and three children carried bunches of early hellebore, pale pink petals resting against their woollen, gloved hands. The wild cry of a kite made everyone look up as it sailed above the valley in search of a meal, its feathers flashing red in the sunshine. Ben and Stacey walked at the back of the procession behind Jack and Heidi; Ollie, Elsa and Tegan in front of them. Even CS Warren had put in an appearance. After five minutes of gentle walking, the mourners arrived at a deep hole dug into the top of a grassy bank. Geraint, assisted by his great uncle Edwin, looped straps around each end of the ossuary and gently lowered it into black, peaty, Welsh soil. They stepped back and Edwin wrapped an arm around the shoulders of his nephew.

'Go on, lad,' he said. 'Tell her.'

Geraint took a breath and cleared his throat. 'I'm sorry, Mum,' he said, voice breaking, cheeks wet, 'and I am ashamed that I didn't listen to you or Dad. I promise I will learn how to listen, to be better, and I will always love you. You will be safe here in this beautiful place, and I, Rowan Randall, am proud to be able to call you Mother.'

He wiped his eyes, dropped to his knees and with bare hands began to push the earth back into the hole; a gemstone set in a gold bangle he wore on his wrist sparkled. Edwin rested a hand on his nephew's shoulder. Rowan got to his feet and watched as Rhys and John filled the grave with shovels, and covered it with turf. The children placed their flowers on the mound together with a single stone of white quartz. Stacey was sure she saw Heidi wipe her own eyes, in a rare and brief display of emotion.

The procession back to the settlement was less sombre. The young girls ran ahead, their breath reflecting the sunshine and floating in clouds above their heads. Will walked behind them and lit a rollie creating clouds of his own. The others followed, chatting quietly. Stacey squeezed Ben's hand.

'If I go before you, I want something just like that,' she said. 'No weeping and wailing or meaningless dogma, just a hole somewhere beautiful.'

'Yeah, me too. Do you think there's room for us in the back garden at Noddfa?'

Stacey smiled. 'I reckon but we'd be nearly on top of each other.'

Ben stifled a laugh. 'Suits me. You know,' he said, 'I'm glad Katrina was able to return to this place, that things could be returned to the way they should have been.'

'I love it that Rowan reclaimed his name and has decided to leave the shadows. Any news regarding his father?'

'We've been able to prove he left the country as he told Edwin he would, and he flew to Kathmandu, as Rowan predicted. Realistically though, trying to trace him from the UK is needle-in-a-haystack territory.' Ben shrugged. 'The bosses are reluctant to spend any of their budgets on an expensive manhunt, when the only charge Peter Randall would be looking at if we caught him, would be unlawful burial of a body. Given the circumstances he might get a fine, probably not much more than that, or a suspended sentence if the judge had argued with his wife over breakfast.'

'Such a shame her husband couldn't be here to see this.'

'I agree.'

They walked in silence until they drew closer to the settlement.

'Any word on Shirlee Lloyd?' Stacey asked.

Ben nodded. 'Poor girl, she doesn't seem to have had much of a life. She's always suffered with severe bipolar disorder and according to her doctors, never seemed to receive much support – if any – at home after her father died.'

'Will she go to court for attacking Will?'

'Very unlikely. Will has refused to press charges, says he can't see it will change anything and she didn't kill him. Very philosophical man, Will North. No, Shirlee will probably be detained under the Mental Health Act. I'm sure she'd never survive in prison and might just get the help she needs, and of course the chance to pick up her life again in a few years.'

'Do you really believe that?'

'It does happen. Secure hospitals like Broadmoor aren't all padded cells, you know.'

'I suppose. What do you think about Rowan's chances? Will he get over this and be able to forgive himself for not believing his mother?'

'He certainly has the perfect opportunity to do that. Sally told me he's been offered the house he walked away from and he's accepted.' Ben squeezed Stacey's hand again and whispered, 'The hobbits and the trees will take care of him. Living here, like this, he can have a happy, healthy life and I'm sure he'll work it out.'

THE END

If you enjoyed this book, please let others know by leaving
a quick review on Amazon. Also, if you spot anything
untoward in the paperback, get in touch. We strive for the
best quality and appreciate reader feedback.

editor@thebookfolks.com

www.thebookfolks.com

More fiction by Nicola Clifford

NO REFUGE (book 1)

Reporter Stacey Logan has little to worry about other than the town flower festival when a man is shot dead. When she believes the police have got the wrong man, she does some snooping of her own. But will her desire for a scoop lead her to a place where there is no refuge?

THE CONSORTIUM (book 2)

Whilst reporter Stacey Logan is investigating illegal raves in the Welsh countryside, her boyfriend DI Ben James is dealing with a suspicious death. When drugs enter the picture, their two separate inquiries will collide. Can they find a way to collaborate and catch a dangerous killer?

NOT FORGOTTEN (book 3)

When journalist Stacey Logan's policeman boyfriend disappears with little more than a note, she suspects he has been abducted. But his colleagues refuse to pursue her leads. She'll have to go it alone, but must brace herself for the worst.

RIGHT OF SANCTUARY (book 4)

When DC Heidi Holtz's sister Greta joins a cult, she has trouble convincing her superiors of foul play. And there is nothing the detective can do if Greta went by her own free will. Holtz will have to find evidence to discredit the sect, or risk losing her sister for good.

CODDLING MOLLY (book 5)

A teenager is found dead after a fall from a bridge on a winter night in Brecon. Nobody knows who she is and identifying her proves a challenge. DI Ben James and DS Erica Bevan manage to connect her to someone else with ties to a drugs gang. But when these crooks bother someone dear to ex-detective Heidi Holtz, she too will jump on their trail.

GONE TO THE DOGS (book 6)

Reporter Stacey Logan is looking into the case of a missing teenager, but she can't help but put her nose into Detective Ben James' murder investigation. Tensions within the community reach fever pitch as events come to a head.

MURDER SPIKE (book 7)

Reporter Stacey Logan lands a scoop when she discovers the body of a man placed on top of a statue in the town square. But that's just the first in a series of bizarre crime cases that hit her small rural town. What is causing the crime spike and will she get to the bottom of the matter before the police do?

RIVER OF BODIES (book 8)

When a woman and a man's bodies are found in a flooded car showroom during the night, detectives guess that they are the victims of a cuckolded husband. But once their relationship is explored, strange details begin to emerge. Namely the illicit activities of the woman and her brother, who has mysteriously disappeared. Once again the cops will rely on the increasingly dangerous investigations of reporter Stacey Logan to reach the truth.

Other titles of interest

The eight-book Welsh mystery series by Cheryl Rees-Price

Having been brought up on a hippy commune, DI Winter Meadows is not your ordinary detective. You could guess from his name, really. But will a cop with a sensitive side have what it takes to police a remote Welsh community with more than its fair share of crime? Or will he be seen as a soft touch by locals who have all manner of skeletons in the closet?

Pippa McCathie's Welsh mystery series

Having left the police following a corruption investigation, ex-superintendent Fabia Havard is struggling with civilian life. Nonetheless she sets to her new career as an illustrator. However, when a girl is murdered in her town, old instincts kick in and she is desperate to find the killer. Her former colleague Matt Lambert will have to decide whether to stop her or allow his former boss to assist the floundering inquiry. So begins a series of cases in which Havard, with her local knowledge and experience, will play a pivotal if unconventional role.

Sign up to our mailing list to find out about new releases and special offers!

www.thebookfolks.com

www.ingramcontent.com/pod-product-compliance
Lightning Source LLC
Chambersburg PA
CBHW061808190726
48289CB00007B/2117

Praise for
L.L. Bartlett's Jeff Resnick Mysteries

BOUND BY SUGGESTION

"This fast-paced paranormal thriller will keep everyone wanting to see a LOT more of Jeff Resnick. If you love a good mystery, especially a paranormal thriller, this series is one you need to tune into!"
—*Feathered Quill Book Reviews*

CHEATED BY DEATH

"This psychological thriller with a paranormal thread will keep the old wheels spinning trying to figure out the culprit. This tough, but somehow vulnerable, psychic detective has just the right amount of edge to his personality to make him extremely appealing. However, the reader won't find the time to discover a "psychic signature" in the pages of this book because it just sizzles hot, asking to be read in a single sitting!"
—*The Feathered Quill Reviews*

"Cheated by Death is a poignant mystery that explores the question of what really makes a family? The book is all about family members gained and family taken away, and the way people cope with these life-altering events. Author L.L. Bartlett shows a lot of compassion in her theme and created believable characters."
—*Deborah Purdy Kong*, author of Fatal Encryption

ROOM AT THE INN

 L.L. Bartlett has done it again. The action never stopped in this gripping tale of murder. I applaud the author for delivering a riveting read. Can't wait for the next book in this exciting and wonderful series.
—*Dru's Book Musings*

DEAD IN RED

"Bartlett's hero is complicated and mesmerizing, making for a gripping and energizing mystery."
—*Booklist*

"Bartlett has a deft touch and makes psychic abilities very real."
—*Library Journal*

"A wonderful mix of hard-edged characters and scenarios with a touch of heart-moving details. There is no guaranteed easy resolution or happily-ever-after summation, but WOW, what an ending. Now, when is the next Jeff Resnick mystery out? I'm hooked!"
—*Merrimon Reviews*

MURDER ON THE MIND

"This is a high-powered drama filled with interesting characters that add dimension to a tightly paced story with a good kick at the end."
—*RT Magazine*

"This fine paranormal amateur sleuth will send readers shuffling off to Buffalo to accompany Jeff on his investigation."
—*Midwest Book Review*

"Nicely written and quite twisty."
—*The Book Bitch*

"I sincerely hope after reading Murder on the Mind by L. L. Bartlett that I've just witnessed the birth of a new mystery series."
—*Books N Bytes*